WINTER'S LABYRINTH

Dana Alexander

ISBN-13: 978-1733300575 (paperback)

Winter's Labyrinth, Arizona
Printed in the United States of America

Cover design by Bespoke Book Covers

*For Mark, and all who inspire, love,
and are generous beyond measure.*

1

The point of the gun jabbed into the side of my neck, proof that the man holding it was serious about pulling the trigger. Again. Shallow puffs of air were all I could manage. It might have only been a stun as opposed to a bullet, but given the chance, I'd be drawing my breath and his blood at the next opportunity.

"I'll explain everything later, Sara." C-05's familiar voice filled my ears, causing my blood to boil well beyond a low simmer. The rage I was feeling would likely cause me to shift into the hawk, as a means of protection. That was the result since I'd been injected against my will with a serum to alter my DNA. While I didn't like the result, it had been useful on more than one occasion. "It must be hard to believe I'm here to protect you this time around, given our last few encounters." He moved beside me.

Or because you're holding a weapon against my neck?

"I don't blame you," he said at my ear. "I'd have a hard time believing me, too. And that I'm no longer working against your effort to recover the last key." He placed a hand on the top of my head. Rage melded with a new sickening sensation.

Did the stun affect the ability to shift? Can't move equates to not being able to fly.

"The evil that hunts you has already arrived." He angled his head so I could see him. "I can't have them find you. Not now. You didn't have to open the gateway to this realm like you did in Scotland and in the Yucatan. I gave the dark forces the location this time." He stood and looked right and left before ducking down again beside me, returning the gun to its original position at my neck. "Oh, it's true that, given the proper coordinates for the initial passage, it opened an entry point from one realm to another. This one, with its *advancements*, shall we say, took a bit more effort to track. It didn't take long for you to find the path leading to the temple." He glanced around at the trees above. "Egypt. Strange how it resembles more of a jungle instead of a desert, huh?" My stare answered him with imaginary daggers, as the gun slipped down my neck an inch. "It was only a matter of time before the dark forces homed in on your energy and our immediate location." His gaze flicked back up to the sky.

How exactly are you helping me?

C-05, a man who'd once been sided with me, had put me on my back one too many times and never with my approval. Over the short time I'd come to know him in this life, I'd given him a fair show of strength that ended up drawing blood. A single chance was all I needed to put him down for a good long while. He was, after all, a man who'd turned against the mission to rescue Earth and keep Ardan, the world where immortals resided, safe.

Enemy number one to the immortals, the Dark Lord, Tarsamon, had used every bit of information C-05 held before pinning him to a wall and leaving him for dead. He'd marked his body so his soul would be forced to wander the realms, unable to reincarnate or find solace. On our last quest in the Mayan jungle, I had cut C-05 free from the necromancer spirit drifting over his immobile body, waiting to take his soul. I never thought granting him one last act of mercy would haunt me. The man should be grateful, not repaying me with the element of surprise and a weapon pressed against my neck.

"Where's that team of yours? They'd never leave you alone for long." His eyes swept across the landscape and back to the area where the portal had opened up.

Should be here any second to string you back to that wall. For good this time.

"Now, now. Don't let our past get in the way of me trying to hide you from the evil that hunts you. Both of us now, I suppose," he said, hearing my thought. "Better keep that mind quiet, too. Can't risk any of your energy being detected."

Maybe C-05 was trying to rescue me now. From whom or what, I had yet to actually see. But I'd be damned if I didn't want him out of my way once and for all, dead preferably, so I could finish this quest. I had enough to worry about with the demons and magic that had met me at almost every turn as I searched for the last two keys.

He crouched beneath an overgrown, leafy bush, further concealed. "Stay quiet," he said. "They're near. Feel the shift in the energy around us?"

I couldn't answer. The initial stun had blocked my vocal cords but not my thoughts that he had already warned me to keep quiet.

Is he hiding from Tarsamon?

The Dark Lord was well into a crusade to consume the life force of humanity and stop me from recovering the third and final key that would put an end to his assault. He'd become as strong as I had in this lifetime, harboring shadows that fed off the negative energy of the humans until they were so weak the wraith-like beings could consume their forms. His faceless demons were set on tracking my energy, often arriving with packs of rabid-like dogs with one mission—hunting me down and delivering me to Tarsamon. To kill me meant he'd release the power of the two keys I'd collected into the world, effectively undoing his efforts to extend his reach into another realm.

What is taking my team so long to arrive?

Another press of the gun at my neck reminded me of the previous instruction to remain quiet.

A shadow crept over the daylight as if the sun had been blanketed in a full eclipse. The graying of stones and trees swept the landscape with all the speed of clouds in a windy, storm-filled sky. I prayed that in that blanket wasn't the deadliest of Tarsamon's forces, the dark angel. For the first time I could remember, I felt fear as though I was vulnerable prey, hiding from her predator above. The safety of the immortals and the lives of billions in the hands of a traitor. C-05 would pay for that, too.

The dark pattern shifted direction, its veil lifting as it glided beyond the two stone-carved faces I'd almost run into before being caught by C-05's grip at my throat. His approach had been a perfectly timed attack, as my hand slipped through the faces to discover they were only an illusion. I watched as the darkness coasted farther away toward a building in the distance.

"They're scanning the territory for you," C-05 said, letting the gun fall away. "They'll be back."

I made an effort to shift to my side and found that I'd recovered some movement in my legs. The stun was wearing off but still left me without all motility.

"Why are you helping me?" my voice scratched out. Sweat started racing down my back, despite the cooler temperatures one might expect any place other than Egypt. *A reaction to the stun?*

"Let's just say I was able to convince the Soltari that you needed my help." He glanced up to the sky. "I made a deal with them."

"And let's say I don't believe a damn thing you have to say after what you've put me through. I don't need anything from you." He'd gone against the Soltari, the all-powerful entity that governed the balance of good and evil in the realms, the Alliance who made decisions to carry out that leadership, and he'd stood in the path of me and my team at every turn. "You have zero credibility."

He huffed out a breath but didn't move to strike again. "I fully expect that."

"Why would the Soltari, who gave you to Tarsamon, listen to you, much less believe anything you had to say?"

"Because I gave them the coordinates of the portal that led *you* here, to where the last key is hidden. I helped them get you to the key. The Soltari shared the location with the small group you left in New York."

The Inner Society. Leahnan, their director. The group of thinkers, telepathic introverts who protected the remaining light of Earth in a high-tech underground city in the heart of New York. The base of which had been carefully crafted to hide such energy beneath a fully charged metropolis above ground.

"You gave the Soltari the coordinates?" Sheer disbelief sounded as the words fell out.

"Yes, before I shared the location of the key with Tarsamon. There was no choice in that."

"There's always a choice and you made the wrong one."

He let out a breath of frustration. "Look, there's no time to explain and even less time before the shadows circle back this way. The real question is why the darkness didn't sense your energy when they passed overhead."

I shook my head. "Wish I knew."

He was assessing whether my reply was a truth or a lie. The ring I wore, made of chiastolite, had been strengthened by the elves on the quest for the last key. It was meant to block my energy from the keen detection of any one of Tarsamon's forces, including the dark angel. But I hadn't seen her flying in the blanket of evil that had crossed our path to test it, and I sure as hell wasn't sharing any information with C-05 on the matter of my energy. At his suggestion to keep quiet, I'd blocked my thoughts from his perusal since the shadow passed over us.

"We're going to have to start moving soon."

"I'm not leaving without—"

A crack of electricity signaled the opening of the portal and I turned my attention to the open space, barely visible in the daylight. *My team.*

C-05 took a couple of steps back.

First to come through was Kevin. Better known in the immortal realms as Cerys, and the Last Great Warrior. We'd spent lifetimes fighting alongside each other and loving one another. Most of the memories of said lifetimes, however, had been withheld from me by the Soltari. They were believed to be a distraction to completing the mission, and a point of contention I harbored with the Alliance.

Kevin took two steps forward, his eyes meeting mine before drifting to C-05. His brows closed over his gaze and he charged.

Had he read my thoughts that quickly about the events that

brought C-05 and me together here? Was there time to find a wall to pin C-05 to before the shadows returned?

I'd managed to get to a standing position and waited, finding some satisfaction in allowing Kevin the chance to release the frustration he'd been holding toward C-05. He'd put me in harm's way with Tarsamon by giving up our locations after he'd decided to side with him. His efforts had nearly cost the lives of the team more than once, and had caused me to be consumed with an illness that only the elves could cure, after being held by him in the Dark Lord's realm for too long.

The two men rolled off the path and into the brush, as the other members arrived. Before being called to this mission, Juno and Matt had been Special Forces commandos. They glanced at me and to the brawl, assessing what was happening. After determining no intervention was necessary, they stood silent, waiting for the guardians of the last two keys, Mac and Topetine, who would lead us to the location of the next key. The small, older woman arrived first, carrying with her all the grace and strength of the jaguar she could shift into. Once Aria, Elise, and Jade arrived, the scuffle was nothing more than several heavy puffs from both men as they glared at one another. C-05 had come out on the bloodier end of things with a split lip and abrasion on the side of his head.

"I had that coming," he said, swiping the back of his hand below his lip and shaking it off.

"You have a lot more due," Kevin replied.

For someone who'd taken an oath to save lives and had done so for a living as the director in the ER at a top New York hospital before this quest began, Kevin's eyes and pulsing veins suggested for one man, he'd gladly set aside the pledge to do no harm.

"He hid me from the shadows that scanned overhead moments before you arrived." Why I'd decided to mention the fact at that moment escaped me. It certainly wasn't to protect C-05. But if he was indeed planning to help us, my team needed to know that he already had.

"Tarsamon's forces shouldn't be here," Juno said. "Something went wrong."

I looked at C-05 and back to Juno and Matt. "It seems he gave them the coordinates to this location."

A tic at Juno's jawline twitched and his eyes centered on C-05.

"Why are we wasting time with him then?" Aria asked. Her flaming-red hair caught a breeze and lifted before resting on her shoulders again.

"They're coming back." Matt pointed a gloved finger in the direction I'd last spotted them. "That way." I couldn't see any indication of the shadow, but that didn't mean he was wrong. Matt and Juno carried the unique ability to see coming events. And they'd been right on too many occasions to doubt either of them now. "Our entry must have signaled a break in the energy."

"Head for a large building about a mile or so that way." Topetine lifted her head in the direction we should go. "We'll be safe there." She shifted into her black jaguar form.

"Jade," Kevin said. "Take Sara."

"I can't trace her to the location without an energy path to follow," he said. "It would've already had to have been set by one of us."

Topetine growled out a call. Her emerald eyes looked over her shoulder before she bounded off.

"Let's move," Juno said. He turned to me. "Don't give any indication of your energy by lighting that ball of fire you use for protection. We're going to have to hope the ring will hide you, even though they may be drawn to the rest of us. Use the shield if you must and run like hell."

"We don't have to run," C-05 said. "I have two vehicles over here." He started to move but Juno pulled the gun slung over his shoulder and aimed it at him.

"How'd you manage two?"

"I could explain it, or we could get the hell out of here."

"Stay in front of us," Juno said. "Keys."

"Don't need them here."

Kevin gripped my hand in his and, with his other, wiped away a bead of sweat. His eyes, every sensation from him reflected concern, but with no time to assess further.

"I know," I said. "Stay close." I'd learned to squelch my instinct to lead and follow direction from him when it came to safety. Not having done so in the past had led to putting myself and my team at risk.

C-05 took off into the brush, with the rest of us close behind. Juno lowered his gun but still kept it pointed forward. Kevin and I, along with Mac, piled into the back of an open-roofed Humvee camouflaged to match the trees and lower-level green scrub, instead of the expected desert oasis. The remaining five fit snugly into the main cabin and headed in the same direction as Topetine. There was no way Matt and Juno were going to break us into two vehicles with a man we didn't trust and the storm of evil moving our way.

I shed the jacket I'd arrived with, feeling the sweat beginning to soak the back of my cotton tank and wishing I could trade out the heavier pants for the shorts I'd had in the Yucatan. No sooner than I had the thought and with only Kevin taking notice, the wish became a reality.

Our thoughts are that powerful? Is that how this beast of a car drives without keys?

The skies clouded again in the ominous gray, denying the light of the sun and hinting at the masking of good over the approaching evil, as the shadows drew closer.

We'll lose her.

"We're not going to lose Topetine," Jade said, hearing my thought. Commander himself of what was left of a small army of men purposefully left behind to keep our pace faster, he had the skill to trace anyone's energy path. "I can track her. I already see the pattern ahead. Right turn at the clearing," he called out.

Clearing? Wide open for…

The screech I'd prayed not to hear earlier cut through the sound of the engine.

"There it is," Matt shouted. "Gun it!"

The back wheels dug into the sandy soil and propelled us to tall bisque-colored walls that extended in an L shape of what looked to be a palace of some sort.

"Duck down, Sara," Matt said, tossing a gun to Kevin and jumping in the back with us. They were already blocking my view from the eerily beautiful but powerful demon flying above and the shadows that flanked either side of her.

Several shots rang out.

There was only one way to put down the deadly angel. I'd seen Mac do it once, allowing me the chance to escape her. Her strength and ability to reach beyond the otherworldly protections we carried made trying to overcome her a dangerous task. At the time, it had been a risk we had to take. At this speed and over the terrain, there was no way for him to jump on her shoulders and stab her in the back of the neck, the one location that could still her for what was believed to be a matter of minutes. No one knew for sure how long such an injury would paralyze her because we'd never stuck around to find out. The little information we had was from the elves who guarded the boundaries in Ardan. Their word could always be trusted.

"You can't kill 'em with bullets," I called out to Matt, watching in the space between two arms as several more shots rang out and a few of the shadows fell from the sky and swirled upward, a sign of their deaths.

"Not with average weapons or average bullets," he said, taking aim again and firing.

I need a damn weapon. My sword offered little protection against the greater powers of evil we were expecting to face, and so it had been left behind with the Inner Society. With Juno not wanting me to use the inherent abilities I carried, I was more or less a sitting duck. Nothing like feeling useless in a fight.

"She's there. Topetine. She's arrived," Jade said.

"Get Sara out of here!" Kevin shouted, firing another round of bullets in the direction of the shadows.

Jade wrapped an arm around me as the demon angel shifted and took a dive in our direction.

A flash filled my vision as another screech sounded against my ear and a searing pain clipped at my shoulder. In the blinding light, one thing was certain—I was out in the open and no longer under the protection that guarded me.

2

I fell with Jade onto the marbled floor in the foyer of a room large enough to launch a battle. Cathedral ceilings with ornately carved beams stared back at me.

"You okay?" he asked.

"She looks pale," Topetine answered, her voice echoing nearby. I turned toward the sound. She had shifted back to her human form and was walking toward me.

"Better than ever," I replied to Jade.

"I'm going back to help the others."

I nodded. "Wait," I said, putting a hand on his arm. "Won't the dark angel track the same energy path you did to get here?"

"She could. But she's searching for your energy trail and it isn't detectable with that ring. I couldn't see it when I came through the same portal you did to get to this realm. If I had seen it, I would've run into C-05 seconds after you. She would have to search for my path, following Topetine. It should confuse her but not for long. I've got to get back."

"Go," Topetine said. "Sara's safe in this house."

I almost laughed. *House? Mansion, maybe. Palace, definitely.* I pushed myself to stand.

A woman draped in white was walking beside Topetine. An intricately woven, silver-colored seam traced the edge of her silken garment. She lowered herself into a curtsey and bowed her head. In her hands was a small wooden box, similar to the handful I'd collected over the years and equally elaborate in carved detail.

My gaze drifted around the room. Unlike numerous historical pictures that had reflected so much of Egypt in gold, there were only a few statues with anything resembling the precious metal. The spacious area was, for the most part, vacant of anything flashy such as jeweled trinkets or collections that might have revealed an overabundance of wealth. This, coupled with the unexpected weather and landscape, had me second-guessing that I'd traveled to Egypt, even if it was from another time.

"This is Amun," Topetine said, redirecting my attention. "She may choose to speak in the native Coptic language or in English."

I smiled and nodded once to her. "Egyptian is not a language I've learned to speak."

"And yet, you would understand her perfectly well. Your spirit, leading you through this mission, knows no language barriers in the realms we travel."

"That may be so, but I can't possibly imagine how we would communicate otherwise."

"Welcome. Your arrival has been expected." The woman of medium stature and sleek black hair stood and met my gaze. A sign of strength. "May I?" She reached toward my arm.

Blood was trailing to the elbow and dripping on the floor. "Oh." I cupped a hand beneath it, reminded of the gash where the dark angel had apparently made contact. "Sorry." The shirt had been ripped at the back, evidence of an attempt to grasp fallen short.

Amun shook her head, dismissing the apology. "Not at all. This way, please." She led me to a wicker-type chair, which seemed so out of place given the opulence of the room.

"Amun has a similar gift as Juno and Matt to see coming events." Topetine turned her attention to the woman. "Will the wound require additional care?"

A whisper of air and a mist wound its way around the upper part of my arm, held, and disappeared, taking with it the residual blood from around the wound. "No," she answered, pausing. "I can attend to this. It's not been infected by the demon."

From the box, Amun pulled a long, thin needle. "Not to worry," she said. Her eyes met mine. "Closing the wound will not be painful."

"It couldn't possibly hurt more than when I received it." I smiled at her kindness and watched as the needle pulled the skin together with transparent thread and without the guidance of her fingers. The magic in the realms we visited still left me in awe. She was right. There was no pain and the job was finished in seconds.

As Amun tied off the ends of a long strip of clean white cloth, Kevin and the rest of the team poured through the entrance.

I jumped up, quickly looking for injury.

"They're okay," Jade said, huffing deep breaths in and out. "Damned evil chased the vehicle. But didn't try for another grab. The firepower was too much."

"Thank you." I turned my attention to Matt and Juno. "What are those bullets made of? I've never heard of a gun that could kill the shadows."

"Won't work on the dark angel, except to piss her off," Juno said. "Leahnan had the weapons ready for us before we left New York. The bullets were constructed by the elves. They contain an energy to alter the ions that make up the shadows' composition."

"Without the vehicle, it might have been a lot worse," Matt added.

"Like I told Sara"—C-05 flicked a glance in my direction and back to Matt—"I'm here to help."

"That has yet to be determined," Juno said. "The vehicle was convenient." He unloaded the pack and weapon he carried from his shoulder and set them beside Matt's gear. Aria leaned against the wall close to Matt, while Elise holstered her gun.

"The only way to be sure of your intent," Jade said, "is to confirm it with Eldor."

The leader of the elves held a seat on the Alliance, and was actively defending Ardan against Tarsamon's forces. Kevin and Jade trusted his word above anyone else's as one of only a handful of aides to us.

"Are you sure we're safe here?" Kevin asked, stepping closer to where Topetine and I stood. He slipped the gun he carried off his shoulder and handed it to Matt.

"Quite sure. This home, or as some might refer to it, palace"—the corners of her lips lifted—"is protected by a spell from the goddess Norul, keeper of the underworld."

Keeper of what?

"It's why you've been able to rest since arriving. Our energy is entirely invisible. Step outside that door, and I cannot guarantee the same assurance. There is an alarm, however, set at about one hundred fifty yards beyond the perimeter of the property, as additional protection."

My eyes drifted back to C-05. And before I realized it, I was already in motion toward him.

"Sara?"

"*Here to help?*" My blood boiled again at the recollection of who had immobilized me. I pulled back my arm and hurled a solid right hook at C-05's chin.

"Never touch me with any weapon. Got it? You call making me vulnerable, leaving me open to the shadows looking for me, unable to defend myself *help*?" I shook out my hand.

C-05 rubbed the spot on his chin with two fingers and nodded slightly before looking at the small smear of blood on them, where my ring had evidently cut into his skin. A wound to match the one Kevin had left at his lip. "You didn't know they were looking for you when you stepped from that portal."

My eyes narrowed. "I shouldn't have to tell you I'm a person to be reasoned with, not to be controlled, and never with a weapon."

"Fair enough."

Silence filled the space as I considered whether the boiling point was going to roll over the edge again. Likely not, having expelled my frustration into his chin. It wasn't like me to hit anyone. But C-05 had too many times put me and my team at risk, inciting such a well-deserved reaction on more than one occasion. I could feel the silent support of the action from my team. The satisfaction contained in that single connection was long overdue.

A touch at my arm caused the rage to fade. Kevin had a few otherworldly gifts. Unique to him was the ability to heal. He also had speed on his side and, like me, the ability to feel what others felt. To what degree he could heal, I wasn't sure, or if he could alter such feelings. Possibly either Juno or Matt, with their ability to manipulate emotions, might have had a hand in it, too. I couldn't tell who initiated the change in mood and it suddenly didn't matter. As if the anger was a single wave on the ocean, it passed on, met and conquered.

"And you." Kevin cupped his hands around my face as though we were alone. I heard the shuffle of bags and soft spoken words from where Juno had been unloading his gear beside Elise. "How are you?" His eyes pierced me with a stare, assessing what he could feel from me. He slid his fingers over my shoulder, just above the bandage.

"I'm okay. It's just a scrape," I said, glancing at the area. "A deep scrape. Nothing serious."

His hand moved up the side of my face and he swiped a long, smooth thumb over my forehead, kissing the spot and putting his arms around me in a protective hug.

His deep sigh of relief would have gone unnoticed had it not fallen just above my ear. *Thank God you're safe.*

It was his thought that had me feeling grateful for the same. While I worried little for a man who'd earned the title "Last Great Warrior," I was no less in tune to the fact that the dark angel wanted me, and would use or hurt anyone I cared for to get to her target.

"You are well?" I asked Kevin.

"Yes." He eased back. His pants still held the smudges from wrestling on the ground.

"If you'll follow me," Amun said, "I'll direct you to the Chamber of Tombs and on to your quarters, where you'll find some comfort and a change of clothing."

Tombs?

We walked past the statues to a set of stairs that went beneath the floor, through a group of three corridors before arriving in a room constructed of solid block. Against the walls were stacks of gold bricks, cloth bags of what looked like coins, and more statues.

"This is the chamber you mentioned?" I noticed nothing resembling a tomb in the vicinity. "What are the stacks of gold for?"

"Gold is reserved for the afterlife," Amun replied. "For royalty, like yourself." She lowered her head.

"Royalty?"

"Pardon me. This is the passage into the next realm."

"What passage?" I asked.

"This room opens a doorway that will lead you to your quest for the key."

I looked at the blank wall, feeling the frustration of riddles from another journey settling in. Knowing the answers would be provided didn't ease the irritation. It was the earlier comment that held my interest above the mystery of the Chamber. "You said royalty?"

"Of course." She lowered her head again.

"I'm a doctor." Or I had been a doctor of psychiatry before I had abandoned a passion to help ease the pain of others for a mission to save the world. "Not royalty. Please, there is no need for any formality."

The woman lifted her head, looked to Topetine and then to the others.

"Looks like our secret is out," Elise said.

"What secret?"

"Go ahead," Topetine said to Amun. "It's okay to explain. Sara isn't familiar with all the aspects of her past."

It's true that when I'd started the quest, I'd learned several facets of the mission including past lives that had been hidden from me, primarily those having to do with Kevin and other missions I'd served. While the Soltari had given me back some of my memory—how to fight, where I'd learned the skill, even some of the previous battles I'd been engaged in with the team—I'd noticed that several pieces of my supposed long existence were still void from memory. The one relating to royalty was apparently one of them and obviously deemed unnecessary to my current task of finding the keys.

"It is not for me to speak in such a manner to a queen," Amun said, further adding to my surprise.

"Queen?" A tiny laugh burst from my lips. "I assure you, you're quite welcome to speak in such a manner," I added in all seriousness. "Queen of what?"

Her eyes shifted from me to Elise, Topetine, and Kevin to be certain. At a single nod from Kevin, the woman bowed again.

"Please. No formality is necessary," I repeated.

"All of it?" Amun asked, glancing at Topetine.

"It's okay, yes."

With a deep sigh, Amun said, "You all are royalty in Egypt. That's because you will eventually return to residing with the Enlightened Ones."

"What does she mean, Enlightened Ones? She means Ardan, right? Or does she mean with Leahnan and the Inner Society?"

"For crying out loud," Aria said, impatience getting the best of her. She started to open her mouth to say more but snapped it shut at Matt's hand on her shoulder.

"It's not for us to remind her," he said.

"We're on the same side, right?" I asked. "I put all of my trust in you. Like you, I left everything I had to follow this quest through to the end. You've been by my side. So?"

"I don't care," Aria said. "I don't care if we aren't supposed to tell you anything because it might interfere. This secret we've been carrying is that we, all of us except Jade and his men, are part of the Soltari. We've assumed identities, roles in the realms we fight in. We allowed certain rules to be implemented prior to our arrival on Earth that were meant to ensure our safety. As you know, your memory and the blocking of it was part of a decision by the Soltari, enforced by the Alliance. We chose this quest as a final mission to rebuild a broken energy in Ardan because it, too, had been corrupted, possibly infiltrated by evil. We didn't know for certain or to what extent until Tarsamon brought his forces across the boundary that had once separated him from the rest of Ardan."

"So the evil does run deeper..." My thoughts trailed off. "Kevin," I said. "You once told me you'd never met with the Soltari."

"It's the only white lie I've ever told you, to keep the promise I'd sworn to uphold to never share our past with you. If I didn't, the remaining force that is the Soltari would never have let me stand beside you on this mission."

There was a long pause. "How long were you planning to keep this secret?" My eyes scanned each of their faces.

"If you fulfilled the quest and recovered all three keys, we were to take it to our grave in this life," Aria said. "There was no need to share it. Does it really change anything that you know your spirit is an extension of the entity, the Soltari?"

I suppose it didn't. There was one issue that needed tending to, however. Jade had recently discovered the Alliance had been infiltrated by evil. Key players had been identified in a conspiracy to disrupt the governing order and weaken it, giving more power to the darker forces in Ardan and with the intent to eventually dismantle it completely.

"And Tarsamon?" I asked.

"Discovered a weak point in the order. When we learned Tarsamon planned to move to Earth to grow his forces and absorb the energy of humanity, the loyal Soltari entities, like us, decided it was time to recover the keys hidden thousands of years ago. It's only with Jade's recent confirmation the Alliance is compromised that we suspect the possibility the Soltari is, as well. We have to clean house and really well."

"If I may." The tiny voice of Amun lifted, barely audible in the break of Aria's resounding strength. "The final key is the acceptance of all things."

"Well, if anyone thinks I'm accepting infiltration, especially after the work we've done, someone's got another think coming," I said.

"Damn straight," Elise shot back.

"With all due respect, there seems to be some confusion. The key of acceptance can restore the current imbalance to a peaceful state. That is its power."

"That means it can restore peace to Ardan as well as to Earth," I said. Amun nodded. "Okay. But this"—I splayed my palms—"the Chamber of Tombs. What's our purpose here?"

"To pass through to the Duat. The underworld. This room leads beyond the protection of the palace into the realm where you'll find the key."

Flashes of blood, skulls and spirits raced through my head from our last quest for the second key.

"Generally, the Egyptian belief is that you must meet with the approval of a series of gods," Topetine said before I could object.

"Aside from the fact that it sounds like Greek mythology, there is no way—"

"Not exactly," Mac said. "The belief is that to make it to the afterlife, ye'd need to pass through a series of gates, guarded by a god at each one, seekin' approval for your soul and actions in life."

The rolling of his *r*'s in that Scottish accent was almost enough to distract me from his description of a world I wanted no part of. Almost. I'd entered Topetine's underworld in the Mayan jungle and I had no intention of doing the same again. No way.

"The underworld is where the key is, Sara."

"Another world of the dead," I said.

"This is not like the Mayan legacy." Topetine turned to Amun. "Has the *Book of the Dead* been collected?"

I scrubbed a hand over my face.

"Only the guardian of the key can hold the book," Amun replied. A stare from Topetine granted a *yes* reply.

"Where can we find the guardian?" I asked.

"The book is a guide that allows passage through the underworld and yes, the guardian holds it," Topetine said. "Since he's already come for it, we're ready to locate the key. But we would need for him to contact us." She looked at Amun.

"He's aware you're here," she said.

"Maybe there's time to clean up," I said, pulling at the rag that was my shirt and seeing that one side of my pants was covered in dirt.

I'd already entered the Duat when I'd fallen into the foyer and the spacious palace of light. Underworld or not, this last part of the mission had to be completed. *Suck it up. Swallow what you can and keep moving.* The thought of more treacherous hidden caverns like those

I'd left in the Central American jungle only a couple of days before coming to Egypt was further exhausting.

"The quest for the third key is nothing like the one you faced in the Mayan jungle," Topetine said.

"Of course not. There's sand instead." I moved some of the granules beneath the tip of my boot. My short fuse over C-05, the mild throbbing wound on my arm, tattered clothing, and now hunger were grating on my nerves.

"Patience, my dear. Access is already granted to you through Leahnan."

"The algorithms," Kevin said, reminding me of the formulas I'd received, studied, and locked into memory by way of the orb that Leahnan kept in a room secured like Fort Knox. The layers of code were meant to unlock many parts of this phase of the mission, as needed, or so I'd been told. What was never explained was how or where that need would apply. It was damned frustrating to feel as though I was searching for an opening in the dark. More importantly, it was why I needed to connect with the guardian, as the only one who could shed light on the path to the third and final key.

3

“She shouldn't be in hiding. She should still be imprisoned in the darkest dungeon in Ardan!” Tarsamon roared. His thoughts had swirled around Sara and her team after learning that she'd obtained the second of three powerful keys that would end his possession of Earth. “Weak. That's how she arrived on Earth,” he growled. “How could she have slipped beyond my grasp?”

“You waited too long to get to her,” the voice of the dark angel rasped. “And”—she paused, casting her gaze back to him—“you trusted someone who came from the light. The man who calls himself C-05. Spirits who originate from the light will always return once exposed to the full force of darkness, unless they are weak. Only then can you claim them as your obedient servants.” She fanned her wings out in a stretch that spanned from one wall to the other, then folded them together as she crossed her arms. “Those who are strong remember the power the light holds. The weak souls never considered such strength in the first place, mulling around day to day with limited vision.” She walked in a circle and lifted her eyes to him.

“You also made the grave mistake of exercising patience. While you set your sights on growing your forces on Earth, Sara learned all that she needed to become the strong human who could fulfill the task that you assumed she was too weak, as an ordinary human, to ever fulfill.”

"There was time! I arrived on Earth ahead of her. I was never weakened by the limitations found in a physical world, like those she was exposed to."

"You thought that would stop her?" She laughed and let out a deep sigh as her lips returned to all seriousness. "She was born into her role to rescue Earth and given extraordinary abilities to survive challenges that world would present. You lost sight of her. Patience is used when there is time to stalk prey. With Sara's team and the Soltari aiding her, helping her to grow stronger, you never had the luxury of time. You should have taken her down when she went into that hospital after the accident that introduced her to her mission and her protector, the Last Great Warrior."

A low growl erupted deep in Tarsamon's chest. He understood full well the angel couldn't lie, even if she carried as much evil as he. Truth was a weapon, an honest weapon with the potential to be lethal if the receiver was unable or unwilling to face it. Sara was the truth he had to stare eye to eye with or she would end everything he had worked carefully to build. From banishment to the darkest corner of Ardan to having a worthy army of demons and shadows that could consume the entire population of Earth. He had organized that negative, dark energy to grow a force more powerful than the Soltari itself. To do so had taken a great deal of time and effort, an effort that one woman, one *human*, would not put an end to.

"She's there, in Egypt," the dark angel continued. "She waits under cover of a protective force, I suspect from the elves."

"How can you be sure she's there?"

"Her team is there. They would not have arrived without her."

"They may be trying to throw you off."

"Maybe, but unlikely. So far, I've been able to penetrate every shield the elves have created. Her life energy is faint but detectable. It's masked by a strong force. She's there."

"If you found her, why didn't you kill all of her team? The lives of those who lead or protect her are of no significance."

"And take the chance of missing your primary target? The elves, the Soltari, they'd risk providing their best weapons for the precious keys. Without forces helping her, she would be able to hide much easier. Their presence helps lead me, or anyone else searching, directly to her."

Tarsamon growled as he crossed his arms and burned a path from one side of the room to the other, pacing. Sara was to him like a mouse he couldn't catch. Left to her own devices, she'd destroy everything he'd created. "I need this consumption of life on Earth to be finished. Once it is, the Soltari will never be able to claim it back. They'll never be able to use it as a place of growth and development of the souls that inhabit it."

"That's where patience comes into play. I'll get to the one named Sara. There is always a way in."

"You must get to her before the last key is released. She's untouchable after that."

"Of course, my lord." The dark angel walked to the open window that looked out across the landscape to what was once a lush forest. Nothing more than decayed brittle remnants where thorns and deadly creatures found solace without light remained. A skeleton of what was once flawless beauty. "You must never trust a soul." Her piercing electric-blue eyes, keen to every movement, scanned below before disappearing in a single thrust into the mixed hues of gray sky.

Tarsamon watched her form glide across the landscape in graceful flight, until she was no longer visible.

A string of thoughts played like a scratched record over and over—the disdain and deprecation from the immortals he'd undergone after banishment from Ardan, and all because he'd disagreed too often with the Alliance. So what if the governing order was handing down a directive from the Soltari? He had earned the right to disagree, after years of fighting for the Soltari himself and losing more than he'd ever gained. His disagreement was so often that the Soltari determined it was he who had been responsible for turning the course of the missions and setting the balance of good and evil off-kilter.

The Alliance never saw the bigger picture, never thought about how the rules they set forth would affect the immortals over time. He realized quickly they didn't care, either. What had been the purpose of the Alliance, anyhow, if they were just going to pass along an order? He was so much more than a delivery boy. He had ideas, ways to make lives better and improvements arrive faster. But there was never room for individual thought. He'd been accused and found guilty of conspiring against the entity and had been banished. They'd pay for that mistake. *Let's see how they handle being overcome by the very evil they try to keep at bay.* What a fitting punishment for an entity existing to teach and gather knowledge through humans and their experience, while trying to keep the balance between light and darkness. As if the two could ever have coexisted.

He couldn't afford another miss when it came to catching and holding Sara Forrester. The thought of failure sent a strong, sickening chill through him. As gifted as the dark angel was at penetrating the power of the keys, it was he who had to stop Sara. The task was his to face, his to conquer. He'd show the Soltari he was not a force that could be overcome, ever again. And, there was still one sure way he could reach her, one way the Soltari had not yet considered.

4

I let out a breath to the ceiling, tilted my head back into a cushion, and closed my eyes. The weight of the responsibility I carried, to see the people of Earth free of Tarsamon's sweeping darkness, settled over my shoulders again. If we didn't succeed, not only would we lose Earth but the eternal bonds between Kevin and me and those the members of my team shared, too. It was a punishment for failure, and another point of contention I had with the Soltari. The first being the decision to withhold my memories. I wasn't sure, however, if that had been decided by the Alliance, the Soltari, or both. Either way, the thorn in my side would soon be relieved for good once I had the last key. With the recent visit to see Leahnan and the Inner Society, the heaviness had been lifted, but only for a short while. Now, in the stillness, there was time to contemplate what might come, what might be waiting.

Amun had shown us a group of rooms to settle into before we were to be introduced to the guardian of the last key. The sun had fallen low in the sky by the time I'd finished a most welcome shower to rinse off the first layer of grime, followed by dinner consisting of red lentil soup and bread. Two sets of clothing had been mysteriously placed in the closet. I left the heavier formfitting pants and shirt, along with a hooded, long coat and opted for the more comfortable lounge type, assuming we weren't going to be traveling in the dark after our meal. I was grateful for the few jokes Juno had shared to lighten the burden for all of us while we ate. Kevin, too, had laughed and relaxed. A rare occurrence since the start of our quest. I smiled again at the memory.

As most of us sat in the cushioned comfort of a modern-style sofa, the firelight and a potent liquor hypnotizing me to the movement of flames, I listened to the pure strength and conviction in the words spoken by Topetine. How could she be so confident? A few of the others, including Kevin, had gone off to scout the area in search of potential dangers. Those who remained easily settled into the same certainty we'd be successful. How could they be so sure? Self-doubt could threaten the mission if I didn't reel it in. It also served another purpose—keeping me at the ready should an unexpected evil present itself. For that reason, I'd rather have self-doubt than risk overconfidence and be caught off guard.

"With the algorithms you have been given, Sara, things will move faster than they did for the last two keys," Topetine said, distracting my thought. "There will be no need to search to solve riddles as you might have in the past."

"They were tests of strength." Faith, trust, and the like. I'd just settled into a relaxed and centered state of mind. I lifted my head and peeked under my eyelids, resisting the urge to open them and fully focus.

"Your strength is solid. I think even you can say with some conviction that your faith in more than what you've known on Earth is resolute."

I nodded my silent agreement, swallowed another sip, and continued listening. The sound of Topetine's voice trailed as my thoughts slid into reflection of my so-called faith.

Prior to obtaining the second key, I wasn't sure I had faith in much more than the average person. I went about life, before this mission, as a philanthropist from an adoptive family. A very wealthy family with not only the financial means but an ambitious desire to give back to those in need. Mary Ann Forrester, my adoptive mother, but as close as any caring biological mother could be, hosted numerous charity functions and extravagant dinners by way of the Forrester Foundation, as tools for the cause. Would I ever see that life again? Ordinary existence was so far away, with the infiltration Tarsamon had already brought to the humans, slipping shadows into their forms to feed off the negativity that had passed between them, opening the door to his eventual take-over. We, all of us assigned to the mission, would stop the progress if we weren't too late. The only thing I could trust was what had set me on this path, the blade and ring the skillful elves had provided and the truth of what Aria, Matt, Kevin, and the others already knew about our responsibilities beyond this world in Ardan. Each one of them had always been beside me, even if I didn't realize it in the beginning. That was another point of irritation I carried about the details of my mission. The loss of certain memories that might have provided skillful knowledge. Would they end up hindering the quest?

"Sara. Did you hear me?" Topetine said.

I opened my eyes and shook my head. "Sorry, something about teaming with entities in the afterlife."

Topetine glanced to Mac, her partner on the quest and the guardian of the first key.

"I said, the dark angel can find evil in the afterlife and join with those souls."

I nodded again.

"Are you tired?" she asked. "Maybe you should go rest. You must be focused as we go forward."

"I know." I ran a hand through my hair and tucked it behind an ear. "It's just that, at this point, I can't help but expect the worst. The stakes are too high. Anything you say is likely not going to surprise me."

"It's not meant to, my dear. But as we are here to guide and defend you, understand the guardian of the last key will need to offer you protection unlike anything any of us can."

"If the danger is that much more imminent, let's hope he does." I lifted my drink for another sip, but instead set it down. "If a spirit, good or evil, can join with another as you say, I wonder, can it split its energy, too?"

"It's been known to, in the underworld, that is. It's a realm that operates by a different set of rules."

"Figures. Still, evil is evil. Should it get in my way, my aim to kill will remain steadfast whether it joins or splits its energy. I suppose, in that case, the question wouldn't matter."

Each of us carried a unique skill set of otherworldly abilities in addition to being avid fighters. All the members of the team traveling with me were masters of energy of all sorts. Kevin's skills were similar to mine, but he also possessed magnificent speed, as did Matt. Aria and Elise could manipulate the forces of nature and, in essence, create distraction as a form of protection. Mac, besides his strength and lovely Scottish accent, was also an expert in broadsword. Each guardian had been taught every last detail of the individual key they were to protect, including its power, where it could be found, and the expectation to follow it through to the end of the quest. To my knowledge, Topetine, guardian of key number two, possessed only the ability to shift into the stealthier and stronger jaguar, masked behind her petite, midforties frame. Jade was by far the best at tracking energy. And, as I'd recently learned, had shape-shifting down to an art, at least enough to fool the Alliance by copying the energy of a member so that he could not be detected. He was direct, aggressive, and fearless in the presence of any demon or a number of them. I'd come to really like those features about him, despite the rough start we'd had getting to know each other. And yet, with all the extra protection around me, I still doubted it would be enough to deter Tarsamon's forces at this stage, being so close to the final key.

If Topetine was concerned about the level of that protection, it should make me at least a little nervous. I'd been told by more than one member of my team that my protection was not for me to worry over and settled on not giving it too much thought, preferring instead to put my trust in them.

"When can we meet this guardian and get started?" I asked.

"I'm not sure when, exactly, but tomorrow we will need to leave."

It was an odd reply. So far, this person was as much a mystery as the perfectly sized clothing hanging in the closet of my room.

"We can't leave without him."

"We won't. I expect him to be in contact with us soon."

"I'm going to sleep off the rest of this night. Wake me sooner if necessary."

She nodded as I stood and headed for the room that was to be Kevin's and mine.

As I entered the pitch-dark space, the small but adequately sized room lit as though a thousand tiny lights had come to life, flickering a dim glow. Multiple candles of all sizes were suspended in midair from all four corners of the room. I stepped farther inside.

Always a wonder, these locations we travel to.

"Does it please you?'

I whipped around at the sound of an unfamiliar voice to find the nearly invisible image of a person in mist-like form.

"What does it matter?" I replied. Traveling this far down the road on the mission, I'd become too comfortable with the unexpected. And since I detected no intended offense from the apparition, I remained calm.

"So feisty. I'd almost forgotten."

"Who are you?"

"My apologies if I'm intruding in your space. I'm known by many in Egypt as Horus. The Eye of Udjat? Sometimes Wadjet."

Horus? Eye of Horus?

I watched as his shape changed from that of a human to a bird, then to the familiar Egyptian symbol of the eye and back again.

"That means you're an Egyptian god, if I'm correct."

"I can appear as many things. But in Egypt, a god of the sky is the most specific. I've carried you on my currents when you have shifted into a hawk."

"Yes." I paused. "Well, that's not a change I like to engage in, though I do recognize the value of it."

"Regardless. We've known each other for eternity."

Another memory I have yet to recall?

"You can be sure of it," he added.

Telepathic, too.

"I am an extension of what you know as the Soltari."

"I see. That explains your appearance, transparent as it is."

In Ardan, the spirit entity, if called upon, came together as a collective voice but appeared as several misty-figured faces, suspended in air, causing me to question how it was that he'd arrived alone.

I could recall only fragments of a prior lifetime, possibly two, after meeting with the entity in Ardan that felt like ages ago. After learning of the infiltration of the Alliance and the potential compromise of the Soltari, I started to believe that the effort to recover such memories might have been clipped for another self-serving pretext. All of the other members of my team had perfect recall. *I wonder if this spirit has the ability to restore the vacancies of memory?*

"Is that what you desire most?" he asked, hearing my thought. I'd become accustomed to the quite common occurrence in the presence of intellectuals with ethereal abilities. "I do see the problem it poses for you," he added. "Missing certain connections and the like."

Desire most. I considered the notion carefully. What I desired most was to recover all three keys, hold all the cards, and release the humans from Tarsamon's darkness to claim eternity for me and my team. The memories of the love I'd shared, all battles I'd fought, and connections with my team from thousands of years ago were indeed strongly desired.

"Not that I'm yearning for a taste of sentimental, but yes," I replied. "In fact, it's at the top of my list of things I'd like to have."

He laughed. "Sentimental is not a word I would have chosen to describe you. Not ever." The misty figure slipped to the other side of the room, making me wish I had stopped at two instead of almost three drinks of the potent liquor after dinner. I'd sipped at the one-ounce glass slowly, but Horus's movement winding between objects indicated the care I'd taken not to down a couple of drinks hadn't mattered. I felt my stomach flip over once in protest before settling.

"As the third guardian, I'll lead you beyond the Chamber of Tombs and to the key's location. All you need to do is remember that every code you carry is a key all its own. You hold all that is needed with the algorithms, even if you don't fully know that you do. The answer is within."

"I can't imagine what that means with regard to where I'll use it. But I do trust you if you say it's so." What other alternative was there? "What about the *Book of the Dead*?"

"A mere"—he paused—"distraction. You'll not need the book, unless you plan to travel without the codes you possess. Even then, it would take far too long to decipher where and when to use such information. Access through the gates is buried deep in the text and stories of the underworld gods. What may surprise you most is that you helped create the codes you now carry."

Surprise didn't scratch the surface. I nodded, half in agreement and half in disbelief. Until every memory was returned, I'd have to go along with whatever came my way. In the end, what was said didn't matter, not until I was faced with a specific challenge to relate the information to. There was simply no way to prepare for what might lie ahead.

It suddenly occurred to me in trusting this transparent image how much I'd changed since meeting Kevin and setting out on this journey. I'd had no trust in anyone, much less anything intangible, and certainly nothing that didn't prove itself first in order to earn that trust. I was nodding to a ghost, and only because I'd seen the impossible, traveled through realms to distant places, and been held captive and implanted with evil thoughts and illness from a demon I didn't initially remember from long ago. None of that could've been explained before experiencing it, never mind believed. What this figure said could be trusted as though the sun rising depended on it. Because it did. I'd seen an example of it upon arriving to meet with the Inner Society. New York had been thrown into a perpetual state of night, as dark a place in the middle of the day as midnight with the effect Tarsamon had imposed upon it. I had no reason to doubt the many other cities that existed in the same state of consumption and darkness.

"We'll leave upon sunrise, after coffee. Or in your case, tea." I smiled at that. "Pleasure to see you again, Arwyn. You should take some rest while I meet with the others."

"Wait. Why the name Horus? Why did you choose that if you're from the Soltari? They don't have names."

"The eye symbolizes divinity and the 'I Am' of higher consciousness. But you know this."

"Do I?" *Of course I do. One day I'll know how, just not today.* And with that, I was left alone. *God damn it.* I turned in a full circle to be sure I was alone. *Eye of Udjat. What was the myth again? Was it a myth at all?*

"Hmm," I said. *Think it has something to do with protection, health maybe. The eye was lost, right? Isn't that how the story went?* "Ah, hell, I don't know." Who could care about such a menial fact, or fiction?

I took a few minutes to look around the room. A comfortable enough bed peeked out from a room at the end of a short hall. The glowing candles still hung, but much dimmer than when I'd first entered. Perhaps my eyes had adjusted to accommodate the change in lighting. Whatever the case, I'd put my trust in what guided me, because there was simply more knowledge that existed than I possessed, or was aware that I possessed.

I went to a small, rectangular table to where a slim, delicate pot covered in painted flowers rested. The scent of jasmine steam lifted to my senses and created instant calm as I poured a perfect cup of tea. The fragrant aroma carried with it the promise of a clear head on the warm, smooth taste that slipped past my lips and down my throat. *Wish I had my laptop.* I might research the so-called myth. Tea and my laptop were an inseparable pair at my home in New York, where I could spend a couple hours that felt like minutes researching anything from a questionable scientific theory to a mundane fact, or myth, as I had when this whole quest began. What I wouldn't give for a little internet shopping, too.

Holding my cup, I turned at hearing a slight sound. Beside the pot, where nothing had been before, now rested a small electronic device that looked similar to my iPad, but wasn't. *Who's listening to my thoughts?* The strong desire to ask if Horus was still here swept over me, but I refrained and instead picked up the tablet and folded my leg under me as I curled into an oversized upholstered chair. The screen lit up with a touch. No password or annoying message denying me access. A search window popped up. I typed in "Eye of" and the entire screen lit with information. "Gouging of the eye" and "protection in the afterlife" leaped off the screen. "Wadjet" was another name associated with Horus, referring to "green" and "risen one."

I stopped reading. Was I up for a lesson in Egyptian mythology? Not particularly. None of what I'd scanned mentioned apparitions or an immortal life and a powerful governing entity. I let out a breath and took another sip of tea. *Fade to black.* Before I could press the power button, the screen went dark. I shook my head. How much of my thoughts were really mine? How far could those thoughts reach? Could I wish for the darkness to retreat, to abandon this world and allow me to finish this quest?

The answers lie within.

While I'd heard the thought, it damn sure wasn't mine. *Horus.* I tapped the screen with a finger. "What answers," I typed, "lie within?" Information began filling the screen:

"Algorithms unlock doors, passages to energy. Keys you carry.

Rules of the realm exist and must be adhered to by all."

"What rules?" I waited for a reply. "Which realm? And don't give me a riddle. Or I swear this device will change shape into a hundred thousand tiny pieces."

"The realm of the City of Souls (ref. Advanced Egypt).

"Spirits may coexist with the flesh, so long as they do not interfere with their path.

"Darkness cares not for the path the key holder takes. It has but only one mission, to stop her.

"Evil is exempt from the Rules of Wishes, as a means of protection should the state of the realm be threatened by malevolence or dishonorable souls."

"Protection? You mean wishes cannot be made that involve darkness?"

"Yes."

"Even if it's to request their removal?"

A pause, and the word *yes* appeared.

"Might want to reconsider that one. Put another 'protection' in place."

On the other hand, if this realm had once had a problem with malevolence, a reason forbidding a wish involving darkness, a.k.a. evil, made sense. And so the magic wouldn't work. Damn shame, too. I was granted a generous few seconds to imagine what this mission might look like unencumbered by Tarsamon's forces before another message popped up.

"All spirits are granted the right of existence, so long as they do not infringe upon another."

"That's an impossible rule to live by. It's why I'm here, hiding in this house, protected by its magic. Evil and good cannot coexist."

"Soltari, Soltari, Soltari."

The Soltari's primary mission was to govern the balance of good and evil in the realms, following a rule of law. Apparently, *this* rule of law. But because that order had fallen under threat, the rule was essentially broken. At least I understood how this mess had happened. Again, information that could have helped earlier in the mission. Finding out details as I went along the quest was more than annoying; it was, at times, downright infuriating. Having a passion for what's right, for bringing about some good in the world was all that had driven me before discovering worlds I never believed existed. The span of knowledge I'd gained, the trust I'd had to give, and the willingness to set aside a once limited vision had come in a matter of a few short months. And yet, there was so much more to understand.

A window opened on the screen with items to browse and purchase, as if whomever I was speaking with was apologetic in some way and wanted a peace offering.

I flashed a smile. "Maybe another time."

The screen went black again, and I pushed it aside.

The effects of the potent after-dinner drink, times three weren't fading after a few sips of tea. I strolled down the small hallway and into the bedroom. All fluff and coziness in tame, muted colors of tan, black, and white greeted me. I set my cup on the nearby end table and considered sleep over a long, relaxing soak in the tub while I waited for Kevin. If I dared to go beneath the covers, I was sure to slip under the spell of dreams in seconds. Instead, standing against the side,

I stretched my arms out and fell forward into the down-filled bedding. It was a mistake, I thought, feeling the comfort of partial rest begin to consume.

The faint sound of light classical guitar lifted across the room, drawing my attention away from relaxation to wonder where the music had come from. As I was about to push off the bed, a hand on each shoulder ran a path along my arms in a gentle, slow stroke, and the press of a body against my backside prevented me from lifting up. I angled my head to see Kevin's face at my ear.

"Going somewhere?" he asked. The words tickled at my ear.

"Was considering a long soak in a bath." Had the lights dimmed even more?

I made another attempt to turn around, but the press at my back was a little firmer and his arms completely covered mine.

"Lovely thought. Mind waiting a moment?"

His face came closer to my lips, brushing my cheek. I angled a bit more and, through slanted eyes, met his parted lips to mine. A single soft kiss.

"Let me see you," I said.

"Not yet." His hands, which had been covering mine along with the weight of his body, lifted, and his fingers stroked the length of my arms to my shoulders and down my back, his legs and torso still holding me in place. "I like you like this."

"Vulnerable, I suppose?"

"Never. It'd be a foolish man's mistake to assume such a thing with you."

I flashed a smile. "Can't argue with that." I carefully lifted my foot, angling it back a bit, placed it on the outside of his ankle, and forcefully lifted my torso. My leg locked against his in a twist. And in a single, quick maneuver, sent him to his back on the bed with me leaning over him. I met his heated stare. The slightest hint of surprise and play skimmed over his face.

"I let you, you know," he said.

The corner of my mouth lifted. "I'm not so sure I believe you."

Another sensation rose above the playfulness, preventing my

ability to see past his expression and read his thoughts. The intensity of those eyes was holding me at bay from knowing everything.

"What have you done?" I smiled. He looked a little too much like a boy who had stolen something and was completely proud of himself for doing so.

"Not what I've done, but what I'm about to do."

"What do you mean?"

His hand extended to my back and gently pressed me close against him. His other hand slipped to the back of my head, his lips dangerously close again. "Darling, I don't know how to tell you this, but the guardian of the key is," he paused, "likely to come as a surprise."

That isn't exactly what I expected. How did I misread that signal?

I eased back. "Horus? I met him already."

"He's not... Wait... You have?"

"When did *you* have the chance?" I asked. "You were out looking around the premises, right?"

"That wasn't all I was doing."

My senses sharpened, trying to decipher what had just happened and why. All I could glean from him was that something very important and perhaps difficult needed to be said or done.

"I made a deal for us," he said, before I could ask.

"A deal. For us?

"I think you'll be pleased, or I hope so."

"What is it? Would you have me guess?"

A long pause passed between us before he finally answered. "No." His hand came from around my back and on his little finger was a ring.

A flood of emotions ran through me. Confusion at why he would produce such a token of affection now. Did he really seek to seal the bond between us in this life? Obviously. Fear swept over the confusion and, with it, the thought of saying yes with the chance of losing him to the evil lurking beyond these walls. I lifted myself off him to prevent him reading the fear surely plastered across my face, if he hadn't already heard the thoughts. *Could I handle such a devastating loss and still fulfill the mission? Am I ready to be only his again?*

He sat up and grasped my waist before I could get away, and reached for my left hand with his. My eyes were fixed on his gaze.

"Trust me. That's all I ask. And I know such a request means everything to you."

I glanced down at his hand for a closer look. It was the ring I'd seen in the window of the antique shop when we'd taken the trip to Europe not so long ago. A mere couple of months. Diamonds sparkled in a frame around an emerald-cut center stone. But how? How could it be the same ring? We'd never discussed it, never talked of...

"It's yours. Lady Mara held it for me in her shop until the time was right. Again."

Lady Mara was another immortal like us. Except, instead of fighting alongside us, she created special weapons under the guise of an antique shop owner. Her blades, guns, throwing stars, and the like were unique because they were crafted using the energy or DNA of the person she was creating the weapon for. The final product was essentially an extension of the person it belonged to. The ring I wore, one of them, was one example, and blended with my energy to hide me for a limited time from the dark forces that hunted me.

"Again," I said, repeating his last word.

How many times had he asked me to marry him in the countless millennia that I'd known him? I supposed as many lifetimes that we had shared together. This one, though, was different. I never intended to get married, and he knew that when I had spotted that ring on our outing. Back then, any discussion of where each of us stood on the matter of marriage had been deflected by the ancient skeletonized watch beside the ring that we had ended up talking about. But so much had happened since that afternoon stroll past Lady Mara's shop, the subject had never come up again and I'd never given the ring another thought.

"Well?" he said, bringing me back to the little matter in hand. "I'm fascinated when I make you speechless, but I'm afraid this time I'm going to have to press for your answer."

I opened my mouth and closed it, then let out a breath. "If this is the same ring I saw in Lady Mara's shop, and it's been mine before, why don't I remember it?"

"It is the same one. The gaps of memory you still have are part of the block the Soltari requested to be put in place." He smiled and stood, still holding me. "If you accept it, you accept all that comes with it."

"All that comes with it? That was the deal?"

"Yes. The decision has been left for you to make."

"May I ask who you made this deal with?"

"Let's just say Horus and I have spoken."

"I see." I quickly put two and two together. "This is not only a proposal but also a chance to restore the gaps of memory?" My gaze fell away from his intense stare that said yes.

His finger traced along my jawline, lifting my chin gently, and my attention back to him. The intensity in his eyes was as fiery as the moment he'd shared who he was to me on this quest. "I love you, in this life and any other. Forever. Will you do me the honor of joining with me for another adventure and live the remainder of it as my lovely wife?"

Never, never, never will I be married. It was a phrase I had lived by and intended to keep. I didn't need complications, ever. That was my motto. Besides, we weren't finished with the dangerous nature of this mission. There was too much at stake, too much at risk should I care…as much…as I do. The words I'd lived by slowed to a crawl, as I became all too aware that the foundation I'd built my life upon had just crumbled in seconds.

"Without a doubt, yes."

There they were. The words I'd sworn never to utter.

I'd said what I felt in my heart, not in my head, and it wouldn't be undone. Would I pay a price to the Soltari for it? Maybe. I didn't care. I'd come too far in this mission, being asked to trust the unknown, as a human, that is. The questionable draw to Kevin before I became aware of his role, the pull to follow this mission, despite what didn't make sense to my eyes—shadows having a wingspan extending across a large ceiling, demons with eyes that changed color with their mood, and angels that were anything but good, not to mention the numerous spells and magic along the way, had once been impossible to conceive as real.

All that aside, that reply was the most important one I had ever given, because when it left my lips, it felt more right than anything else on this quest or in my life prior. What those three letters meant was that I could stand against my fear of the danger that surrounded anyone I cared for, against Tarsamon, and the Soltari. I was ready to face a commitment. I just never knew the key to saying yes to a deeply hidden desire was the release of that fear.

I carefully extended my left hand toward the ring Kevin now held. A spark of electricity moved over its surface and reached for my finger, touching it ever so slightly. The magic contained in that little stone did more than twinkle at me, it teased me to hold it, to embrace its power and the remaining memories of us that had been withheld from me in this life. This ring held the recollection of the lives I'd led. Could a specific energy kept inside a stone restore such history? It could if Lady Mara, Master of Spells, had interwoven a magic to connect with my energy. Would knowing all that history be a burden, a worry for his life that would somehow interfere with the mission? I didn't think so. I'd fulfill my duty and obtain what I wanted for us, an eternity together, and not under the threat of an entity that punished. This man was bonded to me as much as I was to him. The knowledge of our history together should not be hidden from my view any longer. And what about the connection to the Soltari Aria had mentioned the team and I having? I'd finally have an answer to every last question.

"Sara," Kevin said.

"Arwyn. My spiritual name has always been Arwyn. And you, Cerys."

"Yes, my love."

His fingertips grazed the side of my cheek. "I've waited for this moment. I'd hoped you would say yes."

"But you were prepared for me to say no, too."

"Truth be told, I never allowed that scene to unfold in my mind."

I smiled. "I wouldn't have, either, if I felt as strongly as I feel from you now."

He slipped the ring onto my finger. The power it held sunk beneath my skin as its weight settled comfortably in place as though it had always been there. The sensation I felt at his every touch or presence raced up my left arm, across my shoulders, and filled my center. I closed my eyes and let that energy consume me in waves of warm tingles. The soft brush of his lips against mine, his hand gentle at the back of my head held me steady as he drove the kiss deeper. Another rush of warmth and tremors filled me as his other hand moved to my waist, causing me to lean into the touch.

A whisper of familiarity floated to my conscience. A scent I couldn't place lingered and left me with an odd sense of comfort. A flash of images raced across my closed eyelids. Could it really be that the memories were coming back? Had Horus, with Lady Mara's help, been able to grant my wish with a ring? Being part of the most powerful entity in the realms had its benefits.

The light sound of music drifted in the air around us, distracting the effort to identify the rush of sensory information flooding me.

I blinked open my eyes to meet Kevin's heated stare. "Are you doing that? Creating the music?"

A soft smile lifted from the corner of his lips. He sat on the bed and pulled me into his lap. "This world is advanced beyond that of Earth or even the familiar history we were taught of Egypt. The mere thought of what one desires can make it so."

"With the exception of getting rid of Tarsamon's dark forces."

"Yes." His eyes lowered to my lips and returned to my focused gaze. "I had a little help greasing the skids to give you your memories."

"Horus?"

He nodded. "He never agreed with the decision to block them."

"That *deal* you made. What did you have to give in return for me to remember everything?"

"A promise that nothing will interfere with you completing the mission."

"A promise? That's it?"

"Yes. It helped when I explained the level of compromise Jade found with the Alliance."

He shifted beneath me, drawing me closer. I caught the faintest hint of his masculine scent, instantly bringing back a memory of rolling over, tangled together in his sheets.

"If I may give you one word of caution," he said, slipping a section of hair behind my ear. "You must guard your thoughts carefully. The physical world of Earth moves slowly compared to other realms. It allows time for decisions and creation of plans that can't be afforded at this stage of the mission. We can't have evil discovering what worries you. It's why the last key was placed here, in this underworld, to help us get to it faster."

"How does that work for the evil that hunts us?"

He shook his head. "Not now. Plenty of time for that later. Right now, I want time with you, and only you. No talk of evil. No keys. Nothing but us." He placed a lingering kiss on my lips, followed by another, and leaned into me, his lips at my ear. The gentle press of strength against me sent a wave of urgency to feel all of him. "What do you desire?"

"I think you already know." I eased back and brought my lips to his, brushing the tip of my tongue across his lower lip, following with a soft, slow kiss as I wrapped my legs around him.

I wondered if all that was needed, wanted, was indeed a single thought to make a wish come to fruition. In an effort to satisfy his question, my mind went to the baths we'd taken only a couple of times in the past. Skin-to-skin contact under the soft, warm water was most intimate, the closest I could feel to him.

His hand glided over my cheek and under my chin, lifting my gaze to his. When our eyes met, it was as though he could see straight through to my soul. There was no doubt he'd seen the vision in my mind.

In a mere blink, the room changed, and the sound of trickling water lifted over the faint music. He reached under my shirt and gently lifted it over my head. His eyes fixed with mine, drifting only once as my hair fell forward. He pushed it behind my shoulder, clearing a path for his touch. His breath grew heavier as one hand held me firmly to him and the other slipped up my side and cupped my breast. His eyes closed as he pressed his lips to the place his hand had been. I released a single breath to the ceiling, as the long fingers of both warrior and physician slipped to the back of my neck and urged me closer.

"I'll never lose you," he said against my lips, fully aware of the only worry I had for him in agreeing to marry before the quest was finished.

He stood and lifted me from the bed, my legs and arms entwined around him as he held me close. He walked to the place where I'd heard the water and lowered me to stand in front of him.

"It's so beautiful," I said, looking past his shoulder to the bath that had transformed into a dimly lit oasis. An in-ground tub, with a tumbled rock surround, had a light waterfall trailing on both ends into a swirling pool. A soft glow emanated from behind the water. "It's as though we stepped outside."

"The walls are still here. Hidden, but here. This is a fraction of what awaits us at the end of this quest. Whenever we'd like." *If we are successful.*

While he hadn't spoken the last phrase aloud, I heard the thought as clear as if he had.

With all three keys, I could ensure the Soltari or the Alliance would never again punish the immortals. We could seek the balance between good and evil throughout the realms without the sting of possible repercussion hanging over our heads.

"Bring your passion back to me," Kevin whispered, placing another kiss on my lips that began soft, growing firmer as he pressed them open to receive more of him. I languished in his taste, his touch, as I gave back that which he sought from me. "I need to feel you, Sara. All of you."

"And I you."

I'd never needed anyone. Survivor was my title. Warrior to anyone who dared come close. Walls against commitment had been shattered by the purity of real love and determination to see all that was possible between us. He'd done that. This man, who to me was much more than any man I'd ever known in this life or any other. He had the patience of a Tibetan monk, will as steadfast as my own, and strength and speed that had earned him recognition as the Last Great Warrior. *A fighter like me.* The passion I held for him was born from the contrasts of such strength and tenderness, too potent a combination not to give in to. Before I was conscious of the fact, I was standing naked before him.

I lifted his shirt and slid my hand across his chest, feeling the pounding of his heart. I waited, then continued the path down along his side, grazing the deep scar to his waist before unhinging the button at his pants.

"My God, Sara. Every time you touch me…"

He stripped off the rest of his clothes, scooped me up, and walked toward the steps leading to the steamy pool. Planes of muscle that would soon be my undoing arched beneath my hands and pressed against me. My breath caught at the first sensation of heat as he lowered us into the water. As I slipped to the side, his hand moved behind to my lower back, holding me firmly to him. He positioned himself over me. His eyes, with their flecks of gold in deep brown, lit with the fire of his intent, holding me captive beneath him. The only sound in my ears was the shallow breaths of anticipation. Close. So close. He'd stoked that fire with an expert touch in a matter of seconds.

Mine. Forever mine.

His thought cut through the sound of heated breaths as his lips fell again over my own, pressing harder as we wrestled to get closer. The fire of his body, the taut muscle holding me in position gently beneath him. I needed to feel him that much more. He knew it. I wrapped my legs around him, the taste of desire too strong for either of us to deny. He drove himself into me, causing me to break free of that kiss and gasp as he crushed me to him. His rhythmic thrusts lifting me quickly, too quickly, to the brink that would send me over the edge.

Just a little longer. Need to feel him a little longer.

"Let go, my love. I want to hear you."

The sound of his voice. The gentle command combined with his movement was too much. I cried out my passion, unable to hold on to that sweet intensity passed to me with each stroke. I closed my eyes to ride that peak with him.

"Look at me, love," he said.

I opened my eyes to see him staring at me. His thrusts had shifted to sweet caresses but began to quicken again with the promise of another onslaught of lustful fury.

My body responded, gripping him tighter, while my hands glided across his back to his neck. My fingers slipped into his hair as I urged him against me. His moan, consumed by our kiss, swallowed in my desire for him once more. The arm that held me to him gripped tighter around my waist as he fought to maintain control under the slick water. All I could see in my mind's eye was him driving deep within me. Was it my thought or his shared? Suddenly, he broke away from my lips, his lungs demanding air to keep up with faster breaths. His eyes lifted from mine as a deep groan spilled from his parted lips and a tremor ran through him in my grasp. He waited until the calm filled him before slowly shifting to separate us, moving behind me to cradle me against his chest as he'd done in the past.

"Not yet," I whispered.

I turned to face him, slipping my legs around him, as he rested against the tub. I leaned closer and kissed just below his ear, and again below that, lingering. Sounds of satisfied deep breathing cracked through the stillness in the room. The music had stopped at some point after we'd entered the tub.

Kevin's fingers trailed down my back.

"I love you," I said against his ear. They had been the hardest three words to say before now. Funny how giving up fear allowed "easy" to come forward.

He leaned back and cupped my face in his hands. "I always knew you did, before you knew you did." He waited, eyes tired and yet piercing my own with his stare. "I love you forever."

"And I you. Always, my love." I pressed my lips to his, softly, slipped farther down, and turned, my back against him. His hands drifted across my abdomen and his fingers linked together. Several moments passed without a word between us.

"What if we could finish this quest successfully and live a full life together in New York and in Ardan?" he asked, breaking the silence.

My eyes drifted closed in thought, only allowing the fantasy for a split second. Mac had once suggested something about my life being exchanged for release of the keys I carried. I wasn't sure that was the only way. But ever since the mere suggestion of it, and the fact that Tarsamon had not killed me when he had the chance, I assumed it was an eventual hurdle we'd have to cross, and one that prevented me from contemplating plans for the future. Living a full life with Kevin on Earth. Was that even possible?

"A life like that seems so far away," I said, "like this mission once did when you first found me. Yet we are already on the path for the last key." I hesitated, the elephant in the room sucking up the space. "What about what Mac said?"

"I'd be lying if I said it hadn't concerned me a bit when he first hinted there'd be a chance I could lose you. But like the possibility of you not accepting my offer"—he stroked a thumb over the ring he'd placed on my left hand—"I've never let that scene play out in my mind, either."

"And if there was a way we could finish this quest and live a full life together, what would it look like to you?"

"Little house, dog—"

"Whoa. Wait just a minute."

"Okay, no dog."

I laughed. "Sports cars need garage space." My hobby of driving and the need for speed were my personal keys to freedom.

He brushed the hair aside at my neck. "That's right. A collection like that deserves proper housing." He placed a kiss on my neck. "Big house, no dog."

I smiled. "Try again."

"Big house, for the cars and dogs, an in-floor tub, with fireplace." He kissed my neck again. "You're shivering. C'mon."

He stood and helped me up. Two robes appeared on a rustic wooden table in the corner as we stepped out.

"It's cold here," I said. "Like winter. I swear the temperature feels as though it's been dropping since I arrived." Or since I'd been stunned by C-05's gun. "Do you feel it?"

"Some, yes. But it feels okay in here, and I run pretty warm anyhow. Let me take a look at that wound from the dark angel," Kevin said. "Let's make sure there isn't any infection setting in."

I slipped the shoulder of the robe to the side, revealing damp fabric tails.

He carefully untied the knotted material and removed the bandage. No evidence of injury remained. Kevin glided his fingers over my skin. "Nice, quick work."

Our eyes locked. I'd learned to read concern in them, despite his effort to hide it. What I could see was that he had no explanation for the slight trembling in my body. I brushed a finger over the ring on my left hand. One thing was certain—with the promise that came with this gift, nothing would stop me from pressing on with Horus at first light.

5

"What are you looking for?" I asked. Juno sat perched on an outside, upper-level deck with high-powered binoculars.

"Jesus, Sara. You startled me," he said, lowering them. He pressed a button on the headset he was wearing.

"If I did that to a former Special Forces operative, your focus must be intensely centered on something very worthwhile."

"What are you doing out here?"

"I wanted a look from another view while I finished the last bit of my tea this morning. Besides, I hate being cooped up inside." I paused. *Where's Jade? Haven't seen him this morning. Did he manage to contact Eldor?* "What are you watching?"

He shook his head. "Nothing to be concerned about. The shadows are congregating just outside a ridge over there." He pointed in the direction he'd been looking. "No movement toward us yet. And yes, Jade managed to confirm C-05 was sent to help you."

I still doubted the fact, despite how much I trusted Eldor.

"And Matt? Is he on the other side of this palace?"

"Yes. And before you ask, the dark forces are on that side, as well."

"Hm. I can't imagine we'd be staying much longer here, then. Do the others—"

"They are prepared to leave as soon as Horus gives us the go-ahead," he said, anticipating my question.

"That will be now," a voice said from behind me. I whirled around to see no one, but felt the same presence of Horus that I'd felt last night in the room. "The other members of your team are already in the Chamber of Tombs."

I swallowed the last of the tea and set the cup on the ledge.

"Juno, let Matt know we're ready."

Juno moved off the ledge, said a couple of words into the headset, and left me alone with the voice.

Once he'd gone, the apparition I'd seen the night before reappeared. "Is this easier for you?"

"To communicate with? Yes."

"Good. I want you to know a few things before we enter the underworld."

I cringed, again, at the thought of entering another world of death. Topetine's words of such a place being different from the last provided little comfort.

"Quite some time ago, I led the Soltari by guiding them to where certain realms would hold places of development, similar to Earth."

My eyes drifted down at the realization that what he said was in fact true. "Yes, you did. I was at your side on some of those missions."

Every memory really has been restored.

Horus nodded. He waited a breath. "The gates are passages into the depths of the underworld. I set them up as a layer of protection against anyone who might want to seek out the key before you were called to duty."

"I remember." And it felt so good to say so. "It should be easy to obtain."

"You might think. You'll have to pass through only one to unlock passage throughout the realm. Once you do, your energy and the ring identifying you as the Light Carrier will allow you and your team an easier path through the underworld. However, with the presence of light, there is also a place for darkness. The creation of such a place means there also exists a choice for one over the other."

"You're referring to the rules of the underworld. I have no desire to choose anything other than what I fight for. You can't be wondering whether I've considered giving up, giving in to Tarsamon and his darkness."

C-05 had once had such an inclination and followed it, after all. I might as well put any doubt to rest.

"I don't have any concern on such a matter with you." He shifted to my other side. "We created the gates in the underworld, to hide the key. But since then, the development of the darkness flows in places where light exists. It wasn't our doing. That evil has drawn its own followers. The underworld is where Tarsamon discovered the strength to develop the force he carries, expanding into Ardan and continuing to build on Earth."

"That means we are playing on his turf, where he's most comfortable." What did that mean to what we would encounter? My thoughts went to all the darkness I'd seen, shadows, illness created, the dark angel with the ability to manipulate and implant heavy, emotional thoughts to cover my own, so focused and intent on her purpose to cripple my ability to fight. That type of negative energy was disabling, pure destruction to a soul. "For how long? And how was he able to utilize a force in the realm?"

"Shortly before you set off for Scotland, in search of the first key. A matter of months is all. As to how he utilized the force, he had to have had help. The Egyptian underworld is just another place of existence, but for souls. It has keepers that often act as guides, protectors, and gods, all in place to maintain the balance. And for the most part, that worked for quite some time. But as with all power, it can become corrupted by want, desire. In order for Tarsamon to utilize a continuous source in the underworld, he had to have sided with a powerful entity. A god. Only two are strong enough to support him—Norul and Aqen. One holds the key you seek; another is a protector of the realm. I suspect it's the latter. Your entrance will likely engage these sources.

"All you need to know is that the knowledge to get to the key resides with you. There is no riddle to solve. No clues to decode."

"Then let's go get it."

"There's one more thing. When this is over, and you're successful—"

"If I'm successful, you mean."

"I'm going to need a guiding force I can trust going forward." He paused, and the sensation in the air around us grew heavy. "I'll need you to lead the Soltari."

What? I can't. I shook my head. *Kevin…our future. You can't ask this of me.*

"Why? Why choose me?"

"I need to be free to ensure no infiltration exists elsewhere in the realms, and that the seed of evil is not left to grow again. I can only trust someone capable of holding the keys of enlightenment. I can only trust someone pure of heart. There is no one but you."

"But—"

"And before you nominate a member of your team as pure of heart, you must know that it will take foresight as well as strength to make the decisions necessary to lead the Soltari. You're that person, that spirit. Whether you believe it now or not."

That was as good a reason as any, I supposed. But I'd had plans. Still did. The words *absolutely not!* were choked off in a cough, the ability to argue reduced to a strangle in my throat.

What about all that I sought to obtain for the immortals? I supposed that could be done if I was leading. What about Jade and his army? He was angry at what had been passed down to his men. Four famines had been their punishment, wiping out a good part of his forces and preventing them from going into the realms, unable to eat, and for what? I paused. Could it be that simple? Rule by fear. That was the course the Soltari had chosen, what had sent me on this mission to begin with. Fear was never a part of the original directive of the authority over the realms. The entity must have changed their direction.

"The Soltari have been compromised by the very evil that's consuming Earth?"

"Perhaps. The energy of the force has changed, but nothing is certain."

While Jade and I suspected infiltration, we wouldn't be able prove it without first obtaining the keys, drawing the Soltari out, and using the keys to evoke change. *Tarsamon. How deep did his poisoned roots extend? When had he threaded them into the Soltari?* As warriors who kept the balance in all realms, my team and I had left Ardan to come rescue Earth. We recently discovered Ardan's boundary had been pushed by Tarsamon's forces, along with Jade's confirmation at least two members of the Alliance were working against us. It all made sense. The governing entity had sent the harsh punishments down to maintain control over the immortals, to create unequal power. And they'd done so in other ways, by separating eternal partners. Combined, they'd delivered a steady dose of strength, given a more powerful hand to the evil that now had a firm hold in both realms of Earth and Ardan. Separation and punishment were never the intention in creating the governing order. No wonder C-05 had turned against us. And what about the four famines Jade had said his men had endured? Why hadn't I been aware of the decision? I had assumed it was a blocked memory, but even now, I had no recollection of delivering such a cruel order.

"Sara." I looked up at the lingering mist, recalling how he often preferred to appear as a spirit entity, but had mastered the ability to transform his energy into the physical appearance of a man, depending on the mission. "The decision for the famines was indeed cruel punishment, made without your knowledge. You never could have known, were never meant to know, or you would have stopped it. I wasn't there, either. We trusted the rest of the order to hold the line while we kept the balance in other realms. We chose to be active participants in the fight."

"But why wouldn't Jade say something? For God's sake, it was four famines, not one. It turned the immortals away from their fight. His soldiers abandoned their missions because they had to."

"Who would he tell that he could trust if, as he suspected, the Soltari had been infiltrated? He was fighting to save his men."

My eyes drifted down in thought because only thirty or so remained. Human years were short in the eyes of eternal life. But the time that had passed for Jade and his men had to have felt like forever.

"We'll make amends later. I need your assurance regarding the Soltari."

"You need my answer now?" It wasn't a request from him but an expectation. I'd have to see about that.

"I'd like it."

"I can't give it to you. Not yet. Not until I have what awaits at the end of this mission, for my team, the immortals, and me."

He waited, contemplating an answer, I supposed. Could he really ask anyone else to lead the Soltari who didn't hold the keys to the survival of Earth, as well as the potentially compromised realm of Ardan?

"Very well." Horus moved ahead of me, toward the same door Juno had gone through to meet up with Matt.

Really? That's all? I'd hoped my answer would suffice but, given the enormity of what he was asking, expected it wouldn't.

"Oh," he said, stopping and turning to face me. "Two things: As you know, Jade managed to find Eldor. He confirmed C-05 had been released."

"The question is why?"

"He's working to help you."

"I can't believe that, not after what we've been through. Not after what he's done. How do we know those who work against us didn't approve his release under the guise of the Soltari?"

He didn't answer.

"You know more than you're saying," I said.

"I know as much as you do."

And then some.

"That's why I need you to lead when this is over. I can't monitor the realms and remain connected within the Soltari in a manner necessary to make important decisions. But I do believe Eldor. He can always be trusted."

That was true, because every experience had proven it to be so. That same truth had always been my guiding force. A rock of strength I could count on, no matter its harsh, jagged edges.

"You'll need this before we proceed any farther beyond the Chamber of Tombs," he said.

Horus lifted his hands to his face and flattened them in front of his lips, fingers pointed in my direction as though he were going to blow me a kiss. A flame lit, like those I created with my own hands as a defensive weapon. Only this one wasn't in the shape of a ball to be hurled, but instead like that from a match, small and innocent in appearance. The blue-white flame fluttered indigo, turquoise, and copper. Or was it gold? The colors shifted so quickly it was hard to tell which, and yet, mesmerizing and vibrant all the same.

"Lapis lazuli," he said. "Derived from a rare mineral with the ability to protect you in the underworld." He puckered his lips and blew across his palms. With the flame extending its reach to my chin, the faint sensation of a small breeze reached me. The feeling was mild warmth before the fire shifted to a fine powder that settled across my neck and shoulders.

"What is its protection?"

He smiled. "The last one you'll need to see you to the end of your journey."

While it was comforting to hear anything related to the end of the quest, the only thought nagging at me was if the blue powder would cause another unwelcome shift, like that of the hawk I preferred not to be. I'd have to wait and see what surprise awaited. The words *last one you'll need* left a distasteful residue lingering with me that could only mean one thing—it would only reveal its purpose in the event of imminent danger.

6

Fog, and a lot of it, filled the once vivid, secure space in the Chamber of Tombs. The secret doorway leading to this frozen world had appeared in the brick wall following a Sanskrit chant from Horus. After stepping over the threshold, I'd taken what felt like a few steps past the boundary of the palace into the location that housed the souls of those who had died. By the way my heart was racing and the sensation of cold stinging my face and hands, I was still very much alive and feeling as though I'd stepped into a walk-in freezer. The trembling I'd felt the night before returned. I stamped out the chill rising through my body and rubbed my hands together.

Despite the recent gaps in memory filled, I still didn't understand how the paths connecting one world to another were formed. The words I'd heard when I started the quest returned as though in answer. Everything is energy, from every thought to its physical or, in this case, invisible transformation.

"Over here," C-05 said.

A hand clasped gently around my upper arm. Instinct at being handled in any way caused me to want to jerk from the grasp and fight. Instead, I let the uncomfortable sensation of trust follow the feeling of no immediate danger, for a minute. *There should be more. Too quiet.* The sounds of the other members of my team were no longer beside me.

"You'd better be damn sure about this."

Kevin. Thank God.

"Where is everyone else?" I stepped out of the fog into a brightly lit but clouded sky to see our breaths falling out in small, ghostly puffs. The grasp at my arm fell away. Clumps of snow clung to the long, leafless branches of the trees around us.

"The team took a separate path," Kevin said.

"Redirected in an effort to throw off the dark angel," C-05 added.

"They can't be happy about it. Do they even know what happened?"

"Horus gave them instructions early this morning," Kevin said. "The split was necessary to ensure the best chance of getting you through the labyrinth of passages in the underworld and to buy us as much time as possible."

"Time for what?"

"To get you to the temple pyramid before your energy can be detected in the realm," C05 replied. "We need as much time as we can get before the proverbial bell sounds your arrival. Your energy is far too strong to remain hidden for long."

An icy breeze caught my hair and lifted it, sending a chill down my neck.

Like the other portals that would clothe us in the appropriate garments for the time, our passage through the Chamber of Tombs had dressed me in more formfitting attire, including a couple of layers, a long, heavy coat, and boots that hit at mid-thigh. A cold, steel gun was holstered on each side of my hips, replacing the swift blade I usually kept. The elves had been responsible for the precision weapons we carried, making me curious about the guns. Our weapons were often crafted for the world we would encounter. It had to be true this time if they were provided in place of the powerful sword so important to me in the past.

"The bullets are specialized, like Juno's and Matt's weapons against the shadows," Kevin said, sliding the magazine into his gun. "Similar to the hollow-point type that are meant to do more damage, these have been crafted to disperse the energy the angel is composed of."

I lifted a brow at that. "The elves?" He nodded. "Do I still have the ability to create fire as a defense?" Not waiting for an answer, I held my palm out to create the tiny spark that would light into a flame. *A little heat, no matter how small, would be nice.* But before I could ignite the spark, Kevin closed his hand over mine.

"I wouldn't do that. Your abilities should be well intact. But this world works off pure energy, meaning anything you create is detected far beyond our location. If you send a tremor of energy out, it reverberates, like an insect caught in a web. No need to sound the bell that we're here, darling, and ruin the small cover we might have." He kissed my hand and released it.

Damn the cold. "Any chance we have a vehicle?" I pulled the long coat tighter around me as a breeze shifted in our direction, causing me to wish for warmth if I couldn't create it. The lining of the coat began to heat. Was I willing it via the Rule of Wishes? Mind over matter, perhaps? What did it matter, so long as it was a welcome temperature?

"We aren't going too far. Besides, I'd like to make sure we remain hidden as long as we can." C-05 had stopped his inspection of the immediate area. "I'm sure this is the right place."

"*Right place?* What the hell is going on?"

"Remember that 'bargain' he made with the Soltari?" Kevin said. "He's following through on it."

"I'm going to need a bit more information than that if you expect me to follow him."

There was silence for a split second as a thought that wasn't mine flitted across my finely tuned senses. Kevin glanced to C-05 for an answer.

"I promised the Soltari that I would show you the path inward. In exchange for helping you, I won't be banned from Ardan." I narrowed a gaze of disbelief.

"I thought Horus was our guide."

"He is. He's with the rest of team right now, to help throw Tarsamon's forces off track. That's why time is of the essence for us."

C-05 turned his back and set off down the only iced pathway as far as we could see. The sounds of our footsteps were swallowed in the layers of snow as Kevin and I followed.

Without being sure who the honest players were in the Soltari, only time would tell if C-05's self-professed help was genuine.

As punishment for C-05's failure on a prior mission, his partner had been banished to another realm, the location withheld from him. To find her would have taken eternity in the multitude of universes that existed. It had caused C-05 enough anger, he'd said, that he wanted to see the end of the punishing force of the order, and why he'd joined with Tarsamon. It was too soon for me to give him my trust.

"Why would the Soltari have needed your help?" I asked after a few minutes of hiking in silence.

Without breaking his stride, C-05 replied, "The dark angel. She's been on the hunt for you since you escaped her in the Yucatan." He paused. "She knows of another entry point into this realm."

"From Tarsamon's connection to someone here?"

"Exactly. The initial plan for you to get to the key by way of the *Book of the Dead* needed to be altered. That's the reason why you carry the algorithms."

That matches what Horus told me. And C-05 would know this because he was once tasked with leading the team.

I glanced to Kevin. "You believe him?"

"Yes. He speaks the truth."

I nodded. Kevin and I could detect an attempt to construct a lie as part of feeling the emotions of others. But C-05 was masterful at disguise, almost as good as Jade's to mirror an identity or to track energy.

Separately, the shadows were certainly a force to contend with by themselves. But the dark angel, beautiful with piercing blue eyes, long jet-black hair, a wingspan the length of her body, and skin the color of smoke, was an entirely different form of evil. The strength she carried was not merely in muscle but in the ominous way she could withdraw memories and emotions precious to someone and manipulate the darkest evil upon them, causing one to feel heavy with sadness, grief, or worthlessness. Her aim was to evoke weakness upon her prey to the point where they had no fight left and then begged for death. I'd never known her to grant mercy by way of ending a life, not like the shadows or demons in Tarsamon's legion of hunters.

"Is the location the dark angel used to enter the realm anywhere near here?"

"No. The only other gate is for the passage of new souls, those recently deceased," C-05 said. He sucked in a deep breath and blew it out. "But she's had a head start."

"Then we sure as hell aren't safe out here discussing it," Kevin added. He pulled his weapon and held it in hand at his side. "Where did Horus want you to lead us?"

I am to take us as far as the Nile and then Horus will need to guide us the rest of the way."

The Nile. Egypt. Really? The myriad of trees on either side of us, also blanketed in white, made it hard to believe this icy realm was in any way connected to Egypt. I glanced in multiple directions, noting the absence of sand, palm trees, and heat. "Are there pyramids around here, too?"

"I thought the Inner Society would have prepared you," he said, shifting his attention forward again. "Didn't they at least tell you the palace is the location of what is known as an advanced Egypt? The existence as it was before the archeologists of Earth discovered the pyramids and remains?"

"Yes. But this doesn't look like the same place Horus and I visited to set the gates in place according to the *Book of the Dead.*"

"A lot has changed since you were here last, mainly because of the evil that has come into the realm. Forget what you think you know of Egypt."

My heightened senses triggered on a feeling that he was hiding information. I felt a block go up to prevent me from reading anything more. "When have you had time to keep track of a death world?"

He was silent. My hand slipped to the gun at my hip but didn't pull it. Kevin's eyes darted to C-05 and then to me. He shook his head and I moved my hand off the gun.

"I had to return, on occasion, for Tarsamon."

A lie.

"Prior to that I had to get information for your team. It required visiting the realm to make sure all was in place for your arrival."

A truth.

The ability to decipher the truth in the words spoken by anyone was even sharper than it had been when I'd set out on the quest. If C-05 was indeed helping us, why did he need to lie? *He must be hiding something.*

"Let me get this straight. We pass through a portal from New York to arrive in what is an advanced Egypt, but it's really the underworld?"

C-05 rounded a corner as if a clear path existed. It probably did somewhere beneath the snow. "This way. Yes. The palace is on the outskirts of the underworld. To reach the location of the key, we had to go through the Chamber of Tombs. It's the only sure way to get beyond the palace boundaries without being detected by Tarsamon's forces."

"Okay. But the Nile, the pyramids. How is it that they exist in a death realm, in a freezing-cold death realm?"

"What is real in the world of the living exists also in the world of the dead. It may look and feel a little different, but the topography is the same. It's a parallel existence. Two different planes of existence mirroring one world—physical like us, and substance, like Horus."

"We have Ardan for spirits like Horus." The answers arrived before I could fully form the follow-up question. "And for those who have left the physical world and need to restore their energy, we have places like this realm."

"You're in touch with the spirit of who you really are, at last, instead of leaning on the limited vision as a human for your information."

Kevin angled his head toward me and smiled.

After a few minutes, I asked, "How did the dark forces discover the *Book of the Dead*?"

C-05 glanced to Kevin, then away. "You ask too many questions."

"You established the lack of trust," Kevin said.

"Some information they had, after making a connection here. But some they obtained"—he waited—"from me. Because I was supposed to lead this team at the onset of the quest, I had key facts about the gates, namely the entry and exit point, provided by the Soltari, creators of the book."

"You told Tarsamon every detail you knew? How could—"

C-05 stopped abruptly and turned to face me. "He read my thoughts," he interrupted. "And not *every* detail was shared." His tone reflected irritation. "He'd grown tired, impatient. He pinned me against a wall and used his strength to inflict pain. A lot of pain. But I didn't volunteer all the information. He was able to read into some of the knowledge I carried."

I couldn't help but lose a little more respect for him, not that there was much left after he'd joined with Tarsamon. It wasn't because he'd been exposed to Tarsamon's strength, energy almost as powerful as the dark angel carried. For that I was sympathetic. It was because he had no reserve, no ability to combat such a force. Maybe the energy he described was so powerful he couldn't. *Jesus, am I making excuses for him now?* He'd only thought he could bargain with a demon and found out otherwise. No excuse for that. In the end, it had been better that he hadn't led the mission for the keys. The quest couldn't survive weakness in a leader. Because of his carelessness, his selfishness, my team and I were at greater risk with the Dark Lord's knowledge of the passageways to the key.

"You're still the luckiest soul I've ever known to be given a chance to rectify one very bad mistake."

"Let's take a quicker path," Kevin said, pointing to a set of sleds and accompanying dogs attached. Their forms appeared somewhat transparent. As I squinted my eyes for a better look, they seemed as tangible as any other physical object.

Making things happen at the speed of thought was a concept I could get used to, especially given the bitter cold. "How could you know the dogs would be available?"

"Part of being successful at managing the energy around us means we believe it conspires in our best interest," he added, tucking his gun into a shoulder holster. "Besides, it's too cold to keep moving on foot."

"How much farther?" I asked, stepping onto a sled behind Kevin's.

"About another mile. Let's hope this aid didn't cause too much fluctuation in the energy to draw attention," C-05 said. "Our final destination is the Band of Peace. Just a few miles ahead."

From the little research I'd done to prepare for an eventual trip to Egypt, I'd learned the Band of Peace was believed by some researchers and Egyptologists to consist of almost one hundred pyramids, including Giza. They were utilized by the Egyptians for technology instead of tombs. But what type of technology? Soundwave? Electricity, maybe? I couldn't remember.

"But first, the Nile."

As we took hold of the reins to the dogs tied to our individual sleds, the inquisitive nature of my mind started turning over angles. Was it possible for C-05 to trick Kevin? He knew I'd follow if he brought Kevin and if I believed our guide would be meeting up with us. I was now separated from the protection of my team with no idea where the entry point might be for the Dark Lord or his forces. What if we were being led into the center of that evil?

7

"I hate caves," I said under my breath, after a good twenty minutes of hiking into one. I was, however, grateful to be out of the direct cold and the single gust of wind that carried on its currents a warning as we'd entered.

We'd followed C-05 to a location he said offered additional concealment from the danger of Tarsamon's forces hunting on our path, and a safer route by way of the Nile to the temple located in the Band of Peace.

The minimal light we'd had at the start of the hike was now non-existent. I pulled out my flashlight and shined it ahead of and behind me. "About as much as I hate entering anything called the underworld," I added. I had learned that much on the last go-round with Topetine and the unremitting riddles of the Mayan glyphs. Not helping the matter, I'd discovered the floor to be a mixture of blood and mud. The musty, metallic-scented memory flooded my senses. I swallowed and aimed my flashlight once at the ground, making sure all was clear. The jungle had also been the place I'd first encountered the dark angel. I could still feel the strength of her leg muscles locked around my neck. I rubbed the spot that held the memory while scanning the walls in front of me. Chiseled detail lifted from the dust-covered floor to the ceiling. I shined the flashlight up and over. Two falcons marked each corner.

"Dark. Closed in," I said more to myself. *A little light would be nice.* And with the thought, the area mysteriously lit enough to make out more of the features, as well as the direction of the passage ahead. The cave walls and ceiling were not made of stone as they had been in the jungle, but instead reflected scattering shades of blue and appeared constructed of glass. *Wonder if I could ask the walls to fade away, or a roof to open up.* That particular desire, however, did not manifest. "What are the walls made of?"

"Quartz crystal," C-05 replied.

"So this is the crystal cave," Kevin said. "I've heard of it. It looks like ice."

"A glacier cave in Iceland is similar in appearance only. This one allows the flow of energy through it."

Kevin stepped closer to one of the pillars on either side of a large doorway and looked up. "How are you supposed to apply algorithms to quartz?"

"It's a maze," I replied, not really sure how I knew. I just did. I hopped off the small ledge I'd found, opting for more secure footing. "Fully enclosed, with no escape. Isn't that right?" I looked at C-05. "The entrance has been shut this far in."

"It has. But where there's a way in, there's always a way out," C-05 said, searching his own corner of detail.

It was a phrase I'd heard since being reintroduced to Ardan and setting out on the quest for the keys. I'd learned from experience that it was also true. Despite how confining an environment appeared, or how limited access to help was, there was always a path out. The trick was finding it. Going back was never an option, either, because as I'd discovered from the onset of this mission, the path would inevitably circle back to the beginning. It felt like a wicked game of Entrapment, in which we were caught by impenetrable obstacles. The reality was we weren't, if we could remember to set our sights deeper. Doing so required letting go of fear and having the willingness to see things beyond what they appeared to be on the surface.

I put my hand on the pillar Kevin stood beside. "The labyrinth of tunnels will lead us to the keeper of the key." I turned to C-05. "What

I need to know from you is where the entry points are. Where can the evil enter?"

"I don't know."

"You said you did." My stare pinned him to the opposite pillar.

"I don't know where they are inside the walls. Only on the outside." *Another truth.*

"Well then, are we near one, on the outside, that is?"

"We passed one on the way up, maybe a mile and a half back. But because we didn't encounter any dark forces, I didn't think it was important to provide that information."

Kevin stepped close to him. "For future reference, it's not only important, it's imperative."

"In that case," C-05 said, "the entrance closest might lead to this maze. There are tunnels that should run beneath the cave. I don't know if they extend as far back as the entrance."

I met Kevin's gaze and looked back at C-05. "And how many other entrances might there be in this area?" I asked.

"There wasn't time to search out every last possible change in the realm." I didn't need a brighter light to see the twist of annoyance at the corner of his mouth. "To my knowledge, there are no more passages on the side we entered. I can't say what exists beyond the Band of Peace." Silence passed between us, as Kevin and I calculated risk with the little information provided. "Horus wouldn't have asked me to lead you in this direction, through these specific pathways, if he thought there was more danger here than where your team is."

"I don't know. I still don't trust you. But if Horus left you to lead us, there must be something he knows that I don't."

I glanced back to the wall, zeroing in on an image of a feathered serpent. "That's got to be a sign we're on the right track." The serpent king was the one who had held the key I obtained in the Mayan jungle. As I stepped through the doorway, the passage lit along the corridor. "Okay, let's see if Horus is right about having all the information I need to unlock this passage."

I reached out to touch a thin, wooden sheet of papyrus embedded in layers beneath the crystal wall. Glyphs and images of figures had been drawn in a linear fashion as though to tell a story. I held my palm flat, pressing the silver ring identifying me as the one person who could hold the power of the keys against the quartz. The tiniest ray of light, no bigger than the tip of a pen, connected my finger to the image. The letters engraved on the ring lit. I felt nothing from the exchange of apparent electrical current.

Before I could attempt to interpret the images, the figures came to life, a still drawing now animated. I jerked my hand back and watched as the glyphs, too, shifted direction, organizing the images into another order.

"I assume that's supposed to happen?" I looked to C-05 for confirmation. "The glyphs are code?"

"The extent of my knowledge is only the entry and exit points. Never had an opportunity to get into the meat of the mission. Not at this level."

"The movement was activated by a certain set of codes," Kevin said, "keyed to identify each fraction of code within the subsystem of where you direct the energy. Like this." His fingers moved back and forth under the line of images.

"But I didn't know to apply such energy to this. It just happened."

"Exactly." Kevin's eyes stared into mine. "You have the knowledge. The algorithms already know where to connect. We just needed a guide." His chin lifted in C-05's direction. "To get you to the point of contact."

"It's also likely that, by triggering the images, it won't be long before your presence will be known to all in the realm."

I nodded and turned my attention back to the panel of drawings.

A falcon was flying over the sun, while a man in an ornate headdress below the bird was holding the sun's rays over his head, aiming them at two helpless figures as he moved his arms back and forth in a repeated fashion, stuck on replay. Water flowed in a calm current behind them and in the same direction the path led down the corridor. I glanced along the rest of the panel.

"Must be this way," I said. As the passage lit deeper into the center of the maze, shadowed footprints began to show on the walls and floor.

The hair on my neck stood up, as my senses sharpened. I tried to home in on the all-too-familiar sensation of the dark forces, but there was nothing I could pick up.

Shadows had always meant evil. C-05's words, *a mile and a half back,* kept repeating in my head about the last entrance point he was aware of. I looked at Kevin.

"I'm not picking up on any indication that those footprints have anything to do with Tarsamon, either," he said, answering my unspoken question.

"We have little choice but to follow."

There was enough light to track the pattern being outlined for us. The papyrus continued the length of the walls. I slowed my pace, carefully trying to decipher the pictures' meaning. "I can't make sense of the message. The sun. The falcon. Does it mean Horus? It could be telling the story of our arrival."

"Or a signal of your arrival," Kevin said. "Remember, your energy is felt—"

"Before I am seen. I remember." He'd told me once that my energy was like a beacon, a potential call to an avid hunter. All of which meant the dark forces had to know, or would know soon enough, where to find us. It was Kevin's subtle way of telling me there wasn't time for me to review the scrolls on the walls.

"Tarsamon's forces, especially the dark angel, have to know you've separated from the team by now," C-05 added. "That particular demon's awareness is extremely heightened."

"I wonder how far before we get to the end of this maze." I huffed out a breath. "Look," I said, noticing a light on the wall where the scrolls told their story. "The pyramid is lit. Looks like you're right. We've got to go there."

"We don't even know if this maze leads out to it," C-05 said. "Besides, my instructions are to bring you through the maze to the Nile, not the pyramid."

"And you have, mostly. You can wait here if you choose. But I'm here to fulfill this quest and as quickly as possible without being a sitting duck for Tarsamon." I stepped past C-05.

"She goes where she's led," Kevin said, following behind me.

I picked up my pace, watching for the footprints as confirmation I was headed in the right direction. For once, I trusted my gut instinct with zero doubt. There wasn't any good reason why I shouldn't. This was dangerous work. Anything could happen in a realm where hunters made it a practice to hide. There wasn't any ominous sensation, no indication of evil. And perhaps because Kevin didn't feel it, either, it gave me more confidence to press on and follow the pattern on the walls as our only guide.

I'd made about four turns, following the path that wound around inside, with nothing but glasslike walls and storytelling scrolls as our companions. It felt like we were getting closer to the center of the cave.

"What's this?" I stopped to get a better look at a stone that was not unlike the rest of the crystal but with script-like writing on it. "It looks like Sanskrit."

C-05 stepped closer. "This doesn't belong here."

"A point we agree on," I said. "Why would Sanskrit, associated with the Hindu culture, be tied to Egypt?"

"Not only that, this writing wouldn't have appeared until at least a thousand years after hieroglyphs. It's much too early to be here," Kevin added.

I glided my fingertips over it. "And yet the chanting of it opened the door to this realm from the Chamber of Tombs."

"It doesn't make sense," C-05 said.

"Unless they are meant to be connected in some way." Kevin paused. "Or unless someone put it here for you to find."

"As a guide, perhaps?"

C-05 stepped closer. His fingers traced the edges of the stone. "Judging by the irregular edges and how it looks forced into the groove, I'd say it was put here recently. And if it was put here as a clue, someone else would be expected."

I shifted my gaze from C-05 to Kevin. "That can't be good."

"There is nothing from my training that would tie this quest to the Hindi," Kevin said. "Horus must know what the tie is if he used the passage to access the realm."

"Likely, I suppose. I never ran across a reference to Sanskrit in preparing for this mission, either," C-05 said. "Some of the texts were known to be scientific or technology based. The Rosetta Stone is the only other tool to be used to decipher the Egyptian hieroglyphs. But this is not in the proper language for translating, and again, the timing is wrong." He shook his head. "It's clearly Sanskrit, possibly Vedic. I suppose it's possible the writings existed earlier than Classical, but this stone just doesn't belong here."

At that very moment, the footprints that had marked our path disappeared. Before I could wonder why, a firm grasp clamped around my ankles, nearly throwing me off-balance. Kevin reached under my shoulders and hooked his elbows under my arms to hold me up, but it was no use. Several hands of the same soot color as the prints guiding us through the maze were wrapped around my feet and ankles.

"Pull her out of her boots," C-05 said. While Kevin held me tight under the shoulders, I lifted my knees, kicking to free my legs as C-05 bent over and tried pulling my boots from the thigh. "She's not budging."

Several airy voices bounced off the walls around us in a single word, "Westing." The sound grew louder until it was almost deafening.

"Hold on to me," Kevin shouted above the noise. He pressed himself against my back and slid his arms farther beneath my shoulders, interlocking his hands at my chest. I wrapped my arms around his.

The ground began to rumble, causing C-05 to give up the attempt to free my legs as he stumbled backward. Kevin took a step to the side to maintain his balance as a crack formed where we previously stood and broke to the right.

I've got to get free. A black hole opened where the crack had widened. *No, no, no. Grab on to something. I'm not going...*

Before I could finish the last thought, Kevin lost his balance and, with it, our struggle to remain upright. The same dim light that had guided us through the maze shined in the depths of the crack and lit the path downward. But nothing was visible except dirt.

One quick glance at C-05 revealed his struggle to free the stone.

Maybe he didn't want to leave it for someone else? Or perhaps he thought we could use it? "What are you doing?" I shouted.

I could still feel Kevin's arms, holding me as if they were the strong straps of a backpack firmly attached. The narrow passage left no place to escape as the crack widened. The grip at my feet released and we both fell into a dirt slide moving straight below the quartz tunnel.

Roots stuck out from the walls as we slid past them, and another group of objects flashed by in a glimpse of off-white. Or was it yellow? I couldn't make out the images until I turned my attention away from the plummet downward and toward the wall of dirt.

A foot, a hand, a forearm, then several, purposefully extended their reach out of the walls of dirt. First one, then another, followed by several more.

No skin. Death. Time slipped into slow motion as skeleton-like arms reached through the soil on the downward trek. It was like a horrible nightmare but with all the sensations of being alive. I wanted to kick the images away, praying they wouldn't make contact, but feared Kevin would lose his grip. How he'd managed to hang on this long was incomprehensible.

How far does this go? Is there anything else to grab on to?

The ground beneath us disappeared, as open air was followed by the icy sensation of water smothering us. Only then did Kevin's grasp release as we swam up for air. C-05 followed with a third crash. The currents were strong, pulling us in a direction we had no control over. I gulped air, searching for an edge to swim to, but found no bank in sight. All of the walls, mostly dirt, held together by numerous outgrowths of roots, went straight up. We were under the control of the currents that carried us into the open twilight of the evening sky. Nothing but hope as our only lifeline to cling to, and one thought—maybe Horus was nearby and the dark forces had not yet found us.

8

"The Nile must be a direct path to the pyramids," C-05 said, brushing his fingers back and forth through his spiky, wet hair.

"What makes you think so?" I asked, casting a gaze upward and not seeing anything remotely close to a pyramid in sight.

We had clawed our way through the currents and floated into a channel outside the caves before finally crawling to the bank of the river. The frigid air was nothing compared to the sensation of pins and needles that stung my body at hitting the water followed by the beginning of numbness, until I remembered I could alter anything unrelated to evil with a strongly desired wish. My clothing was like new at the very thought of abandoning the soaking-wet attire for dry, warm clothing. What we needed was a fire, warmer air, for sure. That wish, however, hadn't come to fruition.

"We can't alter the climate or risk being detected by setting a fire," C-05 said, ignoring my earlier question. He cupped his hands together and blew into them, rubbing them together. "The thermostat here is permanently set to cool. Energy of the dead moves easier in darker, cooler environments."

I sat on the bank of the river, resting my elbows on my knees, catching my breath in short white puffs, reflecting on the horror we'd witnessed as we slid down the long dirt path. "And you know this from your visits here to get information for our quest?" I may have helped set up the gates in the underworld, but I didn't recall snow or icy temperatures.

"Way back, when you and Horus were here to set the gates according to the *Book of the Dead*, you weren't human. You didn't feel this temperature as you do now."

"So long as the clothing keeps doing its job, I'll be fine."

"What the hell was grabbing at us as we slid down?" Kevin asked. The images that had interrupted my thoughts evidently plagued him, too.

"People who've died who didn't make it to the death realm."

Dare I ask why not?

"They're trapped between worlds. Most who end up there refuse to accept they are dead." I narrowed a gaze at C-05. The man had more information than I ever guessed he might. "That's how I understand it."

I glanced up and over, scanning the area. Ribbons of deep orange and yellow stretched along the horizon, separating day from night.

"First time I've ever seen a dusting of snow on palm trees and whatever that other type is." I lifted my chin to a grouping of five trees, the leaves of which were still attached and perfectly still. Not a single current moved among the branches. A certain unsettling calmness in the air had the hair on my neck rising. It was a sign, a reminder that peace could sometimes be an illusion.

I lifted one of the guns and eyed it.

"They aren't affected by water," C-05 said. "Kevin, you still have your sword?"

"I've never been on a quest without it." He paused. "I thought the guns were better weapons against the dark angel."

"They are. It's good to have multiple weapons. Never know how strong Tarsamon's forces are becoming the longer it takes us to get to the key."

"Maybe. I'd be willing to bet he's more interested in intercepting Sara's path than strengthening an already powerful demon angel." Kevin held out a hand to me. "You okay?" I nodded, taking his hand

and standing. "We've got to get out of here. We can't be hanging around in the open." He turned to C-05. "Which pyramid does she need to get to?"

"Like I said, I was only to deliver her through the maze to the Nile."

"Did you recover the stone you were trying so hard to free from the wall?" Kevin asked.

C-05 patted his chest and abdomen in a frantic search for the item. "Damn it," he said under his breath. "You think by taking the stone, I was trying to throw someone off track? Someone who might help us?"

Kevin stared blankly at him. "No one's here to meet us, to get us to the pyramid. And you did shoot her at the onset when you didn't have to."

"Shit." C-05 turned away. "I protected her from the shadows before you and the rest of your team arrived. I could have handed her to them."

"Jade confirmed with Eldor he could be trusted," I said. "Horus mentioned it to me before we left." I turned to C-05. "Your behavior is questionable. Has been all along. What were you going to do with the stone anyway?"

"Make sure whomever it was placed there for didn't find it."

"And if it was meant for someone who could help us?" Kevin asked.

"Not likely."

"Well then, it looks like you were successful, since you lost it."

"Yeah, lost," he said, taking a few steps closer to where the water met the edge of the bank.

The man was a growing annoyance that had been under my skin since my very first meeting with him, prior to recovering any of the keys.

Now, what about the pyramids? I thought, shifting gears toward something more productive. "Isn't the Band of Peace a theory that the pyramids were power generators, instead of tombs?"

"Some archaeologists believe so. But I don't really care about theories. I care about Horus getting you there."

"Maybe we're supposed to meet Horus at the Band of Peace, instead of the Nile?" *Maybe it's a trap? This river must lead to the pyramids. If we follow it through there...*

"Sara," Kevin said, distracting me from further thought. "We've got to find cover."

"I'm going to make use of the ability to shift and take a look around," I said. "Might as well put Jade's potion to some use for something more than escape."

"I don't think that's safe with night coming," Kevin argued.

"He's right," C-05 added. "Once the light is gone, the power of the dark forces grows stronger in the underworld. It's better if we stay put and wait for Horus. You'll create less detectable energy if you aren't shifting into another form."

"Sara Forrester?" a commanding voice bellowed across the early evening sky, the light now barely visible. I whirled with both guns in hand in the direction of the sound. A very muscular, tall man appeared from out of nowhere, stepping toward us. His face was blurred, until he waved a hand over it, revealing strong facial features with a jutted chin and angular cheekbones. What looked like a mass of dark, wavy hair hung to his shoulders.

"Yes," I answered. Caution filled my tone, though I detected no threat. "Who are you?"

"One of the keepers of the City of Souls. Your presence is causing a growing disturbance."

I suppose I should care. "Do you have a name?"

"Names are not important in the Duat. We know each other by our specific energy patterns."

I lowered the guns but held them steady.

Kevin lowered his weapon, too, while lifting a flashlight in the direction of the voice.

"Keep those at the ready," the man said.

C-05 stepped forward. "We're looking for Horus."

"To get this one"—the man extended his open palm to me—"to the temple pyramid. I know."

"How do you know?" I asked.

"It's my job to be well informed of all activity in the underworld."

He had to know that answer wouldn't suffice. Had he been informed by Horus? By Tarsamon? Who else? *If this really is Egypt, and if my recollection is correct, the people here believed in several gods, kind and malevolent.* I suddenly became aware of the blank stare he must see looking at him.

"I've been in contact with the spirit you refer to as Horus. He is with the other humans you arrived with. Your team. You can't stay here long, or you will become weak and at risk of remaining here."

"Dying," I said. "We can die here? I mean without Tarsamon or his forces having anything to do with it?"

The sound of a halfhearted laugh lifted from deep within his chest. "There is no death, only westing, or transitioning, as it is referred to here. Spirits leave the body and travel west in the setting sun to arrive in the world of the afterlife."

"Call it what you like. If my heart stops beating, it's death in my book. I know who I am, immortal as a spirit. But I'm not ready to leave my body, not here or on Earth."

"Let me be clear. The living aren't welcome. In the case of immortals such as yourselves, who can reincarnate and remember your experiences, you're not accustomed to being here. Not for long, anyway. It takes a toll on the energy of the spirit when it's trapped in the living body, especially in a realm where you are aren't supposed to be attached to the body. We have to get you through the realm."

"How long ago did you speak with Horus?" Kevin asked, returning to the more immediate matter at hand.

The man turned to meet Kevin's gaze. "Several minutes. Maybe an hour by now. I told him I'd track you. He was busy with a demon of particular strength and tenacity."

The dark angel.

"She doesn't really belong here, either. But then you both have your sights set on a mission to accomplish. I've offered my services to Horus, to see you to the temple pyramid. I believe you'll find what you came for. And I'd like to get the realm back to a state of normalcy."

The first sounds since pulling ourselves out of the water lifted over the previous stillness in the form of several screams. Are those the cries from the spirits of people who had died? They aren't too far from where we are. Then again, could they ever be far enough away?

"You'll want to follow me and quickly." With another wave across his face, the blur of features replaced the details, causing me to wonder why. Like the omission of his name, were features also not important? He started off inland, away from the river, as we followed.

"Can we make it to the pyramid before the dark angel finds us?" I asked.

"Unknown. Whatever you do, do not shift, either of you." He pointed a finger between C-05 and me. "Do not draw attention by the use of energy. This realm is sensitive to such fluctuations."

So I've heard.

A few minutes passed with nothing more than the soft-padded sounds of our footsteps through snow. Tiny blades of grass peeked through as I stashed a gun and pulled my small flashlight, skimming it over the ground in front of us. The trees provided some concealment from anything above. Little good that would do when we were in a highly sensitive world in tune to energy. The light I carried suddenly went dark. I tapped it against my thigh. Nothing.

"Your light does more to show where we are than to help you see," our new guide said. "Here." He held a palm out and the faintest glow encircled his feet. "My energy is already known here and won't draw draw additional attention to us."

"Best to block your thoughts. Even better, keep a blank slate," C-05 said at my back. "The dark angel is keen even to a shift in thought."

The sun had gone down by now, and a full moon was lifting over the horizon, providing additional light to the figure of the man we followed. It had not escaped my attention that the person leading us had not given us his name. Who was this "Keeper" of the City of Souls?

"What do the spirits call you here?" I asked.

"They don't." He paused. "I lead the spirits of the humans to the final place the soul resides. There is no relationship beyond the travel."

"To the city where we heard the screams?"

"That's one location."

"How many other places are there?'

"Too many to recount here. The locations where the soul resides are based on the beliefs the humans carry. How they live their lives, depending upon those beliefs, determines where they will want to be or transition to in the afterlife. Take this," he said, holding a disc out to me.

Strange. I hadn't noticed him holding anything other than a long staff. I holstered the remaining gun and put out my hand, feeling the weight and coolness of a metallic disc in my palm. "The amulet is a necessary tool to access what you seek. You'll know when to activate it." I tucked it in the waist of my pants.

"Something's coming," C-05 said.

"I feel it, too," Kevin added. "Sara, get behind me."

I pulled the guns again, made sure my mind was clear, and put my back against Kevin's as we guarded each other.

"Not here. Follow me to the white cedar tree," the man said.

Cedar?

We ran into a grove of trees whose limbs were bare of leaves. As we entered, the glow of white was easily spotted and oddly comforting.

We were stopped by a fierce growl steps from reaching the tree, echoed by another, as two beasts, each the size of a large tiger, blocked our approach. The illumination of the cedar reflected what could have been mistaken for a lion from a distance. Their faces, framed in a mane, were reptilian with smooth, leathery skin. They flashed rows of teeth that reminded me of a great white shark. The head rested upon a body of fur.

"You have no jurisdiction in these woods," the man said. "Let them pass."

The beasts shook their heads, ruffling their manes, while they ignored the command and continued to block access.

"There is a spell that has been put upon them," he said to us. "This is not their area to protect. And they would never disobey a command from me."

"The Dark Lord," Kevin said.

"The gods are the only ones with power over them. Only one god in the City of Souls would have wanted to turn them on you."

"How many gods are there exactly?" I asked, keeping my attention fixed on the lizard-lions in front of me.

"Two in this realm."

"Would you happen to be one of them?" I asked.

"No. But these creatures belong to me, help guard the realm."

Something about the beasts, the way they were pacing, was causing me to feel that strange twinge just before I'd—

Another scream broke our focus on the beasts and changed into an ear-piercing screech. Mine.

Kevin's arms wrapped around me but it was too late. I'd already shifted, faster than I ever had in the past. My arms broke free of his hold and became the five-foot wingspan that lifted me high above everyone on the ground. *What happened? I never meant to shift.* Kevin picked up the guns I'd dropped before returning his attention upward.

"Shit," he said as I continued to soar higher.

"Your task grows more treacherous," the man said, watching me fly in a circle above him.

My hearing, like my eyesight, was so much sharper in this form.

"We'd better hurry. If Aqen, the underworld god, is responsible for sending the beasts, he's likely already aware of my intervention." With the staff still in hand, he lifted it and pointed to the tree. *"Ahmet da se un."*

A light from the tip of the staff extended its reach to the tree. The longest branch reached out and touched the glow with its tip. The energy combined and formed a radius of light that encircled the group of us, including the lion creatures. The power of it pushed me forward slightly higher in the sky and sent the most sensational feeling running through my bones, from head to foot and back again. I found a current that made it less work to glide above the group. When I lowered my gaze, the light was gone and the lion beasts were walking out the way we had entered on our approach to the white cedar. "We'll follow them to the temple," the man said.

What was the light that had changed the sensations in the air and the intent of the beasts?

C-05 might still have followed any guiding evil, but Kevin wouldn't have. He would have sensed trouble and done anything but let it lead him. I glimpsed ahead and saw the point of what looked like a pyramid. It couldn't be more than a mile. I could be there in no time in this form. I saw Kevin put his arm out for me to land, throwing an article of my clothing over it for protection. I probably should take the invitation and go along with them. But I couldn't. I had to get to that temple as quickly as I could and put the talisman to whatever use it was intended for.

The talisman. Where was it? I must have dropped it when I shifted. Had I left it in my clothing? Must have.

A flash in C-05's hand redirected my sharpened focus. Indeed it was a disc. But had it sparked with white electricity when I'd held it? I didn't think so. How could I be sure it had not been left behind? I could go back. No, not safe.

Kevin's shout to me was followed by sharp stabs of pain, as though a handful of knives had found their mark in my back, connecting with each nerve. Every thought disappeared in an instant. I lost my ability to focus on flight and realized I was no longer in control of my wings but instead being held by, God help me, the jaws or claws of another creature. I struggled against the grip, but each movement tore through the layers of feathers, piercing skin and digging deeper into my flesh. Ugly thoughts of impending death filled my mind. *The dark angel.*

The call of a bird rang out. I craned my neck to see a larger bird flying higher and appearing to dive-bomb the demon that held me clutched in one hand, with long, razor-sharp claws at the end of those graceful but deadly fingers. At last meeting with her, Tarsamon's darkest weapon had called out in a high-pitched scream during the attack. This time she'd plotted and moved with care not to alert anyone, including a guardian of the underworld.

The dark angel turned sharply to one side, leaving me feeling as though the right half of my body was peeling away from its bones.

The pain was becoming too much to bear. I went limp in her grasp. Below, Kevin ran the same length we flew, his rage unstoppable. But where was C-05? At the sight of the bird from below, I shrieked loudly, startled by the thought of another assault, this time from beneath. I feared the bird would hit me. I flapped wildly through the pain, struggling in a last-ditch effort to get free and risking the loss of a wing as the other bird struck at the neck of the deadly predator that held me.

The grip at my back finally released. The pain and memory of the sharpened claws, still stinging and throbbing, clung to every muscle and nerve ending. The cold air found new, tender spots to tap. The breeze this high up made the air feel that much colder. I flapped harder, feeling a new stab of pain with each lift of my wing, and the ground still was getting closer. It was no use. The right side of my body wasn't functioning. I pressed through the pain for a couple more attempts before settling on a glide and, with any luck, a soft landing.

I caught a second glimpse of Kevin as my feet scraped the ground a short distance from him. With his otherworldly speed, he was at my side before my body had fully come to rest on the ground.

"My God," he said, his hands hovering but not touching me. As an empath like me, he had to feel the pain of my injury. "I don't want to hurt you more."

I could not form a thought for him to read. Another screech in the sky sent my body into a tremble. Despite my weakness, the drive to get to the temple was stronger. We might be safe there. I stumbled forward in the direction I'd been heading before the attack by the dark angel, my right wing open and dragging to the side. Kevin took small steps beside me, willing me to stop and allow him to help. In the time we'd been together, we respected each other's strong will. But the time for independence was not now. *Let him help.*

I made it to a nearby sapling, its low-hanging branches heavy with snow as cover, while the sensation that would change me back into my human form worked its way through my body. The excruciating pain radiated as the bones reformed into a human skeleton, still broken at the shoulder. I was aware of Kevin at my side as the last bits of clothing draped over my legs. I still didn't understand how it worked that the elves were capable of creating spells or magic that could anticipate what would be needed in a realm and when. Blood-tinged snow left a trail to where my arm was wrapped tightly in black formfitting fabric. A heavy coat was provided, too, but my arm had been left free of that part.

"Let me see it," Kevin began. But as he kneeled beside me to get a closer look, he leaped to his feet instead and pulled his gun, aiming straight ahead.

Gray feet and matching legs strode in front of us. *The dark angel.* A new trail of fresh blood followed. Was she injured? From what I could see, the dangling arms she held belonged to C-05. She shifted his limp body, barely alive, so that Kevin could see.

"This is what happens to those who belong to the light."

He did once, but could he still? Would the Soltari accept him again?

A single gasp from C-05 sounded like almost like he'd said yes.

The dark angel moved closer. Kevin fired the gun. But a long-fingered talon slipped across C-05's throat. His body fell from her arms and lay unmoving on the ground, the light of his eyes going dark. A sense of sadness coupled with relief crept over them before they completely faded.

I waited for the collapse of gray legs against the snow. Had Kevin missed? Not likely. The sight of blood spilling into the snow sent my stomach into a lurch. I slammed my eyes shut, waiting for a thud that never came.

The deep roar of a lion sounded a short distance from us and I opened my eyes. *The beast.* I waited for a second call from the other in response, but nothing. We'd lost sight of them. Where was the man who had led us to the cedar? Had he left us stranded? I'd have to shift again to find them. Even if I could, I wouldn't be able to fly.

Kevin angled himself more in front of the dark angel. Why was she still alive? He lifted the gun, aiming straight at her head. She didn't flinch faced with the barrel inches away. Another shot sounded. She stumbled backward but didn't fall. Ringing filled my ears, closing out all other sound.

If her focus was on him, she might fight against him. It was exactly what I didn't want. This was a dangerous creature, capable of inflicting a great deal of pain to the living. She'd given C-05 a quick death. And I was grateful for it. The man had suffered long enough, albeit by his own bad decisions. I couldn't have Kevin fight this powerful demon, or die trying.

"Kevin, don't," I said. I needed to move my hands together to create the ball of light.

"You can't hide her," the dark angel said. "Almost had her…" Her voice drifted off. The color of her skin altered between lighter and darker shades of gray with each step.

Why aren't the bullets killing her? Are they the wrong ones? What if they are for the shadows, that would, what did Juno say, only piss off the angel?

"The killing of this pathetic creature doesn't calm the anger I feel toward your kind." She nudged C-05's lifeless body with her foot. "The blood trail I see from your partner is…mildly comforting."

"Nothing can satisfy that insatiable anger," Kevin said, standing firm against her movement, one step forward, another to the side, positioning himself at the right angle. His eyes locked on her. "Let me put you out of your misery."

Before she could answer, the gun he held dropped with a soft thump into the snow. A whirl of black and tan twisted like a dust devil and collided with a flash of steel, in enough time to take a single breath. Two more thumps, much heavier than the last, followed as the angel's head landed seconds ahead of her body and rolled a mere couple of feet from me, her electric-blue eyes fixed wide in a permanent shocked stare.

I pressed a flat palm into the snow to stand but was pushed to a seated position as a blast of powder coupled with black spray clouded my vision and the space in front of me. When it cleared, the body and head of the dark angel were gone, and in her place was one of the hideous lion beasts. Had she disappeared like the shadows that would spin in a funnel cloud and rise into the air above? Or had the lion… The second option was abandoned as I felt my stomach lurch again.

Kevin's otherworldly speed couldn't have been detected, anticipated. I hadn't even felt his intention. His movement was smooth and swift, to finish the creature before she'd ever had a chance to consider his remark, or reach me. The only evidence he carried of the action was the thick gray liquid that ran the length and dripped from the end of his blade.

A single roar jolted me from further thought, echoing a new wave of ringing in my ears.

Kevin turned to me. "Can you walk?" His words were barely audible.

"I think so." With his help, I stood and took a quick assessment of the pain and overall mobility. "Why didn't the bullets kill her?"

"They would have, eventually. She was struggling against the shots, but her energy must have been more powerful than the elves realized. I wasn't willing to wait."

"Good. I was concerned for a moment."

He flashed a smile. "She never had the upper hand once she landed. Not even close. How's your pain?"

"Can you feel it like you feel everything else from me?"

"Not to the same degree. It comes through as waves of pain running through me.

"It's pretty sharp. Better if I don't move." I shrugged the uninjured shoulder. "I'll live. I can't move my arm, though."

He placed his hands over my ears, warming them. The ringing ceased within seconds of him covering them. His eyes searched mine, seeking confirmation I was okay. "You can't fight."

"She isn't meant to," the familiar voice that sent me through the Chamber of Tombs replied. "She has a sole purpose to recover the keys and defend herself when necessary." Horus showed his ghostly form, which lit under the moonlight and reflected off the snow.

"Horus," I said, looking past him. "Where is the man who was with us?"

"Never mind that. He came to get me once you shifted."

"How did the dark angel know where to find us?"

"Your passage through the tunnel with C-05 altered the energy levels, likely signaling your location. She was probably stalking as soon as you exited the river."

Horus directed his attention to Kevin. "Climb upon the back of the lion. He'll carry you to the temple. No dark force caught in these woods would dare confront them."

"Why not?" Kevin asked. "The dark angel had to know the beasts were here."

"They are destructive to evil when not encumbered with a spell from an angry underworld god."

"Wait," Kevin said as I grabbed at the mane of the beast with my uninjured arm and began pulling myself up. "First, let me take a closer look at that." He lifted his flashlight.

"I'm going to need the guns you're holding," I said, spotting them tucked beneath a layer of material.

He slipped them back in place at my thighs and tossed the remaining garments into the pack he had brought, slinging it in a cross-body fashion before taking a closer look at my arm.

"The shoulder is dislocated, and possibly a broken femur. I'm not sure how severe, though. I want to stop the bleeding first. Hold on, okay?"

I nodded.

He wrapped a large but gentle hand around the area with the most blood. I cried out at the slight movement. My skin began to heat under his hand. He had some ability to heal, but I didn't know to what extent.

"Can you heal a break?"

"There's not enough time. But I can close the wound. Prevent further bleeding. It's going to hurt like hell."

"It already does," I said as he gently released the slight pressure and lifted his hand away. "We need to reset the shoulder and immobilize the arm."

"Allow me," Horus said. The white mist that was the spirit encircled my arm and started swirling around it. Intense pain blurred my vision. I buried my face in Kevin's arm as he held me against him and muffled my cry in his shoulder.

In a matter of moments, the knife-stabbing pain had subsided. I turned to face Horus, stunned that the only feeling that was left was a dull ache and soreness.

"It's still going to need time, but at least it's not causing you to be distracted."

"Amazing." I gently stroked my fingers over the area that had hurt the most. "Thank you."

Kevin slipped the arm of my coat over my shoulder. "Wrap your arm around me and I'll place you on its back," he said, referring to the lion beast.

I did as he instructed, placing the uninjured arm around him as he lifted me onto the beast's back. Kevin settled in behind me. I held on to the mane with one hand, as we started back on the path toward the temple pyramid.

"Wait," I said. "We can't leave C-05 here." I turned and looked past Kevin. The only sign of the body that had been there was the blood stain that had been under it. Had it disappeared with the dark angel? Who had taken it? "I don't understand this world," I said more to myself.

"You will when it's your time to pass from the living into the City of Souls," Horus said, his transparent image floating beside us.

"But I thought we could remain in Ardan. You gave me your word."

"You can. But everyone who has lived must pass through the Duat first."

A long silence settled between us, along with contemplation of what was lost and what had almost been lost in a short period of time.

"Where is the rest of the team?" I asked after a few minutes.

"They're meeting us at the temple," Horus said. "Along the path you were traveling before we had to alter it to throw off the evil."

And yet, the evil still managed to find us.

"Tarsamon is in the realm. The demon angel that reached you is not the only one he has with him. The shadows and other demons didn't want to risk coming near the white forest. The cedar was placed in this location for cleansing of an overabundance of evil."

"Then why did the dark angel chance it?"

"She was the one you escaped on your last mission. She was willing to risk the forest, so long as she stayed in flight. We can't look back on what was. It doesn't matter anymore."

Tell that to my arm.

"Our focus needs to be the temple."

"What about the talisman?" I asked, looking at Kevin. "C-05 had it when I took off."

"When he shifted to aid you…"

"What?"

"The bird that caused the dark angel to release you was C-05. She killed him for protecting you. I thought you knew."

Of course. C-05 had only to brush against another person or animal to capture some of their energy to become a mirror image of it. He'd only done so three times since the quest had begun. Once to hide, once to escape, and the last in an attempt to trick me into believing he was Elise.

He'd come to my aid and now he was dead? A wave of guilt washed over me at doubting him, and the words I'd said to him that now seemed more than unkind in death than life.

"He gave me the talisman before he shifted." Kevin paused. "You can't hold on to any feelings of regret, my love. All that happened is as it was meant to be. To keep you alive."

9

"Guard her well," Horus said to Kevin as we pressed past the snow-covered foliage outside the entrance and into the pyramid temple. "Those who reside in the City of Souls are already dead. They have nothing more to lose. Their loyalty, however, belongs to whomever they believe to be strongest in the realm. But your team..."

I nodded. He didn't have to finish the sentence. The fact that our team had plenty at stake was well understood. Our team needed to come together to be as strong as possible.

"How far behind us are they?"

"Close. A matter of minutes is all."

The large room of the temple pyramid was in no way a resting place for tombs but an active building, humming with electrical current and a strange stuttering click sound every couple of seconds. The scent of the air in the room was ionized. Not sterile, like one would find in a hospital setting, but instead as though the water vapor was energized.

I scanned the walls and ceiling covered in the same sparkling quartz as in the crystal cave. Unlike the maze, there were no writings or glyphs telling a story, and only very few smooth surfaces. Instead of muted shades of blue, there was the addition of color, so many different hues, everything from bloodstone and turquoise to citrine and smoky quartz. A deeper layer of purple amethyst rested below the lighter jagged edges. A beautiful kaleidoscope of color without being garish, illuminated by an unknown energy.

"What is this place used for?" I asked.

Horus's transparent form slipped beside me. "It's a healing temple." He drifted higher, to another level above us.

"If it works, why don't the elves use it?"

"They did once, long ago," Kevin said. "Eldor says it's 'old magic' to them now."

Information for the task I'd come to fulfill flooded my senses, drowning out the influx of color. The algorithms I'd been provided could arrange a set of crystals to operate at their highest potential by maximizing the energy within the chemical composition of each crystal. But for what reason? What does it have to do with the key I needed to find? In seconds of reflection on the creation of this mission, the memory surged forward.

Yes. The correct combination, like a lock, releases the specific crystals housing the key.

"There should be a specific set of colored quartz somewhere in here," I said. "Correct arrangement of parts to make the reconstructed whole. That's the key."

I set off in one direction with Kevin close behind. Voices could be heard not too far away, echoing off the walls. The sound of Horus's reply was returned. But that was of no concern to me. The magnetism within these walls drew me to the purpose I'd come to fulfill.

The rise of multicolored crystal, in all shades and varieties, lifted high to the ceiling in a dimmer room off the main hall. I'd found what I was searching for. I reached a hand to touch a blue crystal that conformed to my palm as I rolled my hand over it.

"Diasterism. The stone that has light transmitted through it," I said more to myself. "This one." I placed my other hand upon a piece of rose quartz. The wall of color lit softly in sections beginning with the blue stone, moving its way upward as it came to life. A small, painless electrical current could be felt, moving through the stones I touched. The intensity increased and the center of my abdomen grew as warm as when the Druid priests had given me the key of light. A bead of sweat ran down one temple past my ear.

Could it really be that the energy I carry syncs with the crystals?

The stones began filtering the connectivity as the current made a circular pattern. I held my hand steady, watching as the energy highlighted the stones and traveled into me as though I was another component to the operation of the machine. The ground rocked once beneath my feet.

"It needs this energy to engage the mechanical function. I'm part of the access point."

Kevin, who had been standing off to the side watching the strange process unfold, turned suddenly at the sound of voices that had grown louder. "What else needs to happen? We've been tracked by Tarsamon's forces. I've got to get you to safety."

"It should be engaging but seems stalled. Maybe it is, maybe not. But I can't rush it."

"There isn't any more time left."

I glided my hands over another set of stones, but nothing happened. The light that had been incorporated into the energy of the stones ceased to move, its brightness faded back to normal.

"Wait. The talisman. The man who gave it to me said I would need it."

Kevin dug through the small sack he kept strapped across his chest. "Here," he said, handing it to me. "Hurry."

I could feel his desire to see about the commotion, to aid in the fight I could hear my team engaged in. But his need to stay with me was greater.

"The man said I would know when to activate it."

"Well? Do you?"

I paused, searching for the answer, trying to ignore the increasing sound of fighting getting closer. "No." I looked over the wall of crystals. "There's no place for it here. It must be out in the main corridor area."

"I'll follow you. God willing, we can discreetly find where it belongs and quickly."

As we were leaving, Horus appeared. "The temple is surrounded. The dark forces know you're here."

"The team?" I asked.

"Inside. It didn't take long for them to find you once you connected with the energy in here."

"The crystals are activated. But the talisman... I don't see any place for it."

"That's because it belongs with the underworld god."

"What? Which one?"

A look of confusion fell over his face.

"The nameless man who met us at the Nile said there were two in this realm," Kevin said. "We've got to hurry." His eyes were fixed on an area in the main hall.

"Only one is expecting the talisman. This way," Horus said. He moved to the arched doorway, back to where the commotion was.

The room was very different from when we had first entered, darker somehow, and the ionized scent in the air was gone. My team was fully engaged in fighting the troll-like fiends that had been set free to hunt the trail of my particular energy pattern. Among them were the faceless demons who sought out anything that didn't mirror the energy found in the dark world. The shadows roamed over the once brilliant walls, now dulled behind their gray and black forms. At seeing or scenting me, the creatures stopped.

So many sets of yellow eyes.

A slight movement drew my attention to a ledge where Tarsamon stood gazing down, his red eyes like lasers homed in on me. His appearance, a void of black with beads of red. On other occasions, he'd transformed into the shape of a respectable man, one who offered civil conversation once. But now he wore only a hooded cloak. No face, no visible jawline. All that was present was the pure evil energy that he'd become over time. Though I'd seen it several times, it always reminded me of renditions of the Grim Reaper. This was the form I'd come to know in my history with him, the one he preferred when preparing for battle or a show of strength. What would he do now, with all of my forces and his in one space?

There was no way he intended on letting me get to that last key. He'd laid claim to the energy found among the humans and wasn't about to let that go.

My fingers clutched at the talisman even tighter. It was the one piece that held the promise of the end of this mission. The key was so close I could almost touch it. But holding the talisman meant there was no way I could fight the numerous souls seeking to stop me. As though he knew it, the Dark Lord pointed a long, black finger in my direction, ordering all the forces he'd brought with him to attack.

"The shield, Sara!" Juno called out from somewhere. "Now!"

I did as he said, imagining the force of light wrapping around me, strengthened by the first key I'd been given. But it wasn't there this time. I was only able to create a small band of protection that would never stand against the power blazing in front of me, held at bay for the moment only by the defense of my team. Had I lost the gift from the Druid priests that enhanced my energy, gave me additional protection, when I'd touched the quartz and activated it somehow? And did I still hold that first key if I didn't have the warmth in my abdomen as a sign it was with me? That sensation had always been proof of the existence of the power ever since it had been given to me in a Druid realm hidden in the forests of Scotland. And now, it might be gone.

I looked at Kevin and shook my head, fully aware that he was in tune to my thoughts, feelings. He created a shield and pulled it around us as several of the shadows leaped off the ledges while others that had been hiding began peeling themselves from the quartz, revealing the crystal's true light again.

The winds began to howl through the temple's opening. Elise and Aria were at work manipulating nature and atmospheric energy, to make it difficult for any more of the Tarsamon's forces to enter, while the remaining ones drew closer.

"We can't wait under this shield for long," I said. "There are too many of them."

Where the hell does this talisman go? Where is the underworld god who is supposed to take it? And where did Horus go?

I scanned the wall between the crevices of shadows and demons that clawed at us from outside the shield, in search of a disc-shaped crevice or anyone that might look like an underworld god.

Couldn't get her alone. The Chamber of Tombs. The power in the realm prevented getting close. It had been a cluster of random and obscure thoughts that entered my mind, and not my own. Had I been able to receive a thought from Tarsamon?

A large growl separated from the numerous calls and screeches of Tarsamon's army, filtering past the shield to my ears.

"Topetine," I said, lifting my gaze to see her jaguar form and her glowing green eyes calling to me.

"It's not safe to take down the shield so you can get to her," Kevin said.

"Then don't. She wants us to follow her."

"Which means all of them will follow because they want you or what you carry."

"They're coming whether I stay or follow her. What choice is there? We've got to get this thing to the right place."

"That place is here."

"Then she's only trying to get us to safety. I'm going up there, where Tarsamon is."

Another group of beasts struck the shield, cried out, and recoiled. A show of anger to pin their mark filled their eyes. Their lips curled in fury.

"And do what?" Kevin was reluctant to let me get any closer to danger than necessary. I understood. But my drive to move forward despite that danger was stronger than any need to remain safe.

"I've got to find where to deliver this talisman. There isn't time to wait for Horus."

I pushed past him and ran up the only slope in the cave, with Kevin at my back. The rough grooves of the quartz with some edges sharp enough to cut aided our traction, allowing us to climb faster.

"How strong is your shield?" I asked.

"It's not fading yet. Just do what you need to."

Those words gave me strength. He had my back, and we weren't going to argue over who knew best. There wasn't time, no place for it when our task was this critical and this close to completion.

My injured arm was no more than a dull and throbbing ache as I pushed harder up the steep climb, making sure I was still under the protection of Kevin's shield. As long as I could move, I had to. I could worry about pain when there was time or if I could no longer climb.

We reached the top. Unsure just how long his shield would hold, I lit the spark and watched as it changed instantly into the ball of fire and went out. Something was definitely wrong. Very little shield, no ability to hold the flame as a means of defense. It made no sense.

"I don't have enough energy to fight him," I said. "I don't know why. It must have something to do with the energy in this place."

"Stay beside me."

We angled ourselves against one side of the wall, opposite from where we'd last seen Tarsamon.

"This energy, Tarsamon's, doesn't feel like what I've encountered before."

"That's because not all is as it appears."

"You sound like Cerys, guiding me in Ardan. Why would Tarsamon's energy be any different?"

"This is a different kind of place, Sara. More advanced technology. More advanced energy. It works differently."

"Yes," I said, creeping around the corner. "If only I knew what it was I'm sensing."

Feels dangerous. Which must mean Tarsamon is nearby or plotting a step ahead of us. Where the hell is he?

"Get rid of those thoughts," Kevin said, still right behind me. "They'll weaken you."

I pulled the guns and flattened my back as best I could against the jagged wall. The ledge became more narrow as we inched our way around. "Can't ignore a warning."

I took aim and began firing at the beasts closest to us. Those hit turned into black smoke and rose into the air in the same manner as if I'd struck them with my sword. Caution continued screaming a repeated warning in my head, closing out all other thought. I aimed at the next closest target. *How much ammunition is contained in each weapon?*

"Limitless," Kevin said, hearing the thought. "I've got plenty."

The crackle of electricity pierced the shield. My body slammed against the wall opposite Kevin and beyond his reach. One of the guns clattered the rest of the way down the slope. I stowed the last one, needing my hands free to break a potential fall. The dark angel? At that, my footing broke through the extension of the ledge and I slid down the wall, clinging to a narrow edge, testing the strength of Horus's medical intervention.

"Hold on," Kevin called. "Coming to you."

How? There was no path to the ledge I was on, short of taking some large leaps and hoping for a sure landing.

I fought to pull myself up, but the jagged edges of the crystals were cutting into my fingers. I looked down. Another hard ledge and several feet farther, nothing but solid ground.

No way out but to shift. Dark thoughts. Need a good one to become the hawk. But the talisman…

"Hold this," I said to Kevin. I held tight to the rock cutting into my left hand and tossed the talisman and remaining gun to him, just in time to grasp another ledge with my right hand. My arm throbbed but was still functional. Was Horus's medical work temporary? Or perhaps just a fresh heal being put to a limitless test? *Shift, damn it. Dark thoughts.*

"Sara." A call to me rang out from below. I couldn't look, or risk losing my grip.

The shadows descended to my location, detecting a new sensation to feed upon—fear and the possibility of capitalizing on my slightly weaker state. In the midst of the gray migrations over the crystal, a white mist moved up the side of the wall where Kevin and I had been trying to find where the talisman belonged. *Horus?*

I watched, caught my breath, as it sunk beneath the stone and revealed the hidden shadow of the hooded figure of Tarsamon, uncovering him from his disguise in the wall.

The Dark Lord angled out of reach, jumping closer to a small alcove above me as the white mist lifted from the crystal and extended toward him. A maroon color encircled him. Was that his defensive shield? The last time we'd been this close and he'd tried to touch me, a painful current of white energy flowed from my veins into him, causing him to immediately release his grip. It had been a warning to him that it would take more to uncover the secret of that particular key's strength. Each of the keys held some additional benefit to me for the quest, and by far, keeping a demon lord at bay had been the most useful.

The dark thought I'd been searching for, the memory of Kevin's pain as the witness to the loss of his mother to a killer at age seven, finally arrived, joining with the pain in my arm. I let go of my hold on the rock edge and flapped wildly away and over the fighting below, farther from the shadows that had been closing in.

Midway into circling back to Kevin with the intention to shift back to my human form and retrieve the talisman, I felt the stinging of a thousand fiery needles piercing me. A cloud in the same maroon color that had surrounded Tarsamon engulfed me.

I heard Kevin utter a slew of expletives while realizing I could no longer fly. He raced below me, but the Dark Lord had been faster, closer. I fell to the floor amidst the fighting, my body already shifting back, unable to hold the transformation. When I landed, I was already clothed. So much faster than ever before. Evil thoughts, the dark ones that made one unable to see a way out or any light beyond the nightmare, covered me in a heavy blanket. The pain intensified. It had to be the work of the filthy colored residue that still covered me.

"You may collect that last key," the gravelly voice of the Dark Lord said over my head. "But I won't let you die to release them. You hear me? Suffer. The light will not endure. The time has come for its end."

The back collar of my coat lifted, pulling me several inches off the floor. With what energy I had, I kicked, wished for the dagger the elves had made for me once before, and found the weight on the inside pocket of my coat, along with another at the lapel. Could it be?

I reached inside the coat, pulled the heavy-handled blade, and jabbed the space over my head, hoping the aim would strike the hand or arm that held me tight in Tarsamon's grip.

A scream that wasn't mine ripped across the cave, echoing off the walls. When I blinked again, the black-hooded figure of the Dark Lord was gone. I was lying facedown on the ground, head turned to the side and the dagger gripped in my fist. The maroon color over my body was no more than a thin line.

Despite my fight against it, my eyelids closed in longer increments. *No, not now. Got to get to safety.* I was beginning to slip out of consciousness. Shifting was weakening to a body, but perhaps, too, I couldn't endure his energy any longer. Was losing consciousness a defense mechanism? No way. I wouldn't have trained to be a fighter for a millennium to end up knocked out and at the mercy of any evildoer. But why weren't the other forces in his army capitalizing on his release of me?

I looked up to see what the source of the call had been. The white mist encircled the area of Tarsamon's throat, locking him against the wall. The demons and shadows smothered the area, the scent of fear enticing them, drawing them closer. Fear was what had drawn them to the humans, after all. The very same fear often revealed in the form of anger, a sense of power or control over something they didn't understand. But whose fear was it? Mine at being caught by the evil or Tarsamon's at being caught by Horus? Who was more powerful right now?

Got to move. Got to get out of here. Find Kevin, the talisman, the underworld god. That's the task. Find one thought that will close out the blanket of darkness over me.

Another shriek followed by a chant that had started at one end had me wanting to close out the noise. Why hadn't the demons attacked? Was the maroon energy Tarsamon delivered hiding my own? *Where's Kevin?*

"I'm here. Hold on." Had he spoken over the chaos? "Over here," he shouted.

"Where?" Maybe he was caught or stuck in a battle. I could try to get to him, but I couldn't see well enough to find him.

A small, quick flash burst where I'd heard Kevin's voice and then disappeared.

From the corner of my eye, I spotted Aria and Matt fighting another set of shadows. They ducked as a black, mysterious form, much larger than any of those Tarsamon kept, rolled through like a dark storm cloud, filling any remaining space. My arms were stretched above my head. I pulled them in and planted my face into my hands, still holding the dagger, and said a small prayer to anyone who would listen—the Inner Society, Eldor, Cerys, anyone.

In the darkness, I crawled on my elbows, feeling my way across the floor, as though the weight of ten men pressed upon my back. The pain of the fiery needles was still present but had dulled after the initial sting. The words *no fear* flooded my thoughts, along with a mental picture of the small boy with green eyes and auburn curls I'd met on my mission for the first key. Why him? Back then he had held a light and directed me where to find the Druid priests, but I didn't know him. I had no connection to him. He'd never even told me his name. And yet, for some reason, I held on to the image of him and the small flame as though it was the single factor willing every muscle to move forward toward the voice I'd heard, to a safer place so I could finish this mission.

I couldn't have crept more than a foot or two before I felt a pull at my legs that at first dragged me through the random screams and barks of the demon forces before I was lifted and tossed over a shoulder. There were too many entities to see anyone specifically, much less who had lifted me. My ankles were held tight, preventing me from kicking. I beat my fists upon the strong back of the person holding me and opened my mouth to shout for Juno or Kevin, only to find it quickly covered by a hand.

"Shh. If you keep quiet, I can get you where you need to go."

I stopped fighting. *Who is that? And how the hell does he know where I need to go? Say something else.*

"Shh. Your thoughts, too."

Jade. He was the only one on our team who could trace energy and quickly.

I locked down every thought and word. Silence felt like eternity, until we sat quietly in one of the alcoves away from the main room. I'd tucked the dagger away in my coat and began to feel at the lapel for the additional suspected weapon in the clothing I'd been provided, sliding the chisel-ground two-and-a-half-inch blade out and back into the sheath miraculously sewn into the collar. I'd never used a tactical, surreptitious weapon like it, not in this life, but was well aware of what it was when I'd felt its weight—convenient in an emergency. It just hadn't been the right tool for the job this time around.

The tips of my fingers were beginning to tingle from the cold as I let go of the lapel dagger. Were we outside? The temperature felt as though it had dropped by twenty degrees. I rubbed my hands together and stuffed them under my arms, taking notice of the walls of the alcove. The entire area was surrounded in amethyst-colored crystals. Just how many corridors were in this frigid temple?

Jade put an index finger to his lips. He had the ability to transform energy and hide it, sometimes even the identity of another person. Immortals were keenly aware of shifts in energy, especially their own, making the task almost impossible to successfully carry out without being detected. I didn't fully understand how he was able to accomplish such concealment, but he'd been skilled enough to convince members of the Alliance.

"Horus said this was one refuge set aside if it became necessary. I'd just like to be sure these crystals can block energy." I nodded. After a few moments of silence, he asked, "Do you think you can stand?"

I shrugged my shoulders. "I think so." My shoulder was the most bothersome to me. Still injured, it continued throbbing, but at least I could move it. I wouldn't try climbing anytime soon.

"Trust me?" Jade asked.

"Sure." I stood to find I hadn't injured either leg in the fall. The weakness that had kept my movements to no more than a crawl was gone, free of Tarsamon's blanket of immobility. I could feel my strength returning with each passing minute.

He signaled for me to follow him, peering left and right before he led me outside and around to another alcove.

"This room leads back to the main temple. Don't worry," he said before I could ask about Tarsamon and the demons. "Horus is taking care of that in there." He jutted a thumb in the direction we'd just come from. "I masked your energy to move you out."

"I hope it works."

He placed a hand on either side of my shoulders and held them firm. "Tarsamon might try to track you, sure. Like I said, don't worry. It's being handled. We'll be fine so long as you don't use that strong will and energy of yours to undo the effort. Don't try to shift again."

I flashed the scout's honor symbol and nodded once. Never before would I have listened to anyone telling me what to do, least of all Jade. The man had tried to take the first key from me, and it hadn't mattered that it had been for a good reason. He'd meant to use it as a bargaining tool to make sure no one from the Soltari harmed his men ever again. Very soon after that, and after my anger had been tempered, we'd made a pact to work together to get resolution for him and all of the immortals, agreeing punishment was not incentive. It was crippling, creating anger and resentment where it had no place.

"We have to move quickly. Put your hand here," he said, tapping a set of white crystals in one place.

"Why?"

He cocked his head at me and raised his brows.

"Okay, okay. But Kevin has the talisman," I said quietly.

"This one?" He lifted the disc from his pack.

He'd somehow confiscated the relic from Kevin in all the confusion.

I did as he instructed, placing my hand on the quartz, again feeling the crystals warm beneath my palm. They lit in response to the sensation of heat, however little I carried. That illumination began to transfer to the other crystals around the grouping I'd touched. A crack formed midway to the ceiling, opening large enough to put my hand through. Smaller cracks extended from that. A door to the alcove I'd not seen prior to entering suddenly slid shut. I lifted my hand from the rock.

"What's going on?" I said, no longer caring who might hear. The only sound was the same low *hum click* I'd heard when we had first arrived in the crystal cave that emanated through the temple pyramid.

"Not to worry."

My eyes narrowed on Jade. *Impossible.*

"You said you trusted me," he added.

"I've never heard you say 'not to worry' in, well, ever."

A smirk pulled the corner of his mouth up.

A tiny crack in the quartz had me following it with my fingertip, until chunks began falling out and over my feet. I backed up a step as the crystal began self-carving in a series of semicircles and grooves.

"Here," Jade said, handing the talisman to me.

"How did you know to…?"

"Sara, it's the way it was always meant to work."

But whether he meant where the talisman should go or the fact that he was the one assisting me, I couldn't be sure.

I centered the heavy metal disc into a space mirroring the size and shape of the talisman, turning it to the right until it clicked. The talisman lit.

"Enter the code."

It was my turn to give him a look.

My fingers went to work without a single thought about what the code was, as I spun each of five circles configured on the edges of the disc. Once finished, a small current of electricity moved over its face, as it came to life with the same energy I assumed was contained in the crystals.

The quartz around it began to grow in response—multiple vibrant arrays along with pale hues of blue, green, pink, and clear formed a crisscross pattern over the face, until the talisman was hardly recognizable beneath the layers. The ground trembled, as it had when the crystals had been activated. The previous clicking noise stopped. The device had somehow been the mechanism needed to turn this crystal palace into a place that sounded like a well-oiled machine, creating a hum as smooth as molasses. Electricity flowed across the quartz crystals, uninterrupted and consistent as power streaming over electrical wires.

"Quickly. We've got to get back to the others."

"Is it safe?"

"I told you, Horus has the dark forces under control. He brought a reinforcement."

Reinforcement? "And that's where the key is hidden, right?

Jade didn't answer, only turned for me to follow.

Of course it is. Right in the middle of Hell's creatures.

Jade led us through a narrow hall to a crevice that opened into the main temple. I turned to the side and squeezed through into what had been a battleground of screams and evil. A strange and eerie quiet, not right for the seemingly short time that had passed, filled the temple where my team and the legion of darkness had been fighting. My eyes widened to the size of dinner plates. Every one of the beasts and shadows were locked in a fixed animation, frozen where they stood.

How? I've never seen anything like it, not here or in Ardan.

Another cloud, smaller than the first that had engulfed the temple, made its way across the room, moving like a version of Horus, transparent but dark. I lifted my palms to see if my ability to create the familiar fireball of protection had returned, but Jade put a hand over them.

Everything I'd learned since being reintroduced to my immortality was that all bad things came in the form of darkness. My heart sank. *Why would Jade bring me back when it isn't safe? I trusted him. What if this figure is here to stop me from getting the last key?*

I felt Kevin behind me, his hand at my back. A soft touch. *No one else is alarmed?*

I narrowed my eyes on the length of smoke crossing the room, watching as it transformed into the size and shape of a woman, with one realization—this was the "reinforcement" Jade mentioned. One person had been capable of stopping all of this?

10

It's said by some the eyes tell all. In my experience, that had been true. For as long as I could remember, I could read plain truth or the spinning of a lie in someone's eyes. As I stood motionless in front of this woman, entity, underworld god, my senses detected no hostility, no evil. Only worlds of knowledge stared back at me, and a whole lot of power contained within her being.

Gone was the thick cloud of black that had muddied my vision while I crawled across the floor trying for escape. Instead, a thick cloud of opaque white rested a foot or so above our heads. The open space once filled with screeches, grunts, and fighting had been replaced with an eerie silence. Since I'd locked the talisman into place, the only sound that could be heard was the same smooth hum, without the click this time.

My gaze lifted to Juno and Matt standing just outside the entrance, with Aria and Elise only steps away from them keeping watch.

I turned my attention back to the shadows and the faceless, flesh-colored demons suspended in motion. So many twisted grotesque forms—crawling, arms raised to strike, and the yellow eyes of smaller demons fixed on specific targets. One of the trolls, a gray-skinned creature, held wrinkled hands to his dough-like face, lines of claw marks running the length above and below them. Evidence of Topetine's mauling. Even the black trail of blood pouring from the gashes in his side had halted on the trek downward. Strips of freshly torn flesh hung locked in time. My instinct was to take the creatures down, as if the power that held them immobile would fail at any moment.

What about Tarsamon? I glanced to where I'd last seen Horus holding him by the neck, but there was no sign of either of them.

I didn't trust what I could see. The danger, after all, lay in what was hidden. Yet I had not even the slightest inkling to pull the guns. *The guns! Where are they?* I quickly scanned the floor. Kevin hopefully still had one. The other was nowhere in sight.

"Sara, Light Carrier of the Soltari." I returned my attention to the voice in front of me. "I am Norul, guardian of the underworld." She shifted her gaze to the team that fought with me. "With the talisman in place, you've restored a valuable energy source to this realm."

Technically, a man who resided in this very place had the talisman all along. Couldn't he have restored the power?

She laughed lightly. "A keeper of the City of Souls could not have enabled the crystals to move," she said, evidently hearing my thought. "The talisman is useless without the power you carry from the two keys working in combination with the algorithms."

"Norul, the underworld god?" My question sounded more like a statement, daring contradiction.

"I don't care much for the term *god*, or *goddess*, just as you prefer not to be referred to as *queen*."

I narrowed my eyes, studying her. *How could she possibly know about that conversation?*

"Everything is known in the underworld, except that which is reserved for the keys, of course, like the the algorithms you carry. Once you cross into this realm of life from what you know as death, all conversation, all feeling, anything once hidden from the eyes and ears of the living is revealed once the soul is freed. Only truth exists."

"Revealed to whom?"

"Anyone seeking to know. May I see your right hand?"

I placed my fingertips in her waiting palm. Her other hand extended behind as she touched the crystals glowing with a light of their own. She reached farther to grasp my wrist in a solid grip. A sensation penetrated my skin, to deeper layers that began to warm in a mildly distressing sensation.

What more energy could remain, after it had been drained into the crystals?

"You carry a very powerful life force." Her stare pinned me in place and I saw something shift in her eyes.

What does that have to do with anything? The nerve signals to my brain were on high alert, warning not to exceed the threshold of pain.

The grip on my wrist tightened a little more. I broke the gaze and glanced down to see the color had changed from a once healthy glow to an inflamed patch. A pattern was being created. Was this another mark to indicate passage of the key, like the one the Druids had placed on my abdomen? Whatever it was, it was starting to sting in a most uncomfortable manner.

Before I could withdraw my wrist from Norul's firm hold, a set of strong hands I recognized as Kevin's was on either side of my shoulders.

Distracting. Comforting. Could he feel the pain of this, too? Was he able to displace some of the discomfort with his otherworldly gift of healing?

As if in answer, the prickling beneath the skin diminished.

"You'll want to step back," Norul said.

A small commotion filtered to my ears from behind me as Topetine and Mac shifted. Kevin's hands remained steadfast against my arms. *No danger. All is well.* I couldn't look at the distraction, mesmerized by the eyes of this woman, this ruler of a death realm. *I have to trust everything is being handled.*

The quartz crystals started to crack, all of them this time. And not just in a single line to the ceiling but in a web that extended up and across in every direction. The humming sound grew louder while larger formations pulled back. I captured the movement on either side of Norul as softer stones crumbled around us.

"Your acceptance of the key, the exchange of energy between

you and the stones, has opened the channel for the machine to work properly, as it was intended."

This time, I broke the stare and looked behind her. The wall of crystal had been hiding a deeper mechanism within. A channel of water, from the ground, raced down the center of a newly opened aisle, a hallway, separating one half of the temple from the other. On either side were open doorways to passages. Where they led was a mystery. A dim light shone at the entrance of each, but nothing more was visible. The entire chamber behind her seemed like one massive machine, like the stokehold or boiler room of a ship. My team and I were at the opening, the mouth of the beast.

Like the drop in temperature in the alcove, the sting at my arm cooled, much to my relief, and my gaze drifted back to Norul.

"What does it do?" The words fell out in a sort of slurred mumble. I wasn't even sure if she'd heard me, or if I'd actually said them.

"The temple and its energy are the healing power for this world. It restores balance to a spirit upon arrival. The amount of force created in this pyramidal machine can heal through sound and is shared with other pyramids in the area. Its purpose is to restore energy and a higher state of being to those who have allowed their energy to diminish in life. The force it creates is the connection to all things."

"A part of the whole," I murmured. "As everything is. Nothing is ever truly separate."

She smiled. "No. It's not."

Different notes of the most clear, melodious type rang out, reminding me of the perfect pitch and tone of each individual octave of a large set of wind chimes.

"You've been gifted the last key through the energy of the temple." Norul released my hand. I glanced to see the familiar image of the infinity symbol cooling at my wrist before letting it fall to my side. She turned to Kevin. "The immortality of her spirit will endure with you if you so choose. There is no power strong enough to break the bond you share."

Not even the Soltari?

I blinked a few times out of what felt like a trance, now fully alert and in time to feel the riveting pain hit from behind, collapsing me to the ground. My legs were immobile, preventing escape. I glanced up. Norul's eyes had changed in color and shape, narrowed in rage.

Kevin's arms wrapped around me tight. His body covered mine, hunched over for protection. I turned my head to see what had struck me. *Tarsamon.* He stood at the entrance to the temple, flanked on either side by two more dark angels. One alone was equivalent to the most powerful forces of energy I had ever contended with. *But how?* How had he escaped the death grip Horus had held around his throat? My thoughts raced from the still-frozen beasts and the false sense of safety I'd been surrounded by seconds ago. *What happened?*

My team. They had to be close but I couldn't see them. I didn't know if that was because they were out of my line of sight or because there was a new symptom plaguing me—that of a very bright light closing out my peripheral vision.

"Their thoughts are centered on obtaining you or your blood, whichever is easier to get," Norul said. "Let me deal with this. You"— she pointed to Kevin—"stand behind me."

Kevin gave the orders. He didn't take them. And he sure as hell wouldn't stand behind someone, even at the command of a god, not when my safety was at risk.

I felt his fight—pull me to safety or do what he was instructed— and the quick processing of information that led him to determine the best course of action to stay beside me. If I went down, he'd go with me.

Norul's voice lifted above the commotion, calling out several phrases I didn't comprehend but sounded like commands. A flurry of small shadows fell from the cloud of white and began racing back and forth across the hall, bumping into and around the still-frozen demons.

Could I still shift? And risk a sudden takedown by either of the dark angels? Not a chance. Fighting one was hard enough. Two would be next to impossible, especially in the form of a hawk I was still learning to master.

"Follow me," Kevin said, reaching for my hand.

I stood, took two steps and fell as another lightning bolt of pain rocketed my shoulder. A warning not to move? Screw that. I wasn't anyone's sitting duck. I rolled to the opposite side and pushed myself up. The searing sensation, coupled with the consideration my team was perhaps under the same attack, had rage and the desire to protect rising quickly to the surface. My sight closed in so that it was narrowed but intensely sharp, like the hawk. I waited for the full effect to consume me, but nothing happened. Instead, a tiny blue spark flickered in my line of sight. I held out my hand. The flame lit in my palm and lifted higher, begging to go to work as the fireball weapon I'd utilized in the past. Had this key altered my abilities, enhancing my strengths and eyesight? There was no other explanation for how quickly the energy moved. Expanding the tiny flame, I created the defensive shield to block another hit and felt Kevin's arm wrap around my shoulder.

"I'm okay. Get us out of here."

Kevin released my arm and led the way past the new arrival of Norul's strange little shadow men. They were clumped together in small groups consuming the previously frozen demons and trolls that had followed our team into the temple. As we passed them, they stopped the massive feast and turned. Low growls erupted at either being disturbed or as a warning not to interfere. Likely both, I guessed. My stomach leaped into my throat at the sight of the feasting of half-eaten beings of any sort. I shifted my attention back to Kevin.

That must be death for the undead, the spirits, or at least for the evil in a death realm.

We were steps away from the entrance of the temple, our freedom within reach. Tarsamon and the dark angels were no longer visible. The once empty pyramid was more than cramped with Norul's additional underworld creatures. With the aid of Kevin's speed, we dodged the few additional beasts Tarsamon had brought with him as our team fought against those remaining. It would be an easy finish. *Why had he come back to the temple, anyway, if he had escaped Horus? My blood?* He had to know he was too late, having missed the opportunity to stop me from getting the last key.

The Dark Lord didn't want the keys I held. He had no use for them. And now that I had all three, he wouldn't want me dead if what Mac had once said was true—that I might have to exchange my life to release their energy, the power I held. I had yet to confirm the fact, but that would be the only reason to come back for me, to make sure I never released them.

"Whatever happens, stay with one of us," Kevin said, referring to any member of my team.

On the surface it sounded like a good idea. A safe plan. But that only meant if we were caught, the other person would most certainly be killed. There was a better chance of survival if I separated from them.

A movement near the ceiling caught my attention. I flicked a gaze upward in time to see one of the dark angels sweeping her long wings out in approach. Her head angled to the side. There was no way I would be able to tolerate another encounter of their specific brand of undoing.

Kevin put a hand over my head as we ducked and maintained our course for the door.

Norul called out again, and a sweeping white mist swirled between the dark angel and Tarsamon, rising between the two and lifting into a serpent-like form. Tarsamon disappeared in a veil of maroon as the serpent mist swept upward and twisted around the dark angel like a funnel cloud. The gorgeous turquoise-blue stare widened in shock as the energy that gave her immortality was squeezed from her. Kevin grasped my wrist and pulled me against him as we exited the temple. The wings of the first angel fell limp in the grasp of the ghostly white cloud.

I risked glancing back to see the remaining demon angel break through the white mist just above us, her claws out and ready for attack. Kevin's arm slipped to my waist as he gave one solid yank, tumbling us into the snow-covered brush. I rolled to the side and readied a fiery sphere to hurl, its flickering blue flame reflecting off the snow as it danced in my open palm. As I took aim at the dark angel, a streak of light caught my attention. It had followed the same path from where she had taken off in flight and was at her back before she could adjust her angle to where we'd fallen.

Oh my God, Jade!

The dark angel crash-landed on the ground feet from us, her eyes meeting mine in a fury as she fought to get Jade off her back. She was no match for an immortal with his level of skill with blades, coupled with the angle he'd chosen at the exact right moment. He drove one of his long knives into the back of her neck, the most sensitive area known to have a detrimental effect, and plunged his weight into it so that it angled to the side, severing key nerves and any chance of recovery, before rolling off her. Her shoulder twitched against death before succumbing to the force.

I blew out the flame I held ready and let the shield fade.

Kevin stood alongside me, watching for any movement from the angel.

"You all right?" Kevin asked. Jade let out a deep breath and nodded, resting his hands on his knees. "I owe you one."

"You owe me more than one," he huffed. He lifted his head slightly. "You two had better get out of here. Get back to the Chamber." He looked over the dead creature, kicked at her with a boot, and went to retrieve the knife still lodged at the back of her neck.

"What about Tarsamon?"

"He must have escaped. There's no way he can go in there now," Jade said. "The energy inside is too powerful. But I don't trust that he hasn't got another plan." His attention shifted back to the knife as he wiped it in the snow.

Kevin stood beside me. "Jade's right. We should get back. Are you okay?"

My head felt light, a little dizzy but otherwise okay. "Yes. Are you?"

"Fine."

"He's always fine," Jade added. "Except for that incident back at the little township in the Mayan jungle." He smirked. "Then, not so much."

Back then, Kevin had gone to the aid of a villager who'd asked for his help, claiming to have fallen ill. Only then had he learned

Tarsamon had inflicted a curse on the people of the village and created a trap to capture him, which had very nearly caused Kevin to be severed in half and put on display along with others who had not joined the tormented. The Dark Lord's effort had been a foiled attempt to ensnare me at the point of his rescue. In fact, with magic and spells not being part of my repertoire of otherworldly gifts, saving Kevin had required the skillset of a J-man, better known as a medicine man to the Mayans.

"I don't understand what happened," I said. "Juno and Matt can see coming events." I paused, searching the ground for an answer, before returning my attention back to him. "Their ability has been hindered in other realms in the past, but with a power as strong as the dark angels', how is it that they didn't see them coming?"

"The dark angels can penetrate the defensive power of the keys you hold. You can be sure they can distract lesser energy, like Juno's and Matt's. They did that, and more."

"What do you mean, more?"

"Their abilities were disabled before they could get a warning to you. It's why two of them were here, working together." He let out a deep breath. "Juno and Matt were paralyzed temporarily."

I nodded, still concerned. "I saw them fighting." *I think.*

"They've taken harder blows than that. They've recovered. See?" He pointed the tip of his blade to the side of the pyramid entrance where Matt and Aria were talking, and where Elise brushed a thumb over Juno's brow.

I turned to Kevin. "What about Tarsamon? I could swear I saw Horus hold him in a death grip before Jade pulled me to a safer location. How did he get free?"

"Horus went to get Norul," Kevin replied. "He never had Tarsamon."

"My eyes don't play tricks on me. Not usually."

"The power in there"—he tilted his head in the direction we'd just left—"is more than either of us knows."

"Maybe. But I know what I saw."

"Don't be too sure," Jade said, stowing the blade. "Can't trust anything when the ruler of death is at work."

"Your energy feels different," Kevin said, shifting gears.

"Must be the key. I feel it, too."

"It's something else."

"It's different," Jade said, stepping closer to us.

"I can detect the key, but I sense an energy I've not felt before... that you aren't...well, I think," Kevin said.

"I feel a little dizzy but that's all." *Maybe some residual shoulder pain.* It didn't help being struck by the dark angel after getting the key from Norul. "I'm fine."

"We'll see," Kevin said. "I'd like another look at that shoulder." His hand stroked down the side of my face. "I wonder if your eyes will stay like that."

I shook my head. "What?"

"Tiny sparkles in the cornea."

"Don't know. Could be the same stars making me light-headed." I smiled again.

"We've got to get back to the palace."

"You can say that again," Aria's voice carried from a short distance away. I glanced over to see the rest of the team, including Topetine, still in her jaguar form, with Mac beside her. "Fighting demons is ugly, sweaty work."

"I could use a long soak in that huge jetted tub," Elise said.

"Me, too," Juno added, winking at her.

She shook her head.

I glanced back to Kevin. "Do you know the way?"

"I think so, but from here—"

"I've got it," Jade said. "The path back, that is."

"Is Tarsamon gone?" Matt asked.

"He is." The voice of Horus swept between us, taking shape beside me. "But he's not left the realm. Not without you," he said, angling his head toward me. "He's grown stronger than I anticipated, and there's only one way that could have happened—he's joined with Aqen."

"What? Who?" I asked.

"Aqen, the second god of the underworld, and the only other one with a tie to the demons in the realm. He's usually a protector in the City of Souls and has been known to manipulate time as well as devour condemned souls."

Hmm. What might cause a protector to do harm?

"Wait," I said. "Norul is responsible for getting rid of the frozen demons. She wouldn't have joined with the evil."

"No. Norul is the keeper of the key you released from the crystals in the temple, and yes, she helped clear Tarsamon's forces. Her power overrides any other god in the realm. But only Aqen could have led the Dark Lord to the temple. No one of lesser strength would have dared defy Norul."

"But why? What's in it for him?"

"I don't know yet."

"And the man who led C-05, Kevin, and me to the temple?"

"He assists Norul by transitioning the spirits from life into the City of Souls."

"Yeah, where's C-05, any… Oh…" Aria said as Kevin sent the images of the battle to her.

Jade turned to Horus. "You're saying we have another god to deal with who is *helping* Tarsamon?"

"It appears so."

I let out a heavy sigh. "But you had Tarsamon in a death grip," I said. "I saw it." Would we ever be able to stop him? My head suddenly felt heavy, as though I was trying to balance a bowling ball on my shoulders. "How did he get free?"

"I never had Tarsamon in a death grip." He looked closer at me. "I wonder if he caused you to hallucinate, maybe believing it would distract you. If Aqen's involved, I don't have the power to kill a demon of his strength. I sought out Norul to ensure you had received the last key. It's dangerous for Tarsamon to be in the pyramid with the powerful energy it contains. The energy counters his own, like a repelling magnet."

"Do you know where Tarsamon is now?" I asked.

"With Aqen, I suppose, plotting another attempt to get to you." He leaned closer to my face. "Your strength is growing weaker."

"Why?" Kevin asked.

Horus moved around me and shifted again into his translucent form. "Let's get you back to the palace and see if we can help you feel better."

A sudden sense of concern washed over Kevin. I felt him block it from my view.

"Jade," Horus said, "you can find the path we took to get here?"

He nodded. "I've got it."

"Take her and Kevin first."

I stood, took three steps, and fell. "What the hell?"

"The dark angel?" Kevin turned to where Horus had been. "You have healing powers I don't possess," he said. "Help her."

"If this symptom was from the dark angel, I could. But it's not. I can't help her."

"The elves can heal her," Jade said.

"They can't."

"Impossible. They have a spell to counter any evil," Kevin said. "I've seen it myself."

"They won't interfere with the path of the key. Go now."

Path of the key?

Jade bent down beside me.

"I'll carry her," Kevin said. He looked at me. "Don't worry, we'll make this right."

I had no doubt he would. He was a determined man, used to getting what he wanted. What concerned me most was I couldn't read his thoughts. The look upon his face said more than the thought I feared he was hiding—that Tarsamon had made me ill again. But if that were so, if the illness was from Tarsamon, Horus or the elves would have been able to help me. Why couldn't the strongest powers in Ardan heal me?

11

"This is nothing more than fatigue," I said to Kevin. The bed was full of pillows, and I used every one to squish into a wall of comfort. "My body went through more than it ever has. I've used up all of my energy. I just need to rest and I'll be back to myself." *Maybe.*

The concern I'd not seen before in Kevin's face and the fact that Horus wouldn't be specific about why I needed to be rushed back by Jade were a little unnerving. But it would take a lot more than a worried look and no answer to rattle me. Nothing a good solid sleep and food couldn't rectify. But sleep first.

Kevin nodded and settled in beside me in the room we shared above the Chamber of Tombs. I was still curious why it had been given such a name if no actual tombs were present. Maybe there was a plan for them to be one day.

"You don't have to watch over me," I said. I felt a twinge of a sensation from him that I didn't need him. This life had not afforded me the feeling of needing anyone. Not until I'd almost lost him in that last voyage for key number two.

"It's the only way I can be assured you'll sleep."

True. I had to admit since we'd begun sleeping together, I settled in for rest much easier than without him. His six-foot-two-inch frame wrapped in taut muscle brought a sense of security I couldn't deny.

The gentle touch of his strong hands sweeping my hair back before gliding up and down my back was most effective at lulling me to sleep.

This moment was no different. After he gave me a tender kiss and another at my neck, I reached over to stroke his chest, only to have my hand clasped in his and held over his heart. As I lay in silence beside him, listening to his relaxed breaths and feeling the rhythmic beating of his heart, my eyes grew heavier, and within a matter of minutes, I'd crossed into unconsciousness and into a place that felt like Ardan, but an area I didn't recognize.

Going to the realm without any intention was a sign someone wanted to communicate with me. I couldn't have taken more than two steps before sensing a presence. I stepped closer to see a set of eyes glowing from behind the shadows of lengthy bare branches in the dark.

Not red. Not Tarsamon. Then who? And why?

Golden eyes shifted right then left, and a large, furry head pressed up from beneath the lower arms of the trees. *Karshan.* The great wolf, guarded the boundaries of Ardan and, from time to time, had been known to do the same for me from a distance.

"You're in great danger, my dear. Where is the warrior who travels with you?"

"Possibly close behind." If he was planning on sleeping, that is. "Did you summon me?"

"No. I don't summon. I protect."

"Then who?"

"I imagine the Dark Lord is following you. Now that you have the last key, he wouldn't want you to release them."

"Where is this place?" I glanced past him. "I don't recognize it."

He lifted his nose to the air. "Ardan grows colder, darker. It desperately needs the release of the keys. Why do you wait?"

"I was told by the guardian of the first key the only way to release them was upon my death. I question the accuracy of his information." What trusted source could confirm such a fact? It wasn't that I didn't trust Mac, but this was my life. What if he had been misinformed?

I glanced at the sky behind Karshan and back to him. "I couldn't have been away from here for more than a week. How could it possibly have changed so much?"

The area indeed resembled the darker, vacant landscape where Tarsamon had been ordered by the Soltari to live the rest of eternity in seclusion. New saplings at the base of their larger counterparts were already gone. Some of the adult trees still held their leaves. Those that did, along with the brush, were faded in color.

"While you've been at work, the evil that seeks to consume all life has extended its reach across this realm and Earth. Those of us who guard the boundary can no longer contain its growth. We believe the Dark Lord has another source of power aiding him. The only answer is to release the keys."

"Is it true I must sacrifice my life to fulfill that task?"

"It's what has been foretold. The Dark Lord, should he get close enough, will seek your blood."

"I've heard this before," I said, remembering Norul had said something similar.

"But not to kill, you understand? Now that you have all three keys, with only a sample of your life energy, he can prevent your release of them, or so it is written in the *Book of Spells*."

The memory of the magical book returned. While I didn't know all about the spells contained within the pages, there was one I had become familiar with long before I'd chosen to come to Earth to fulfill the quest. The spell I believed Karshan was referring to stated that, with the blood of an immortal queen, otherworldly power she might hold could be transformed, her energy reworked. There had once been whispers in the realm that it was even possible to manipulate it in favor of the entity who had been able to collect the blood. I never gave much attention to such rumors, but now I wondered if there was any truth to such tales. The spell hadn't been written for that purpose, of course, but rather had been created as a means to enhance the abilities of a powerful, trusted source in Ardan to make that entity stronger. *What if, instead, that composition could be changed into a potent poison against the energy I carry, so that it would have a reverse effect?* The words *disabling* and *weak* swirled through my head.

"My dear," the wolf said, "Tarsamon doesn't have the power to change the energy of the keys. With the growth of his forces, Tarsamon has little interest in your current strengths. All but one. He would have a greater desire to create an antidote to prevent your death as a human, to keep you from releasing the keys."

"If my death is called for, I accept it, to rescue the lives of Earth, to save Ardan. I don't want to live forever as a human, only as the spirit I am after I've left my human form, just as it's always been. But I can't release the keys yet."

"You must. It's the only way you can save our worlds."

"I know. Believe me, I know. There is business that needs to be resolved with the highest entity. The Soltari needs a new leader, or at least reforming."

"You can claim your place when the keys are released."

"I don't give a damn about my position in the Order. I need to be sure changes will be made, whether I claim a place, as you say, or not. The best chance of that happening is while I hold the keys."

A wind picked up, resonating a deep *whoa* sound, raising the fur on the powerful but gentle wolf's back. He flicked his ears at it. Wind didn't move in Ardan. The fact that it did now was further proof the world of the immortals had changed. Karshan lifted his nose higher, seeking all information that could be carried on the current.

"If you didn't summon me, how did you know—"

"I guard the perimeter of Ardan. But the boundary has moved. The elves have joined with the wolves, to kill the shadows and demons seeking access to maintain some stability in the realm. I track the evil and, wherever possible, your presence in relation to it. We all do. For the cause we fight for. Deliver the keys. Finish the quest."

"I intend to." *When the time is right.*

He lowered his head and turned before bounding off, disappearing into the gray shadows.

I had to restore balance in both realms and soon. It was the only way any semblance of peace could be recovered. With the light of understanding, the veil of unknowing would be removed. A respect for all life, the second key, would reflect as love. And the last key, the acceptance of all things as they are, as they were intended to be, would reduce the personal and widespread struggle among humans. Even for an immortal like me, who remembered such possibilities existing in other realms and after hundreds of missions, visualizing the effects was almost impossible.

The realization that my life might need to be exchanged to accomplish the task was quickly becoming a growing burden to carry. I might not want to live forever as a human, but I also didn't want to leave Kevin in this life. Did I have to? Was there another way?

The first order of business had to be the Soltari. I hadn't met with them since discovering the Alliance had been infiltrated with members who, in fact, desired to see it fail.

Jade suspected there might also be individual spirits working within the Soltari that were steering me and my team in the wrong direction. How could that have happened? How could spirits have been compromised to the Dark Lord? What could they gain in power that they didn't already have? While I supposed the notion was plausible, it seemed more unlikely.

As though having the spiritual order in the forefront of my thoughts had summoned them directly, the ghostly white mist drifted in and swirled around me like sea spray, gradually at first and then as a mass of white. When it had finished, the image of a hundred or so floating, transparent faces mingled within the mist.

I didn't wait for them to initiate conversation. "By now you must know I have my full memory restored." A mild buzzing sound like that of a swarm of bees passing over one's head was all that was returned. "I am aware that not all who were once for the success of this mission remain so. Some have turned against the quest. The Alliance is compromised with those who work for the Dark Lord. That could only have happened by a similar path that had been opened on Earth also being opened in Ardan. Or"—I considered the thought regarding corruption at the highest level—"at your approval of their appointed seats on the council."

Since obtaining the second key, and the doubt that had grown from a seedling into a real possibility, the words were finally out in the open. The accusation hung heavy in the stillness around me. How many, exactly, were against me? I had to take a shot that the majority was on my side.

"I'll not release the keys without changes. Changes that work to aid the immortals going forward." If they were all against me, they would not find a problem with the challenge, possibly even encourage no release.

The hum grew louder and a single voice rose above it, as the entity collectively put the thought into verbal form. "What is it you wish from us, Arwyn, Light Carrier?"

"There will be no punishments for the immortals who work for balance in the realms. It undermines their loyalty and weakens them. There will be no separation of eternal partners, no famines to be endured by the soldiers or other penalties imposed for those working on behalf of you. You've opened a path for darkness, this infiltration, by implementing such a rule of punishment."

Tarsamon had once been part of the Alliance, as had C-05. Both had turned against the order. How many other souls harbored resentment or anger in the realms?

The hum grew louder, ceased, and picked up again. "We will consider your request."

"You'll do more than consider it if you aim to have me release the keys and have balance restored."

"You have no power over the release."

"Oh, but I do."

"Your humanity, your weakness as a human will force the release."

"What do you mean, *force* the release?"

The heaviness I felt in my body right after the fight returned as if in answer. How could I be feeling this way in Ardan? The realm had always been a place of strength, growth, healing. Like the visual landscape, had that, too, been compromised?

"You can't control what your human body feels, not even as an immortal."

Wait a minute. A sense of betrayal punched me straight in the face. "You've made me ill? You've forced an early death upon me?" *Not possible. I would have remembered that at the onset of the quest, or at least in the planning of the mission. There had to be another way to release the keys.* But as I raced to find options, blocked passages were all that met me.

The mist pulled together, the faces disappearing. A sign they were finished with the discussion. All without a single note of agreement. How many of the souls had been compromised to Tarsamon? How many like Horus still fought for this quest?

"I will not release the keys without your promise of protection for the immortals!" I shouted to the swirling mist. "They will not fight for you again without your assurance!" A rush of rage, feelings of unfairness, flooded me. I suddenly had a clear understanding of the drive the Dark Lord had for revenge toward the Order. What I also understood was that retribution wouldn't solve the discord. And I had no intention of living forever in the dark state of death that was quickly consuming Ardan and Earth.

Had coming to the Soltari been a mistake? What if they were more powerful than my ability to command the power of the keys? What if they were right that as a human I wouldn't be able to control whether or not that power was released?

"They're right. In case you were wondering." The booming sound of Tarsamon's voice replaced the temperate sound of hundreds of spirits. He startled me with the interruption and with the surprise that he was likely telling the truth. I didn't detect a lie in his statement. Because he'd once been part of the Alliance, long, long ago, he would be fully aware of how the order might have planned the release of the keys. That is, unless they had made changes since he'd been exiled to a small area of Ardan, away from any other immortals.

The sensation of heaviness in my head settled like a lead blanket over my shoulders. *Given all the chaos, could he be lying and I wasn't picking up on it?*

"You should know better than that, Sara," he said, hearing the thought. "Lies aren't possible in Ardan, even though the environment has changed more to suit me. But admittedly, truth can be one's undoing or set one free. Isn't that what they say in that world you care so much for, or something to the effect?"

The power of all three keys was enough to rid the world of a plague. The energy I carried in my veins lifted to the surface in response to the Dark Lord's presence and evidence that all three keys were still present. The pain of it, however, was more dulled than I remembered. I lowered my head and pulled the strength I had to my center, trying to shed the imaginary weighted blanket from my shoulders.

"Fate works against you," he said. "You're not going to win this."

"As long as you haven't fulfilled your takeover of Earth, and evidently Ardan, too, I possess all the opportunity of someone who can."

I lifted my head just in time to see a swirl of black followed by a blaze of energy coming at me. A red cloud sent me sailing across the landscape. Negative thoughts clouded my mind. I replaced them with the image of the light I'd once seen the little boy holding on the quest for the first key and found my strength. With every intention of hurling an equivalent response in the form of a ball of blazing fire, I opened my palm. The tips of the blue-white flame lifted off the edges of the sphere on its path toward him. Instead of a single immobilizing blow, the fireball surrounded him in a cloud of energy and held him in its clutches. When he fell to the ground, it dissipated.

"That's the fight I expected," he said, slowly standing. "But I don't want to fight you. We would both grow tired from the effort." He paused. "You know as well as I we won't kill each other."

Want to bet? "Yeah, I often fight for the sheer fun of it," I growled under my breath.

"You can't kill me because we come from the same source of energy that created us. We are of equal strength. You know that now. We will exist always."

"You could kill me because I'm human, but you don't want me dead."

"No. I don't. For obvious reasons pertaining to that energy you carry. I can help you, though."

"You don't want to help me, either." *So, one could tell a lie in Ardan. The realm had changed more than I thought.*

A deep sort of laugh rumbled in his chest. "You do remember. Truth can be altered while not being a blatant lie."

"You want to help yourself."

"I have a mission of my own to protect." He paused. "And yes, I'd like very much to terminate your assignment. If you were hurt in the process, well..." Without finishing the sentence, he threw out a long, whip-like rope. I tucked my body forward to flip and missed the strike.

The sensation of electricity returned without my command, and another cloud of crackling energy filled my palm and thrust toward him. His whip flew out again. I whirled to the left as a sharp sting caught at my shoulder on the turn. The energy I held demanded release, clinging to the rope before fading.

Where are the elves, the wolf that followed the evil and my position?

"You've gone against the Soltari, dear lady. They aren't going to allow your energy to be protected by the forces that work for them."

"You're lying again." *Then again, the Soltari want me to die to free the keys' energy.*

"That's right," he said. "But don't worry. I'm not here to kill you."

Which must mean the Soltari haven't been completely infiltrated by Tarsamon. They hadn't fought to keep me alive like he is. He's still trying to gain a foothold in the Order. If he doesn't, so what if he loses a few of his own forces to abandon the cause?

"This mission you are on finally has the chance to work in both of our favors."

"Impossible. The Soltari would never have set up an outcome that would allow light and darkness at its full strength to exist together."

"True. But what if you could live out your life with him, your love? What if I could give you what you want?"

"You don't possess such a power."

"Perhaps not at this moment. But with the help of this," he said, picking up the end of the rope that had tagged me, "and my connection in the City of Souls, I have an offering."

"Only a god of the underworld could deny entrance into death."

His eyes changed to a pale yellow, a sign of satisfaction.

So, it's true. He's working with Aqen.

Why would the rope have anything to do with… And then it occurred to me. I looked at my shoulder, bleeding from a gash expertly placed approximately six inches down my bicep. *Caught on the turnaway.* Could what Karshan said be true? He'd seek my blood to prevent my death? But I knew the answer before I'd finished the question. Of course it was. My guides and those who protected me never misled me.

"What offering?"

"I see I've piqued your interest. I'll be in touch." He turned to look behind him.

The energy flowing through my veins lifted again, demanding another release, as though directed by an unseen force that sought to search out its opposing energy and strike.

I opened my palm. *I could kill him. End this once and for all.* I lifted my arm to release the energy that had already formed and was sent to my knees. The flame was diffused as it hit the ground. My legs had given out. I needed to wake from this place and soon, to get back to the palace where I'd fallen asleep.

He turned and shifted his image into the civil man I'd once spoken with early in the quest, flashing the same satisfaction, again, in the form of a poisoned smile.

Just behind him, several sets of eyes twinkled like low-rising stars on a would-be horizon. Karshan's pack?

I picked up on another slight movement beyond the branches of a nearby tree, between the gazes of wolves. Metal-tipped arrows glimmered in what little light still remained in the realm.

"You offer nothing to me," I called out as he shifted back to his shadowy, cloaked form.

"Give it some thought. You may decide otherwise. But don't wait too long. That weakness you feel is very real. You fight for more than you and your love and the pathetic humans."

What did he mean, more?

And with that, his image dropped into a black shadow that covered the ground like a murky puddle, as glowing sets of eyes disappeared and the arrows flew with exceptional precision past my head in his direction.

"Sara. Do you hear me?"

I looked to where I'd seen the wolves, but the voice had not been the same as Karshan's. The elves were invisible, vanishing as quickly as they'd appeared.

Who had spoken?

12

"I'll never deal with you!" I shouted.

"Sara."

I blinked open my eyes to the room I'd fallen asleep in.

The soul traveled to other realms while asleep, because it didn't need the rest a physical body did. And yet, any injury sustained in those realms carried back to the physical world to be felt and remembered for the lesson it often was.

As Kevin sat beside me, candles the size of fence posts burned in the corner of the room, flickering light off the walls. Slowly, my recall of lying beside him and dozing in darkness returned. Gauze padding tinged with bright red blood lay on the table beside the bed.

"What the hell? How long was I asleep?"

"Only minutes. But long enough to get this."

I glanced down to see the fingertips of one hand pressed against my skin while the other held a pen-like device against the wound.

"Is that surgical glue?"

"Mm-hm," he said, his eyes still focused on the closure. "The cut wasn't too deep. Did you meet up with the dark forces in Ardan?"

"It looked like Ardan, but nothing like what I remember. And no dark forces, but Tarsamon himself."

"Jesus, Sara." He lifted the pen and met my stare.

"He must have summoned me there. The wolves showed, and the

elves. We battled a bit, but he…I don't know…said he wanted to hurt me, had some offer."

Kevin's eyes narrowed as he tried to make sense of my ramblings. "What offer?"

My eyes drifted down to the side of the bed, recalling. "To live out my life with you, on Earth, as opposed to dying."

"He can't make an offer like that. The keys must be released so that Earth can be preserved and we can remain together. This life"—he splayed an open palm—"is just a small part of our existence together."

"I know."

He shook his head. "It doesn't make sense for him to summon you for an offer he can't make."

"He's also joined with Aqen, confirming what Horus suspected. But I met with Karshan and…" I paused, this time trying to hear the wolf's words exactly. "Something about the blood and an antidote or…I don't know." I was rambling again and, instead of continuing, stopped talking.

"Okay, slow down. Antidote for what?"

"I met with Karshan."

"You mentioned that."

"He said it's written that I must die to release the keys. That the Dark Lord was in the realm and he was tracking him. That's how I ran into the wolf. He said Tarsamon could create an antidote to prevent me from dying."

"Karshan told you about an antidote to prevent you from releasing the keys?"

"Yes. I suppose."

"Did he say where it's written?"

Was he that specific? "The *Book of Spells.*"

"Karshan is a long-time protector of the immortals. His knowledge is trusted." He paused. "And Tarsamon wanted to make a deal with you regarding this antidote?"

"Yes. I think so. I can only assume the deal for us would mean we would remain together if we allow him to consume the energy in humanity and to finish growing his forces in all of Ardan. But to make that happen, he would've had to have fully infiltrated the Soltari. I'm not convinced he has."

Silence passed between us.

"There's something missing. Why come to you with a deal for us to stay together in this life if what we fight for is eternity outside of it? He knows that's more important to us. That's no deal for us."

"Fight for," I repeated, recalling more of the conversation. "Yes. He said I fight for more than my love. I didn't understand what he meant. We fight for all the lives on Earth, to preserve that world."

"He already knows that because he's fighting to keep what he's claimed of Earth." Kevin shook his head. "No. He knows something more. His deal is weak unless there was a way to ensure that we would want to stay on Earth more than we'd care about eternity together in Ardan."

I put a hand on his cheek. He shifted out of the trance-like state. "I do love you, and I want to stay with you in this life as well as any other."

"I love you, too. What we want is to be sure what we have exists forever, not just right now."

"Norul said there is no power strong enough to separate us. That must mean even the Soltari couldn't do so. That threat must no longer exist."

"Maybe," he said, folding his arms and rubbing an index finger beneath his chin. "How would he make an antidote anyway?"

"Karshan said with my blood."

"And is that how this happened?" Kevin motioned toward my shoulder.

"He had some whip or something. I moved out of the way, but the tip caught my shoulder. It could have been much worse, I suppose."

"Maybe it was enough."

"What do you mean?"

"The laceration would have provided DNA, your blood, on the rope for him to use. Lady Mara, the old woman in England who created one of the protective rings for you"—I nodded—"she uses DNA to create specific weapons for the immortals to match with their energy."

I recalled the ring she'd given me on the first quest made from chiastolite, a stone with tan and black coloring set in silver. It provided protection from the evil seeking the energy I carried, but only for a short, unspecified time. She had shown me her stockpile of weapons and had even asked for a donation, a lock of hair, to build more of them for me.

"She was an expert at potions, like her mother and grandmother before her," I said. "She told me about them. And if she could do that, Tarsamon could do the same or has access to someone who can. But why would he think I'd deal with him?"

Kevin shook his head again. "I don't know. And it damn well bothers me."

I threw the covers back and swung my legs over the side of the bed. "We need to find Horus. He might have more answers." As I stood to get my boots, I fell into Kevin.

"You're not going anywhere yet." He helped me back to bed and sat beside me.

"Think you'd better tell her," Jade's voice sounded at the doorway. He'd cracked the door open farther. "I knocked but there was no reply."

I looked from him to Kevin, my patience hardly able to stand the sudden hollow of quiet that felt like minutes passing between us.

Kevin huffed out a breath. "The key you were given in the temple isn't like the others."

"In what way?"

"It doesn't give you additional protection moving forward like the others did." The look on his face turned solemn. He lowered his gaze.

"What he's trying to say is that the key can't give you protection because you don't need it anymore," Jade said.

"I get that."

"No. Not completely," Kevin added. "Instead of protection, it's given you an illness. A means in which to release the power of the keys."

"A death sentence. I know." I paused, suddenly realizing the reality of what I'd said. It was one thing to know a fact, another to have the truth of it, the mortality of it, dished out and served cold. "It's what the Soltari meant when they said I had no control over the humanity I live with. That it will force the release of the keys."

"You spoke with the Soltari?" Jade asked.

"I promised you I would uphold my end of our bargain." *Did I need to share with him they hadn't agreed to it?*

"I told them I wouldn't release the keys until I had their guarantee there would be no more punishments against the immortals, including famines." I looked at Kevin. "And no separation of eternal partners for those who fight for balance in the realms."

The silence in the room emulated that of a mausoleum.

"Their answer was?" Jade said finally.

"There was none. They seemed quite sure I had no power over the release of the keys."

Kevin and Jade shot a glance to each other.

"But you do?" Kevin said.

"I may have been given a death sentence, but you have my solemn promise that, with every fiber of my being, I will not release the keys without a guarantee that permanent changes will be made."

"Your promise isn't strong enough to keep your heart beating if it isn't meant to," Jade said.

Kevin put a hand out to Jade, effectively stopping any further discussion on the matter. Jade turned and left the room without another word.

Was it true? My fate was imminent death *and* no control over the keys I held? I had to be damn sure of what I was pressing with the Soltari. Because if I was wrong—My thoughts were cut off as I glanced to Kevin. His brows furrowed in worry, or was it anger?

"What is it?" I asked.

"You can't risk this, Sara. We need to finish the quest, to rescue the humans from Tarsamon, to keep what we have. Nothing more. Not Jade and his men, not the other immortals who fight for balance in the realms. And you sure as hell can't agree to deal with the Dark Lord."

"More than anything, I don't want to lose us in this, or let humanity die. But there's a rare opportunity to create a better existence for the immortals, too. Don't you see? If that can happen, we reduce the resentment that is shifting the balance, planting the seed of the Dark Lord's anger and his path of retribution." I paused. "I don't want to make a deal with him. I want to end the creation of such evil."

As the words left my mouth, I couldn't believe how I'd changed from hardly accepting Ardan as anything other than a dream following a bad car accident, to fighting for what the immortals needed, deserved for their service to the entity they worked for. There was no way I could ever go back to the way things used to be, a way of life I once wished I could return to. The words that defined my existence prior to this quest—doctor, philanthropist, daughter—didn't matter.

"I can't stop you," Kevin said.

I had to be certain about what I was doing, who I was testing, or all of us, the loyal team that stood by us, would lose their bonds to each other, as well.

"Do you want me to stop?"

He waited before answering. "I told you I trusted you long before you had the first key." His eyes dropped to the floor in a single blink and returned to my steady gaze. "I meant it. I'll stand beside you if you feel this strongly about fighting for more. But I don't see how you're going to overcome a death sentence to release the keys."

"To tell you the truth, I don't know, either. But I am sure it's a path I have to take."

"You're that confident?" I nodded. "I've followed you down the road of uncertainty before, where the answers were not so obvious, and it's led us all the way here successfully." He paused, then nodded. "I'll do it again. For you. For all of us."

"Thank you."

He sat beside me and pressed his lips into a smile.

The thoughts being exchanged between us, no longer hidden for the sake of the other, swirled like a storm around us, busy as a swarm of bees. His thoughts of our pending future along with my loss of one with him, in New York, possibly with children, slammed together with all the violence of the collision I'd been in that had nearly claimed my life and set me on this path.

"If you remembered," he said finally, "every last detail in Ardan we shared."

"I'm not the same person I was when you met me, Kevin. A whole lot more has come to light about our past than I'd ever been granted when we started this mission."

Fleeting visions of our past lives had injected themselves at random points in time since going on that first date with him. After that, flashes of memory came more frequently without ever completing the entire picture, frustrating and drawing me closer to him at the same time. That is, until I received Kevin's proposal for marriage along with a ring that somehow held the key to putting all the pieces of the puzzle together. Before accepting the ring, I'd never realized this had been the first life where my memory had been blocked, answering why I'd been angry with the Alliance about their decision. I drifted into a mild trance-like state, to another place far beyond this one, with one question in mind—had we ever had a family? An unexplained sadness pressed away all other sensations. Before I could delve deeper for the answer, Kevin's words penetrated the thought.

"I wonder if you remember a certain feeling exchanged between us that can only come from a memory of time we've spent in Ardan? You can't feel its full effect on Earth. Do you remember it?"

I considered what memories had come back, feelings of my bond with him, in Ardan and now. I still felt very close. I felt the history, all that we'd been through. "Do you mean the tingling sensation that starts at my neck and runs down my left side?" In Ardan, I'd felt it without him touching me, but simply by being nearby.

"Yes, that's the one."

I shook my head. "It's an intense physical sensation, but what about it?"

"That feeling between us is so much stronger when we aren't tied to the heaviness of our lives on Earth. It's so much more than you've been able to feel. There isn't a word that exists to describe such a connection, that sensation of being free from the physical."

I stared at him, willing that feeling to come through so the empath I was could feel deeper, to no avail. "What are you saying? That if I could feel that much, I wouldn't have any doubt about leaving? I wouldn't risk our eternal future by pursuing more for the immortals?"

"No," he said quietly. "Only to remind you that it's provided comfort to you in the past." He slid his hand over mine and leaned into me. "I felt your sadness."

My heart sank, rocked by his words, embarrassed at doubting his decision to follow my path despite his initial objection. "Oh." I released a deep breath. "I'm sorry," I said, the words sounding out of place and awkward, but still owed. Bad habits were hard to break. Trust issues even harder to mend.

"I meant what I said about standing by your decision with the Soltari."

"And I believe you."

The heaviness in my head returned, and with it the need to close my eyes. I'd have to fight like hell to beat an illness as strong as the one given to me.

It's as though the last key's energy was spiked with a toxin. A toxin, I thought, instilled by the Soltari. The entity was capable of planning every aspect of a mission to its finest detail. And still, with all of my memories intact, I didn't have the one that said I had agreed to give up my life to rescue the world. That wasn't part of the plan. Unable to fight to keep my eyes open any longer, I sank my head into the pillow, mumbling, "I'm not done. I'll find a way."

13

"The Light Carrier is already dead." Aqen's raspy voice grated on Tarsamon's tortured soul that much more. "The last key holds the death sentence to force the release of the keys' energy. You can't change that. *She* can't change that."

"She can't die," he growled. "Too much has been accumulated. The souls, the energy, and the lives collected on Earth will be lost if she does. I won't let it happen!" He waited, daring him to challenge. "A mere human. One who never remembered who she was or what powers she carried in the spiritual realm will never win this war. To allow that to happen…" He slammed a fist on the edge of the table nearest to him, causing a crack to flee to the center. He wouldn't engage in such poisonous thoughts. Doing so was a sign he'd already lost.

Aqen crossed his arms in front of him and leaned against the wall, waiting for the tantrum to be finished. There were more important tasks to attend to. A realm of his own to grow with the influx of spirits entering. Still, there might be something of value to gain, something he could use from this sputtering rage.

For Tarsamon, losing most of the force he'd brought with him coupled with the sacrifice of two of the dark angels in one fight was a blow he never anticipated, not with the strength they carried. They had been the only real weapon able to penetrate the energy and additional protection provided by the keys Sara held, if they could have caught her. Thoughts such as *how* and *never should have happened* shook him like the rattling sound of a knocking engine. He'd received the coordinates to the realm before Sara had even entered, and from a reliable source, or so he'd thought. One of his precious angel demons had even tracked her as far as the crystal cave. What he hadn't counted on was the connection Horus had to have established in the City of Souls prior that helped Sara. It was the only way she was able to make it through as quickly as she had for the third key. The gates referenced in the *Book of the Dead* would have slowed her down, even with the access she'd been given to pass through them. Time was still a factor, and perhaps one he'd put too much stock in. But who? Who, with enough power, would Horus have aligned himself with? The answer registered lock, stock, and barrel—Norul. She hadn't been in that temple simply to stop the fight.

The living had no business with death. And death, the man who revealed himself as a dog-like image to those he met, only dealt with those on the brink of passing. That's why Tarsamon had joined with Aqen. As one of the gods of the underworld, he was well versed in the *Book of the Dead*. He should have been able to meet Sara at any one of the gates and prevent passage. He'd chosen the god over Norul because of his access to those gates.

Tarsamon turned away from the table. "Horus established a connection with Norul. But she's just the overseer of death. What reason would she have to side with Horus?"

"What better place to hide a key than in the trusting hands of a god you'd never expect to watch over it?" Aqen said. "Don't underestimate her. She holds firm beliefs in the proper and just ruling over realms beyond the underworld."

A flash of anger skated over the nearly invisible face of Tarsamon. Only the outline of a jaw could be seen. The slightly brighter flash of red in his eyes signaled the only indication of a change in emotion. It was the sensation of added rage that shifted the current in the room to another level.

"You knew the key was being protected by Norul," Tarsamon growled.

It hadn't been a question but an outright accusation. "Of course not. Why would anyone holding such a valuable item share the information, risk drawing attention to the fact?"

"But how else could Sara have avoided the gates?"

"That's one answer you'd have to get from Horus himself. The gates run according to the way a person lived his or her life. From what little I know about your human, this Sara, she's lived an altruistic life. That alone would have granted her an easier, faster path through, had she not bypassed them altogether, that is."

"Could she have been granted access another way?"

"Again, you'd have to ask Horus. Does it matter now that she has the key?"

Another growl erupted from Tarsamon's chest.

Aqen unfolded his arms and took a few steps away from the raging demon lord. Such energy had the easy effect to overwhelm, even in a death realm. "The illness is meant to pull the Light Carrier's spirit into the underworld, to leave her body. That illness can't be healed by any elf magic, powerful as it may be. I told you, she's not able to resist the power of the keys, only harness it."

"If the illness can't be healed, how does the blood I've collected from her help us?" The growl subsided, replaced with the possibility of hope.

"For every spell in the *Book of Spells*, a countermeasure exists or has the potential to. With her blood, a spell to keep her heart beating can be created. So long as that happens, she can't release the keys."

"And all you want in exchange for this spell is more strength in the underworld by way of the power I've collected on Earth? To transfer my forces here?" He paused, hearing Aqen's thought. "You want Sara's spirit, don't you? But if her heart beats, you won't get that, either."

"Not yet. I'm willing to wait for a soul that powerful to come into this realm. I must admit, though, the notion has high risk involved, even if a spell that powerful could be created."

"How?"

Aqen didn't reply. Instead, he allowed the answer to find its way and settle with the demon lord.

"You can create a spell from her DNA that leads her soul to the underworld. Directly to you." Silence passed between them. "That's why we joined together. We are bound by darkness, only found in the energy of evil, a force unable to be fully contained. What if the spell fails? What then? I can't have the keys' energy released." A funnel cloud of sickening thoughts, including his demise, swirled above Tarsamon's head. "I've heard you described by the spirits in the underworld as the 'mouth of time.' You can control when her heart stops. You have the ability to keep Sara alive, don't you? You can make it so her spirit can pass into the City of Souls and still keep her heart beating."

Aqen eyed the tip of the rope. "Sure. I could, I suppose. But to interfere with such power created by the Soltari would cause serious long-term disruption in the underworld. I never signed up for that when I took you under my wing and agreed to keep you hidden from Norul while you became stronger." He lowered the rope and met Tarsamon's piercing stare. "I'm not interested in battling the entity responsible for life itself."

He had only agreed to protect Tarsamon because the Dark Lord had promised to share a part of his newly obtained power from Earth with him. If he couldn't help create a spell to block against the collapse of his recently acquired empire, he only stood to lose a small interest for growth, as opposed to triggering a war with the entity of creation.

"What kind of 'god of the underworld' are you if you can't create magic?"

"I didn't say I couldn't. I said I won't. There's a respect in this realm I believe you're not familiar with." He didn't want to stoke the anger in the room any more than it was. "We don't step on another's turf or take liberties that can inflict tension and torment to those in charge of certain responsibilities." He moved across the room and sank into a plush-back sofa in the residence Tarsamon had recently established as his second home in the underworld, and far from Ardan. With legs extended to an iron table, he crossed his ankles. "That understanding works well for those who seek balance."

Tarsamon felt more was at play in this game of souls. "But it no longer works to suit you."

The corner of Aqen's mouth lifted.

"In any case, there are plenty of strong spell workers who know how to handle what you're asking for and couldn't care less whose toes get bunched in the process," he said, waving a hand in his direction. "They have little if anything to lose already. But I won't have anything to do with it. I helped keep you from Norul. Your turn to cough up something in exchange."

The sensations from Tarsamon were a violent ride on a coaster, with lows of fury and peaks of interest and hope of attainment. All that he'd built, his army, his plans, his takeover of the human souls on Earth, wouldn't be undone by a god's smug attitude and refusal to help him finish a job.

To put the humans out of their miserable, pained existence was doing a favor to Earth. Of course, that wasn't why his legion of shadows had slipped into their human forms and consumed their life energy, out of mercy for them. He had none. It was a readily available source of energy that allowed his army to grow and grow darker still, feeding off the negativity the humans provided. There simply hadn't been enough understanding, deeper thought, sensitivity, tolerance, factors that would have prevented his passage to Earth. The timing was right and the energy strong. No need to waste it on death and mercy.

The humans had let fear run them. They resisted truth and the demand life threw at them to see beyond the limitations of their circumstances, and instead embraced fear, pain, and suffering until it was too much to bear, passing it on and causing them to see themselves as more separate than alike. In the end, it had been the humans who had chosen the path, one that allowed his entrance and takeover. The whole arrangement had been nothing more than a perfect opportunity. Negativity and imbalance were fuel for his new order of demons and shadows. Good, strong fuel.

Entity of creation. Aqen's words rang in his thoughts, again, like a bad chime. The Soltari's *creation*, the physical life experience, had been bound to fail anyhow, as he saw it. He'd merely sped up the ending. With Sara in position to take everything from him, there was no way he was going to give up what had been a perfect path. No. There was no other way to hold on to what he had created. He had to keep Sara alive.

"What more would it take for you to keep her alive? To deny her death?" he asked.

Aqen laughed at his desperation. "I'm not foolish enough to risk the underworld, the only place I'm guaranteed a place of existence for as long as I care to remain. I've got no beef with the Soltari, and I'm not looking for one. But let me think on it."

Allies, it occurred to the demon lord, were not something he'd calculated into the formula to win, but surely each of them had something in common, something to be exchanged for a single life?

"What if I could give you her eternal partner? One powerful life in exchange for another?"

"The Last Great Warrior? Impossible! They are bound forever by a tie not even you could touch."

"But if she isn't dead yet…"

This time the wicked grin slipped across the god's face. "That's one mighty tall order for you to fulfill." He tapped a finger to his chin. "I could use a strong warrior like Cerys, or what is his Earthly name?" He paused. "Kevin? Yes, I believe that's it," he said.

"What about your worry of interfering with the Soltari?"

"I'd only be carrying out their order of separation by taking Cerys into our world a little earlier than planned. How could they possibly object?"

"All they care about are the keys. Certainly not the life of a warrior."

"Then again, the Soltari may take offense at anything to do with Sara. See it as an intrusion."

Tarsamon had worked a couple forces into the Soltari to enable decisions to be made in an attempt to alter Sara's path, or at least make it more difficult. But that hadn't been his focus. He still didn't have as many entities in the governing order as he would have liked. Not enough to be okay with interfering at the level of taking lives from the Soltari. That sort of infiltration took time and the skillful art of mastering the ability to hide dark energy in a place or group that seeks only light.

"No. My involvement in that regard wouldn't be worth the cost of retaliation. But…" Aqen stood and turned to face him directly. "Your permanent residence here may be exactly the solution for both of us."

"I'm not joining with anyone again." The memory of too many issues, disagreements with the Soltari, and how quickly one could be ousted, like he had, returned.

"Fine. Then work beside me."

Tarsamon saw the play in his eyes. The god had a reputation for saying what one wanted to hear, and an even better one for getting what he desired. But the question was, what exactly did he want out of a partnership? Were Aqen's goals similar to his? Would he be willing to risk his rule to see the eventual end of the great governing order and the light that guided the realms? He'd said he didn't want to start a war. Teaming against the Order would cause retribution to last a millennium. Asking the ruler of the underworld what his intentions were would result in the likelihood of a lie. Whatever Aqen's agenda, he'd never reveal his cards.

"You'll keep her alive?" Tarsamon asked.

"I can't guarantee for how long. Have you considered how much more time is needed to accomplish what you seek?"

"The completion of the armies is nearly finished. The release of the energy of the keys will undo all of that. Everything I've put into action."

"I've got that. But you could have your expansion of forces with me in the death realm. Your shadows and demons would find this residence more than suitable." He flattened his palms to the ceiling in offering.

"The energy of the life force of the humans is what grows the number of shadows and demons of my armies. Death does not have life-sustaining energy. And I need time."

"The question is how much? The Soltari knew time would be a factor when they instilled the power into the last key. They anticipated having to intercede in your mission for the energy on Earth. It's why the death sentence, the illness she carries, is already at work. Finish your task and come join me."

The curiosity was too much for Tarsamon. "What do you gain from this arrangement?"

"A larger army, of course."

Legions always sought more force. It couldn't be a lie, Tarsamon thought. "Let's get to work on that spell." Because if that worked, he thought, he wouldn't need to join in any arrangement. Certainly not under the control of a god. He'd worked too hard, too long, to share the reward of claiming his place as a force to be reckoned with in the universe with anyone else.

"First," Aqen said, "I'll need the help of a necromancer. He cares nothing about crossing Norul's boundary or affecting the Soltari but is powerful enough to alter the energy Sara holds."

"I'm going to need some assurance he won't kill her and release the keys."

"The blood you collected from her is like no other, and it's all the insurance you need when it comes to a conjurer of souls."

14

I woke to the gentle stroke of fingertips down my back, my body curled into Kevin's, the bad dreams chased away by that light touch and his presence. The faint memory of pain, however, still resonated from somewhere deep inside me. Despite the soothing sensation and his ability to heal, Horus had told him he couldn't change a death sentence.

"What if I die, never having said goodbye to Mary Ann?"

His fingers stopped their downward trek.

"You want to go to where the Inner Society is keeping Mary Ann safe? To say goodbye?"

I heard the implausibility in his tone, and the sadness sank deeper. To never see the one woman who had cared for me, loved me as her very own, when my biological parents never had, caused its own pain. But to say goodbye to her, knowing I'd never see her again, would be agonizing, devastating to us both.

"You're right. I can't do that to her. She wouldn't understand."

An uncomfortable silence, the kind that one feels knowing death is upon a loved one without knowing how to change the fact, settled heavy in the room.

As it was, Mary Ann was aware the wicked nightmares she had been having were coming to life, her world growing darker, with sunlight filtering through thick-clouded skies no more than a couple of hours a day. More and more, the Earth was appearing like Ardan and the area Tarsamon resided in. But she wasn't familiar with such a place. I hadn't shared any information with her regarding the quest for the keys or my and Kevin's deep connection. It would have frightened her.

Had she seen the shadows infiltrating the humans? From what I was aware, the Inner Society saw to her protection before she had witnessed the largest change in the humans and consumption of light by the darkness. All she knew about the quest was that I'd somehow be able to help. I'd never told her how, only that I was going with Kevin in search of a medical *cure*. It would never have occurred to her that I'd have to leave her forever. Not unless the Inner Society provided her with information and I had no reason to believe they did.

"It would break her heart," I said under my breath, shifting beside him. I touched his bare chest with my fingertips, pressing a kiss to his warm skin and sucking in that sweet, masculine scent of him.

"If I could change that for you, I would, my love." He kissed the top of my head. "You're afraid. For the first time I can recall, you're afraid, and for someone else." His hand touched where his lips had just been and he inhaled deeply.

"I've also built a life I love in New York. With Mary Ann, my practice, my friends. My life with you is just beginning. Why do I have to leave all of that to rescue so many?"

Yeah. Exactly why did the Soltari decide I need to die to release the keys? There's got to be another way.

"I can't answer that."

I felt a wave of anger coupled with sadness move through him.

"How are you feeling after a little sleep?" he asked.

I tilted my head upward to meet his gaze. "Pretty good, I guess. I needed the rest."

"Any pain?"

What he meant was, is there any pain I was blocking from his keen awareness?

"No," I said, doing a quick assessment and discovering a mild ache in my legs, easily dismissed. "Not really. I felt weak before falling asleep but no pain. Why?"

"You were doing a lot of quiet moaning while you were sleeping."

I laughed a little. "Worried I'm having fantasies without you?"

His smirk said no. "I felt some pain associated with the moan. So, unless you're into sadism, I'm not too concerned about another man. And"—he paused—"I'm happy to fulfill that interest, in a loving manner, of course, should you take an interest."

"Oh, you are, are you? Giving me another reason to hang around longer?"

"Whatever you desire, love."

I kissed him on the lips, then sat up and turned to face the edge of the bed. His hands spread apart, setting me free.

"Careful," he warned. "You're here because you couldn't stand."

I sat on the edge of the bed, looking at the floor, then my legs, and remembered the fall. "I feel strong."

He scooted closer to me, ready to leap if necessary. "Where are you going in such a hurry, anyway? One minute I've got you right where I want you, and the next thing I know you've moved out of our comfy nest."

"I've got to see Horus. As a member of the Soltari, I think he might have an answer to help me." I stood and managed to hold my balance. An ache that radiated from my hips to my legs protested the movement. *Not gonna happen. I'm doing this.* I sat in the chair and began slipping on the knee-high boots.

"Maybe it's too soon," Kevin said.

"No. I can deal with this minor ache. Besides, it might just be the pain from when the dark angel had me in her grip. When C-05 rescued me." *Sacrificed is more like it.* The vacancy of his eyes still haunted me.

"Okay. But promise me that if you feel the least bit worse, you'll come back here."

"All right," I said, reaching for my coat. "If you promise we can continue the earlier discussion about desire."

"Two things," I said, pulling my coat tighter and sinking my hands deep into the pockets as a frosty breeze bit my nose and cheeks with an icy kiss. I followed Horus's misty image as it moved nearby. "Why would Tarsamon believe I would make a deal with him to stay on Earth? Plus, when I spoke with the Soltari, they had no intention of agreeing to release the immortals from punishment. I trusted you."

He stopped floating in a mist around me and took the form of a human in an instant.

I'd found him lingering in one of the most gorgeous flower gardens I'd ever set eyes upon. Located on the premises was a large square courtyard with the palace walls surrounding its boundary. Snow had fallen while I'd slept, layering the ground in a fresh foot of padded fluff. Ice crystals that mirrored crushed diamonds blanketed the top, as well as the edges of every still-blooming flower petal and leaf. A mysterious crystalized garden that seemed to thrive in the cold. I glanced to the sky vacant of sun in mixed hues of gray smeared with white. He said the place brought him a great deal of peace. Which, I assumed, I'd just shaken.

"I'll reply to your last comment first."

Suit yourself.

"I heard that you went to the Soltari with your demand."

"I was justified. And before you tell me—"

"Hold on." He leaned into a row of jasmine flowers strung behind another set of iced lavender blooms. "I miss that," he said, inhaling deeply.

"You will be leading the Soltari. If you want to change the rules, do so. If you don't want punishments to exist, change it."

"It's not that simple." *If it were, the Soltari wouldn't have needed to consider my request.*

"Their reply was a means to consult," he said, hearing my thought.

"They gave no indication I would be leading anything."

"They weren't necessarily denying your request. And it is 'that simple.'"

"Well, they sure as hell didn't seem to welcome it, either."

"The entity and I have consulted on the matter of you being the ruling force, the decision maker, if you will. You have my word that, even now, what you desire to change shall change."

I eyed him for a fraction of a second. How could I be sure? What guarantee did I have?

"I feel your doubt, Sara. You don't have to say it." He stepped farther away and leaned into another colorful bloom. "I told you, I can only speak the truth. You have the choice to believe it or not. But I caution you that if you choose not to, you waste precious time."

"I want nothing more than to believe you."

He shrugged his shoulders. "You decide. I can't do anything more on the matter."

For everything that had occurred on the mission, the absolute most annoying moments were those when there was a riddle to solve, a vague answer, anything that resembled gray area. I didn't think or operate like that. Information was best received in black or white form. Beliefs, faith, sometimes truth, if woven into a lie, were gray areas. I supposed from his point of view, the answers were black and white. I believed he could only tell the truth. From what I could feel from him, the only truth I cared about, my request, or rather demand of the Soltari, was a good thing. Maybe the reply hadn't come with all the reassurances I sought, the warm fuzzy that made everything feel that all was right in the world. Did I really need it? Hell yes. It was my life on the line and I deserved a little reassurance for that sacrifice.

"Your silence tells me you struggle. Is it not enough that I can't tell you any non-truths? *Lie* is such an ugly word," he said. "Your struggle is and has always been your humanity. It causes you to doubt the guidance you receive, whether it be from me, Cerys, Eldor, or any other who looks out for you. Once you understand that, you'll find peace in my words, but never with the Soltari's hum or need to congregate on matters so important. It is a group, after all, that has just become aware of my desire to have you lead. Give them time. But don't think for a moment that time means you'll have to give up what you want."

"I guess I have no choice but to do just that. Still, if you can tell no lie, tell me why Tarsamon thinks I would make a deal with him to remain on Earth."

Horus stopped strolling and turned to face me with nothing more than a blank stare.

"What?" I said, a bit surprised by the reaction.

"He only deals in life. The acquisition of it. Which means he knows. I don't know how, but he does. What did he tell you?"

"Wait a minute. He knows what?"

"What did he tell you?"

"He showed me a rope that he had struck my arm with, said something about Aqen and that he had an offering that would allow me to stay with those I loved."

Silence fell between us, the flowers forgotten, the beauty of their color and fragrant scent all but gone as the icy air grew more frigid.

"What did he mean by an offering?" I asked.

"The *Book of Spells* allows for the creation of magic to empower immortals, but it also allows for the undoing of such, as well."

"Is that what you meant by 'he knows'?"

"Yes and no. If Tarsamon is working with Aqen, who, of course, is well-versed in life as much as death, Aqen would've shared the information he has with him. But he must know he can't bypass Norul's power over him."

"I'm not getting what you're saying. What information?"

"My dear, have you not felt that you are carrying a child?"

15

The blood drained from my face. The words Tarsamon had said, that I fought for more than myself and my love, raced back to me, along with a sick feeling that somehow he'd known I was in a battle to save one more precious life even before I did.

"By the shade of white you've just turned, I can see that Kevin doesn't know of this new life, either," Horus said.

I couldn't speak.

"And you need to keep it so," he added.

My gaze, which had drifted past Horus's shoulder, met his stare. "That's impossible. The man can feel what I feel. Even if I blocked him, he'd sense or at least see the shock I'm in."

"Then you can't see him until you've got yourself under control."

Under control?

"Why can't he know?"

"You must complete your mission to release the keys. If he becomes aware of this new life you carry, it will only complicate the effort."

"You're asking way too much of me, of us, now," I said. "First, it was that if we failed, we would be separated, our team would be separated from their eternal partners. You give me your assurance that punishments won't exist if I say so, but you're willing to take the life I've always wanted to have. You give. You take." I put my hands to my head. "This time you're taking too much." I began to pace. "No, it's not just my life you're asking for but another. You can't do that." I stopped and stared at him. "You can't do that. I won't let you."

"You will save all of humanity."

The words flew past me like darts aiming for another target. I heard them, but I wasn't listening. My mind screamed, demanding defiance. *Damn humanity! Its cruelty, its carelessness, its goddamn hatred!*

"Don't ask this of me. Don't ask me to give up this child for the sake of the keys. It was never part of the agreement to fulfill the mission."

He grasped my hands and held them together. "I am the power that guides health. Your faith could never be as important to your task as it is right now."

"Faith? Faith in what?"

Anger blew over me like a breeze and was gone just as quickly on a search for hope.

"The belief that what you do will not only set right what is wrong but give you all that you could imagine."

"All that I imagine is keeping what I want, while still knowing the importance of what I've been asked to do."

He nodded. "Good. That's all I ask. You won't call it faith, but our understanding is in sync."

"There is one thing I haven't been able to understand through this entire quest," I said. "The riddles, the vagueness of the answers returned for the questions I've had, and the uncertainty of what comes. Tell me something, something straight. No riddles. Do the other members of the team wonder what the outcome will be based on my decisions?"

"Oh, I admit there have been doubts at times, and only because they are human. But no one has questioned whether you'll fulfill this task. They remember who they are, what their responsibility to the quest is, and most importantly, where their faith lies. That is what gives them strength to overcome the doubt."

"I'm not religious. I've never had faith in much."

"That was planned in your decision to take on this mission before being born. You wanted nothing to infringe on your ability to see clearly. This isn't about whether you're religious, Sara. You can have faith without religion. You don't need others to tell you what you can accomplish or what you should believe in. You never have. And yet, you always know the way. What you need to realize is that anything you desire has a path that will lead you to it. The steps may seem small, insignificant at times." He waited, still holding my hands. "Everything is an illusion." He lifted one hand toward the garden in front of us, keeping the other holding mine. The ice crystals melted and a sunlight from nowhere lit the petals, glistening in rays of gold sparkling off the dew that was once crushed diamonds. He waited as I took in the beauty, then put his hand back on mine. As he did, the sun disappeared and the crystal blanket returned. "You have a goal?"

"To finish the quest."

"Another one?"

"Of course. I've already told you I want a life in New York." *More now than ever.*

"There is nothing standing in your way, except your limited vision as a human. All is possible if you choose to see." His glittering eyes were only inches from mine.

"Death stands in my way. You said yourself that not even the elves could heal this illness the third key has put upon me."

"I said they won't. No one can take what the keys have delivered to you, unless you freely give that power away. The path is yours to see."

"But I didn't choose a path to become ill and die. Someone else decided that was how this energy would be released."

"True. The decision as to how the keys would be released was not made by one but a majority of us. But you've forgotten that you control the energy you carry. You've played the role of being human so well you've forgotten the source of your being. You create a labyrinth of possibilities to obtain what you desire and avoid the most direct path to it, all in an effort to follow what seems easiest. Sometimes, the most direct path may be the hardest and not so obvious, but it gets you what you desire. Remember, two things are for certain—one, achieving what you want is always possible, and two, only you can find the path to how that is best accomplished. There is no alternative to releasing the keys, Sara. Start thinking like the spirit you are, and let the human part of you take a backseat for a little while. This is where you'll find your faith. Everything else will fall into place."

He let go of my hands and turned, gently grasping a white flower in his fingertips. "Here," he said. A sparkle fell over the flower, making it appear even more beautiful. "Take this in." He held the center closer to my nose.

I sniffed the most fragrant bloom ever. "It's lovely. But I don't see—"

"You will. Mind over matter," he said, tapping a finger to his head. "Your spirit directs you, if you'll listen." He shifted back into his transparent form and continued through the garden in a mist that mingled among the petals and leaves, until I couldn't make out his form in the distance.

His words sank deep into my conscience and resonated so far into my soul I doubted I had yet opened that door.

"I control the energy I carry," I said to myself.

His information was like a key that unlocked a place I'd either kept hidden or refused to see. But now that the lock had been opened, my focus had been realigned. I had the power to not only see the quest through to the end but to go get the life I wanted for myself and Kevin…and one more perhaps. The only problem haunting me now was the old adage—no one could cheat death.

16

By the time I returned, Kevin was tucked into a mound of pillows on the sofa, sound asleep. Not a stir or a blink of his eyes at my entrance. I'd never really seen him rest before now. He'd always been awake whenever I was, working on notes for the hospital or talking through a security strategy with Juno and Matt. Either way, he'd managed somehow to have an ear into my thoughts while busying himself with other tasks. A man in two different places at the same time if he chose. Even now, as he looked worlds away from the cozy nest he'd settled into, I wasn't entirely certain he was sleeping. I cleared my thoughts, just in case, and set a plate of food I'd collected from the kitchen for him on the table and eased out of my coat and boots, leaving them at the door. All the while, watching for any movement.

Hours had passed since I'd left, lost in consideration in the garden and wandering the halls of the palace. Despite the cold, and the falling snow after Horus had left, I'd needed time to pull myself together before I could risk Kevin's scrutiny or the chance that my eyes might give away my secret. It had taken a good long time to do so, too, much longer than I'd anticipated. Learning I carried a child was one surprise that required adjusting to. The words Horus had said about reminding me to think like the spirit I am had also called for additional space to sink in. That required stepping into a place I'd too often closed the door on. Reconnecting to my spirit was as unnatural to me as attempting a green thumb in Horus's crystal garden, or any garden, for that matter. I had grown more comfortable in my skin as a human versus an immortal. Of course I had. It was my life. But this life with Kevin and the many pasts we'd shared was also my life, and one that could never again be set on the back burner or ignored. My recent thoughts had been consumed with memories, recollections of shared moments, things said.

Assuming everything Horus had said was true, one fact I'd been sure of before I'd left that garden was that I'd need to maintain control over the power I carried. It also hadn't escaped my attention that I was able to stroll for as long as I liked, without a single stumble. *"Power that guides health"* was what Horus had said. Was that the reason I could walk as long as I had? Like the flower that had become something more when it fell into his hands. There was still so much I didn't realize when it came to the abilities of the ethereal beings around me, sometimes masked as humans. What was the full extent of their gifts? Were they kept hidden more often than they were used?

As I looked over at Kevin, I made sure to keep my thoughts blocked from his keen introspection. The candles still burned high above in the corner over his head, dimmer than when I'd left. The tiny lines of his face were softened by rest. The only indication he might, in fact, be asleep.

I'd get what I wanted and still set the balance right for Earth with the keys' power. I wasn't sure how, exactly. But with the hours spent in the garden, a strange sense of confidence on the matter had come over me and still remained.

Keeping my secret was a tiny part of a much larger plan. If I could find the faith needed, it would give us everything we desired. Seemed simple enough, on the surface. But finding a hidden object in the room of my soul I'd hardly had the time or desire to venture into was yet another passage to conquer. My gaze shifted back to Kevin's face. He might have to wait a bit longer than I'd like to know of the child I carried. The fact that it was a larger gift to us long-term set well in my mind. Finding peace in the thought, I quietly sidled myself beside him, easing my way under his arm.

He shifted slightly and blinked open his eyes, staring with a sleepy-eyed look. "That sparkle is still in your eyes. Doesn't look like it's leaving."

I smiled. "Is it too distracting to look at me?"

"Not for a moment. Come here." He pulled me against him as his hand slid down my shoulder, dropped to my waist, and rested over the curve of my hip.

Analyzing. I'd come to learn all too well when he was probing for sensations, feelings to tune into, or my own thoughts.

"You were gone for some time."

"Yes. But I'm much better now. Did you sleep?"

"A bit." He waited, still assessing. "I take it you found Horus and the answers you were seeking?"

"Mm-hm."

"Care to share? You've become quite good at blocking me from reading you."

I shouldn't be surprised he'd picked up on that.

"I know you well. There's never an empty thought in that pretty headstrong mind of yours, love."

"I'd rather get back to our discussion before I was so prompted to leave."

His eyes searched my face. The memory of desire and handling that need, whatever it might be, filled his thoughts.

Could he, would he, rather, let my conversation with Horus go?

"I'm happy you feel better," he said. "I sense something else, though I can't say exactly what."

"I'll explain later. Suffice it to say, Horus's particular kind of magic is in the area of health. I should have read up on the gods of Egypt before entering the realm."

He laughed a little. "When would you have had time, escaping shadows and demons and whatnot?"

"I suppose that's true. Now, about that desire?"

The concentration on his face softened. His gaze dropped to my mouth and returned. A grin danced over his lips. "I'm all ears." He placed a kiss on my forehead, nose, and lingered at my lips, parting them with a firmer press. His tongue swept over mine. A small moan escaped. "Lips, and…" His words drifted off, taking the kiss deeper.

I slipped a long leg over his and, without breaking the bond, placed myself above him.

His hands came around my waist and gently slid beneath my shirt. "Dominance, darling? I do love that about you."

"Shh," I said, my lips grazing his. "Right now, I must feel you. Talk later."

"Here? On the sofa?"

I eased back and nodded, lifting the edges of my shirt. He was faster.

"Hey," I said as he scooped me up and carried me down the hall.

"I prefer a little more privacy."

So much for dominance.

"You'll get your chance," he said at the thought. He leaned into my ear as he placed me on the bed. "Even if I don't make it easy for you, you'll take it." His eyes raked over the length my body. "And I'm thankful for it."

He removed the rest of my clothing along with his and sat facing me. His fingers gently touched along my collarbone, trailing between my breasts. His eyes followed. The path downward stopped at my navel, and his gaze lifted to meet my heated stare.

His gentle persuasion, invitation, was too much. As I reached to pull him closer, he slid beside me and rolled to his back. I placed myself above him and kissed just below his ear.

His head tilted back and a breath escaped to the ceiling. I relished in that simple joy, finding strength in our bond with his ecstasy. It was rare that he would permit me to maintain a position over him, preferring instead to hold me beneath him. I eased back slightly, tilting my head to capture the image and store it for later.

I placed a flat palm against his chest as he aligned himself and slipped into me. My head tilted back and I released a breath, my body assuming the rhythm of our desire. I peeked beneath my lids to see the rise and fall of his chest move faster, the breaths sinking deeper at each movement over him. Would he indeed ride this passion all the way to the end like this?

My passion for him climbed to new heights with each stroke and movement of him beneath me. The intensity etched upon his face, the strain of muscle fighting for control. He had that heated effect on me simply by being near me, as long as I wasn't fighting against such emotion. The truth was, I'd given in to my battle against the type of closeness he offered from the moment we met, shortly after our relationship began, and really at the very meeting of those eyes flecked with gold. I hadn't realized my bond to him then, but I'd felt a deep, unexplainable connection from the moment our eyes had met. Over time, it had only become stronger, closer, as it was in this relished moment.

As though we spoke a language all our own, I adjusted my rhythm to meet his demand for more. His increasing breaths signaling every last ounce of need, desire. A deep groan sounded from him. "Not yet, love." His eyes opened halfway.

In a fraction of a second, I was tossed and lying beneath him under his expert hand as it found its way gently over my cheek, my breast, and locked tight at my hip. His other hand clasped firmly in mine above my head, holding me in place while his lips sank lower and molded to mine as he plunged into me, feeding the same need I so craved from him.

"My God, Sara," he said, lifting his lips slightly, his gaze piercing me. "Arwyn, my love."

Faster he moved, the perfect rhythm that would cause my release much sooner if he didn't ease back. "I'm..." I gasped. "You're so..."

"Say it."

My lids lifted to see the heat in his eyes. The flecks of gold that so often smoldered were on fire.

"Mine," I gasped, lifting my head to his as he bumped it on another thrust.

"Again."

This time the words spoken in the heat of passion, a language from another realm, a realm we shared in spirit, flowed from my lips, breaking the silence in the room between gasps and quiet moans. The delicate sounds that seemed to blend common words into a rolling of syllables and intonation unfamiliar on Earth lifted in beautiful tones between us, with every meaning clear, as though peering to the shallow depths of a crystal-blue lake.

His grip tightened as he wrapped one arm around me and drove himself deeper still, taking me with him. His moan was the final note that called me to him, followed by my own heated breaths as I reached climax seconds after him. He rolled us again, holding me above him. My hair curtained around us and the beats of our hearts pounded together like drums of war. His stare held with mine. A feeling of focused intensity subsided into peaceful calm. His skin glistened with a light sheen of perspiration.

"I adore watching you," he whispered.

"As do I."

"Mmm."

His hand reached up and slid through my hair, moving one side behind my shoulder. His lips came to my ear. "I crave you. Every word, every gasp, the silkiness of your skin as it heats beneath my fingertips. The light in your eyes, only faintly hidden when they smolder in passion. Every. Little. Thing."

A breath escaped my lips at his words. "You're going to start me up again if you're not careful."

I angled my head to see a wicked little grin slip across his lips. "Maybe I haven't finished with you yet."

"What could you have in mind?"

"What is it you desire?" He cupped a hand at my cheek.

I waited a breath and turned my lips into his palm and placed a kiss there. "You. Forever. To feel you in every way." I studied his gaze.

The fire in that stare that had begun to cool started to smolder again.

What was he thinking? He wouldn't let me read his thoughts. Did he already know my secret? Why else would he be blocking me at such an intimate moment?

"Desire has many forms, my love," he said finally, and much to my relief. "I aim to please you in every way."

"You do so very well already."

"You know I'd never hurt you."

I felt my brow furrow. But before I could ask the reason for his comment, he released the block preventing me from reading his thoughts. My concern was replaced with an image of the utmost clarity of me sprawled across the sheets, a silk blindfold across my eyes, hair spilling over the side of the bed, and a lit candle in his hand as he straddled me.

"You're wicked," I said. "So very lovely wicked."

Thank God the smile hadn't meant he'd filtered through my block to discover the secret I held.

Before I realized it, a pink silk scarf had appeared in his hand, reminding me that a mere thought could generate a physical result in this world, at the same time igniting my interest once again.

"I despise the color pink," I said.

The corner of his mouth lifted and his eyes zeroed in on mine. "Then it's a good thing you won't be seeing it." He placed the silk over my eyes, angled my chin to the side, and began tying the two ends together behind my head. His lips went to my ear. "While I attempt to wring from you the reason you're blocking me from reading certain thoughts."

17

Shouts came from beyond the door of our room, in between a particularly shrill alarm. I raced out of bed, with Kevin steps ahead of me. The evening's earlier events were fresh in mind, and that of my stubborn willfulness having for once paid off, as I refused to give away the secret of the new life I carried. I threw on my clothes and found my boots.

Kevin stopped at the door. "One favor," he said.

"Sure." I glanced to him as I finished putting on the last boot.

He opened his palm. I reached him in two steps, to see the silver bracelet he'd once given me as a gift. "You left it in the room at Leahnan's when you stepped through the portal to this realm." The four silver bands joined two diamonds on either side of a deep blue sapphire. But it was more than a piece of jewelry that fit like a second skin. It had been created by the elves for him to track my energy if I was surrounded by too many of Tarsamon's forces. "I don't know what's out there."

"Of course I'll wear it." I slipped it over my hand and kissed his cheek. "Let's go." I drew the guns I'd left on the table beside the bed and followed Kevin out into the chaos in the hall.

Matt barked directions as Juno checked other rooms, calling out, "All clear."

"What the hell is going on?"

"Someone broke the silent alarm on the boundary and—" Mac started to say.

"We've gotta move. Now! No time," Juno called.

"I thought our energy was hidden in this palace."

Topetine crossed the hall to me. "It was. But Aqen has long known where Norul keeps her most precious gifts." She shifted into her jaguar form. Aria and Elise combed their way along the farthest corridor on the search for the evil that hunted us, as Matt followed close behind.

I'd be damn glad when I could get a restful night of sleep again. Not have to worry about a shadow or a demon on the prowl for us.

"This way," Juno said, leading us farther away from the alarm.

"Move outside," I said, raising my voice to be heard. "With more area to scatter, we might have a better chance to throw off whoever has broken the boundary." As it was, I felt like we were being corralled in one area of the palace to be sitting ducks.

"Not safe."

Damn it. It's like we've been breached internally, not just the boundary.

"We have," Kevin said, hearing the thought.

"Where?"

"Unknown yet," Juno said. "You're going to have to shift to remain safe."

"Okay." The painful memories that helped me to shift into the hawk, as Topetine had taught me to do, came and left. I was still human. I tried again to conjure up some of the very darkest, most evil visions I'd encountered, not just in this life but in past lives. Nothing.

"Sara, there's no time," Jade said. "Do it now."

"I can't. It's not working."

"Get her out of here," Kevin said to Jade, who wrapped an arm beneath mine.

"Chambers below ground," Jade replied.

Kevin nodded. "I'll meet you there."

A second later we traced to the location. The muffled sound of the alarm could still be heard, but at least we didn't have to shout.

"What is it? Who breached us?"

"Tarsamon, Aqen, we're not sure. And I don't know how. This place is locked down like the underground haven of the Inner Society. Or, as you like to say, Fort Knox. There's smoke outside."

"They set fire to the palace?"

"Don't know," he said, rifling through the pack he'd brought with him. "It's likely a distraction. But I can't be sure. I've got to get a better look so we know what direction is safe to move to. Stay here. I'll be right back. That means seconds." He gave me one of his stern looks. The kind I'd gotten used to seeing when we'd first met and before I'd known Kevin had asked for his help, as his longtime friend. It was a look that I'd learned the hard way was better not to challenge.

"Put your shield up, just as a precaution," he added, looking me over. "I won't be more than a minute."

I nodded.

He turned and, in a blink, was no longer beside me.

I lifted my hands to create the personal force field of blue-white energy, but only sparks lit. *Jesus. No shifting and no shield.* The defensive spheres of fire wouldn't light, either. "Gone," I said to myself. Fear I'd not felt in some time rolled over me like a wave, while the term *sitting duck* flitted through my head again. Did I sit here and wait? Hope whoever breached the palace didn't already know I was in the chamber? Where was Jade? He was fast. Almost as fast as Kevin. Should be back any second.

Go or stay? Where would you go? I tried leaving my team once, only to find it was a mistake that almost cost us our lives. *Just like it's a mistake to try again. Wait.* The others would be here soon. Besides, time passing always felt longer when alone.

A flash crossed my vision. *Jade, thank God.*

A tight grip wrapped around my throat. Something sharp pressed against my neck. *Not Jade.*

"Now, if I drain the blood from you, we both lose. So, listen carefully."

I remained perfectly still. *Where is Jade?*

A swift movement of air and the answer was clear. Jade had finally arrived, standing in front of me and a second too late. Larger blades normally strapped across his back were now in both hands. A thin beam of light I'd never noticed before ran along the edges like electric current around them. His hood was drawn over his head. The promise of death waiting to take the target whose weapon was still at my throat.

"No shield," I managed to say to Jade, almost apologetic. A flash sensation of his awareness at the mistake of not waiting for my shield to go up before he left reached me. He took one step closer.

The grip at my throat tightened. "Shut up." The veins in my neck and head responded to the restricted blood flow. The other hand dug into my hair and yanked my head back, giving him a better angle for his blade.

I just need a few inches for a leg sweep. Not possible. I couldn't feel anyone standing behind me.

The whisper of breath from my captor was close at my ear. "Your fight doesn't matter at this stage of the game." The voice didn't sound like Tarsamon's.

Jade's eyes looked like daggers zeroed in on their target, waiting for the twitch of one wrong move.

But whoever held that grip held me close enough so that there was no way Jade could touch him without hurting me, too. The creature started backing away, never loosening the grip or adjusting the point of his knife at or very near my jugular.

Jade swept the blades he held in front of him in a crisscross pattern, never blinking his eyes.

Just one right moment.

I could use jui jitsu, a form of defense I'd practiced for several months but not recently. Given that I could feel no one behind me, the action might cause my own death.

The creature holding the cards was right. If I bled out, the release of the keys would put an end to Tarsamon's power while also fulfilling my task to rescue humanity. I didn't know what deal the creature had made with the Dark Lord, but it was certainly no win if his insurance was dead. That is, if Jade didn't get to him first. I, too, stood to lose all that I cared for. I might be an immortal soul, but there was no option to return to a damaged body. Unlike C-05, I didn't have the same gift to borrow the energy of another life by brushing against it and taking that form.

I was led backward, step by step, out of the chamber and across the boundary into the death realm, as the creature holding me captive whispered in tongues.

The look on Jade's face changed into a fit of rage. "Don't listen to him, Sara. For God's sake, don't listen."

How could I help it?

"Let her go, and I won't hunt you down and kill you, understand?"

A curtain of black, coupled with streaks of orange, filled my vision. The vague smell of sulfur followed. From behind a veil, a flash of light that mirrored Jade's energy blazed behind the dark curtain, and the words, "Block whatever you hear…" were faintly captured by my ears, then nothing more.

18

I rubbed at a mild stinging sensation on the side of my neck as the blackness started to clear. Staring down at me from the ceiling were images of wings in bright colors of blue, green, and orange. For every swirl and stroke on the left, another on the right reflected the same, as though a lesser artist of the Sistine Chapel had attempted a similar effort. The flood of visual stimuli coupled with the recent memory of Jade's expression of murder caused my head to throb. I recognized the glyphs below the images, similar to those I'd seen in the crystal cave, telling a story. But this was no place I'd ever been, and certainly not with Horus on a mission to set the gates according to the *Book of the Dead.*

I moved my legs, surprised to find I was free of any bindings, and scrambled to stand from the cold, rocky surface of the stone floor. My head protested the movement as though war drums were sounding the alarm of a coming battle. The sickening smell of sulfur I'd caught a whiff of when being pulled from Jade lingered.

I let out a slight moan coupled with a breath. *Got to get back to the team.* The scent wafted stronger this time, causing my stomach to lurch into my throat.

"You don't have your otherworldly abilities to aid you, so don't try it." I whirled at the sound of the voice of the person or creature who had held me captive before transporting me.

The necromancer. He was standing to the side, not looking at me. The dark, hooded cloak covered a portion of his skeleton face. *Was it the same one who had surrounded C-05 when he was strung up to that wall and left to die on the last quest, waiting for his spirit to be released?* Every bone in my body said yes. Jade had warned me of the magic they carried. But I'd only dealt with them over the course of my battles in other realms a handful of times, and on the rare occasion they'd called the souls of the deceased forward to assist them. I'd never really come face-to-face with one.

"The illness you've received from the key you hold is taking your energy," he said. "There's no reason to immobilize you. It'll happen soon enough." The sound was slurred but spoken well enough to understand.

Not true. Can't listen. Block everything. That was what Jade had begun to say. It helped that I didn't want to hear the words that frightened me most—not having strength, my otherworldly abilities, or the most obvious ones, that I was likely going to die. I might not have my ethereal abilities but I could still run. *Run where? The spirits are faster, stronger.*

After not being able to shift or create my defenses, I had no reason not to believe the evil that spoke to me now. "You look different."

Silence. "You remember," he said finally. The cloak he wore shifted into a black mist as he turned to face me. The skeleton inside that open cloak glowed white.

The appearance was enough to have me taking a few steps in the direction toward the exit I'd spotted. Could I sprint the sixty feet or so and make it?

Necromancers could pass between worlds with ease, taking spirits with them, or let them die trapped in their specific kind of poison. They also had the ability to call upon spirits to serve or fight for them. The stealing of the life force energy before it had a chance to regenerate was what fed them. It's also why Jade had once referred to them as leeches. The feelings being put off by this one were that he was exceptionally strong, possibly a leader. From the odor that traveled with him like a shadow, he'd been around death far longer than any spirit ought to. I'd be damned if this was the way I was going to spend the last moments of my life.

"Where am I?"

"You don't get to ask questions. The answers don't matter. All that's important is the reward for your capture."

Reward?

"May I at least know who you are?"

Silence.

I scanned the room. *Looks like a pyramid temple.* My thoughts moved quickly, trying to assess the location and a situation I had little control over or ability to change. *Is this one of several located on the Band of Peace? If not, how far apart do they span? How close is this one to the palace?*

The scent of the great room was different, too. It wasn't ionized like the last temple. A strange sensation told me it wasn't connected to the others.

"You know about the illness tied to the third key?" I asked. *His presence must be linked to Tarsamon.*

"I created it."

For the Soltari, of course. Definitely connected at a higher level than the average slave demon to a Dark Lord. "Which means you could undo it, for a greater reward, perhaps?" Not that I had anything at the ready to offer. What could the director of the dead need? Possibly the same thing everyone wanted—energy to sustain themselves. I had an abundance of that with the keys, but it wasn't the kind he'd want. There must be a way to negotiate a deal?

"You have nothing I want," he seethed. "I hate you and your kind."

I turned my gaze from the ceiling back to him and felt my eyebrow arch.

My kind. Hate me?

"Do you even know me?"

"Damn fool, you are. Everyone knows you. You may have forgotten who we are, on your fight for freedom from the effects of darkness. What do you know of proper balance between good and evil? You and your keepers of the light provide nothing to those of us in the realms. You preserve a life force on Earth that is crumbling by their own demise. You save those who don't deserve to be saved. You should be made to suffer along with the humans and the dying light you honor."

Someone's in a foul mood. "I can't say I care too much for what you think." I had a task to fulfill and was damn well here to do just that. "What would you want if I could offer something more?"

"Shut up," he snapped.

A smother of black mist blew across my vision, catching me hard across my cheek. Black stars winked in the corners of my vision. A transparent form with all the force of a bar brawler's right hook. Either I still had some lapse of memory or I'd never actually been punched by evil like this. And that was hard to believe given the number of battles I'd been exposed to over the centuries. Maybe too much time had passed to hold such a meaningless memory for recall.

"You don't have the power to create change for those who understand life and death, except for your precious humans. Blind and undeserving as they are."

Not a problem. Offer rescinded.

I rubbed the spot on my cheek, with a promise that even without my abilities to assist, a smack without some sort of retaliation wouldn't happen again.

And yet, I couldn't help but wonder if the animosity this spirit carried was how the Alliance, and subsequently part of the Soltari, had begun to deteriorate. This disease between spirits was much more rampant than Tarsamon's vendetta, whose rage had caused him to set his sights on Earth and humanity. Just how far did this anger reach? And would my leadership in the Soltari satisfy such animosity in time?

I need to get out of here. Where is Jade?

"There you are." I turned at the familiar voice of the Dark Lord I'd come to know all too well on this journey. Beside him was someone I'd not met before. "The sound vibrations in here were distracting my ability to track her. Good thing Aqen knows where to find you."

Aqen. The underworld god Horus mentioned. What vibrations? What sound? Is that why Jade isn't here?

"Never mind them. Good to see the deterrent is working," the necromancer replied.

Without Jade and Kevin, how am I going to get out of here? They are too powerful to fight. Try for escape?

"Sara," Tarsamon said. "It's such a pleasure to see you again."

Outnumbered. Defenses down. Three long strides closer to that exit I'd spotted. I could worry about being caught if it happened. "The feeling isn't mutual, but I'm sure it's no surprise to you."

"I can see in the short time you've been here the negative energy has already begun to work. With your recent weakness, you must feel"—he breathed out a long sigh—"so vulnerable."

And I was. He had to feel that sensation radiating from me. I refrained from meeting the stare I felt forcing me to look at him.

He needs to keep me alive so I don't release the power. With that thought, I felt a strange sense of safety battle to overcome the vulnerability in the presence of one of the most evil entities in the universe. But that sense of safety was nothing more than an illusion. It wasn't real because it couldn't be. Remaining alive was not what I was supposed to do to release the keys. I needed to pass, to cross over into death.

Horus's words came back to me in a rush: *Labyrinth of possibilities. Most direct path.* What I desired was always possible. But to get there, to find that path, I needed to remember the spirit I was and let faith put all the pieces together. Would it, though? There were no guarantees. Then again, that was the true essence of faith—belief that existed where one had no proof. If there were a labyrinth of said possibilities, why the hell weren't any of them coming to me? The success of this mission had been based on whether I trusted the next step. Now, with nothing tangible in hand coupled with being outnumbered, it didn't make trusting those words any easier. And yet, I'd come this far and recovered all three keys. I had managed to stay ahead of the darkest force across this universe.

Aqen stepped closer, stared at me, and turned to the necromancer. "Were you able to reverse the illness?"

Do they want to deal?

"You wanted an antidote. I won't create one that allows her to remain on Earth," the necromancer said. "I would gain nothing from creating such a potent mixture while keeping her from releasing the keys."

"We had a deal," Tarsamon growled. "The *Book of Spells* says an antidote can be created from her blood."

I calculated the distance to the exit and took a few more steps. *One forceful push toward the doorway and there might be a chance to escape.* I still had the guns. Could the specialized bullets meant for the dark angel do enough harm to an underworld god?

"Don't worry," Aqen said, holding up a hand. "She wouldn't be here if there wasn't an alternative." He directed his attention back to the necromancer. "You were able to fulfill the request to keep her from releasing the keys, yes?"

"There is an answer to your dilemma." He swept past Tarsamon. "As her soul begins to cross over from life to death, we will replace her spirit with another newly arrived soul to the realm. One that has enough life force to keep her heart beating, defying the illness. The power of the keys won't recognize the new life. While her heart beats, the energy will have no choice but to remain with the body."

"If *that* body dies?" Tarsamon asked. "That heart stops, and the keys will be released. No matter if that's today or in twenty years."

The cloak of the necromancer reappeared, concealing his skeleton image. "The keys' energy was joined by the Soltari to her specific life force." His dark head tilted in my direction without looking at me. "It was created to work in connection with the heartbeat and the soul, a thread linking all three. The keys' power and illness can't join with a spirit they don't recognize. The Soltari wrote one caveat to how the energy is connected and her control of it. She could give it away freely, assign another keeper to the keys, if it's determined she can no longer hold them at any point in her mission. Since that's not going to happen today, the keys have no way to exit. The energy of them must slowly die, starved of its source of life, her soul to hold it."

My stomach turned at his words. Was it true? I detected no lie. But was I using my gift to hear the truth in anyone's spoken words, or had that ability left, too, along with my other strengths? I couldn't, wouldn't let him undo me, psychologically, emotionally. Those were still the areas I could be reached if I wasn't careful, and if I was purely human and without my otherworldly abilities to aid me.

Tarsamon extended a hand toward me but stopped short of the side of my head. I jerked back, unwilling to allow him the satisfaction of knowing he could touch without the electrical charge of the second key preventing him. The blue energy that had once flowed to the surface of my skin when he'd attempted contact in the past didn't move now. But why? I hadn't yet released the keys.

He smiled, pleased with the result. "It won't be long now."

"What won't be long?" I asked. "What else is there to see?"

Tarsamon laughed lightly. "You really don't know." He turned to Aqen. "She's lost the gifts she had. Fascinating."

"I want her spirit. That kind of strength under my command is worth an army of demons," the necromancer gritted. "You have my assurance she will never be a part of the Soltari again."

Aqen glanced to me and back to the necromancer. "As long as it works as you say, Sara will be under my command. We can make arrangements."

As long as what works? What command?

The necromancer held out his hand. A staff filled the misty palm as he began chanting in tongues.

Without the strengths I'd been gifted in this world, I couldn't block the sound. On instinct, every part of my body engaged as I bolted for the opening of the temple. The odds of escape far from my mind, I ran with only one thought pressing me forward—I had no choice but to get through the doorway. I pulled the guns. My eyes set on the exit. *Still moving. Just another couple of seconds.*

I froze steps from freedom, met by three spirits. Two of them matched the appearance and odor of the necromancer. The third, less ominous in appearance, was flanked by the first two. A bewildered look crossed her face as she glanced to Tarsamon and Aqen. I raised the guns and fired, knocking off two rounds that blew through them like a stone through tissue paper.

"You can't kill what's already dead," Tarsamon said.

My replacement. It was the last thought I had as the guns dropped to the ground in a rattle echoing off the stone surround. Every muscle felt weak. My legs gave out and I crumpled in a heap so close to the exit.

"Kevin! Jade!"

The bracelet Kevin had given me warmed at my wrist and quickly cooled. Had it worked?

I attempted to place my hands over my ears to block out the sounds and found them quickly pulled away and bound in front of me with a black mist that felt every bit like thick-gauge cording.

"You have what you want," I said, angling my head toward Tarsamon without meeting his eyes. "Why is he still here?" I asked, referring to the necromancer, who continued his chant.

The necromancer's skull face stretched in a grossly contorted fashion as he crooned the last chorus.

"To ensure his delivery is protected, of course."

I had to get back to Jade, Kevin, and my team. *The necromancer couldn't have taken me far. Run, damn it. Run!*

But my legs betrayed the command. I didn't recall a temple anywhere near the palace. Would Jade be able to trace my energy with the vibrations that had delayed Tarsamon but not prevented his eventual arrival?

I concentrated every effort and rolled onto my stomach, crawling and skinning my elbows with my hands tied at the wrists. Breaths came in and out in shallow gasps. Sweat beaded over my forehead, dripping down my neck.

"You need to rest," Tarsamon said over the last syllables of chanting. He moved to stand beside me. "I can't entirely control what the keys have delivered to you, Sara. But with my insurance here"—he gestured toward the floating necromancer—"I believe we can manage to keep you with us, so to speak, so your new soul can be here for your beloved Kevin and the life you carry."

The very mention of a child from an entity so filled with evil caused my blood to boil beneath the weakness trying to consume me. A certain protectiveness followed. I wouldn't let anyone take my place.

Kevin would sense it wasn't me. And no child we'd created would be raised by someone else. Tears of rage and fight clouded my vision.

"That's it, bring that desire forward, the one that has driven you in this life. One last explosive fight. I respect that. You can relax then."

No. He hasn't won. He can't win. I won't leave. Not for you!

What I "desire." Horus's image in the garden flashed through my head. Desire. *That's what will determine the control I have and what happens with the keys I carry. I'm not dead yet, and I still have the keys.*

I narrowed my eyes in a glare at Tarsamon. A questioning gaze was returned. "You're sure she has no way out?" he asked, giving me the strength I'd been looking for despite my legs rejecting the effort I willed upon them. I continued to pull myself the few inches remaining to reach the doorway.

Desire. Faith in that desire, which is…

"I said you should rest. And you shall. This will all be over for you soon. The energy you hold, Sara, won't be yours to carry much longer. Let it go." Tarsamon turned to Aqen. "You're quite sure the vibrations, the sound waves you've created will keep her energy hidden?"

"They can't be undone by the otherworldly powers she or her team holds. She's hidden."

"The serum I've given to her is working within her to separate her soul while keeping her heart beating."

Serum? The stick at my neck. It was an injection? I extended an arm the full length in front of me, my fingers reaching through the ghostly figures to the edge of freedom.

A battle was raging inside my body as I began to twist and pull my elbows in and across my middle. The energy of the keys raged against the toxin that was meant to keep me alive. Toxin because it felt poisonous inside me. Unnatural, painful, and wickedly debilitating, separating my soul from a living body joined to the keys. *Death would feel so much better than this.* But the Dark Lord wouldn't let that be.

The spirit that had been bewildered at her arrival was moved beside me by the two necromancers.

My shirt was soaked with sweat and stuck against my skin, my breath no more than micro-breaths, hardly filling my lungs. *No. No. Breathe. No.*

I'd been in this position once, when I'd been introduced to the path for the keys and had come to the end of my training for what I might encounter. What had been the message then?

"Ahh," I cried out as a lightning sensation rocketed through my insides, closing out all thought. My eyes glazed and drifted back to the painted scene on the ceiling. *Focus. I have to focus. The message… it…was about…fear.* Then it flowed readily to me. "Release fear to free your strength." *Fear feeds the power of the negativity, the evil, and the ugliness that brought this darkness forward. I have no fear of this life or the next. I release my fear of the unknown and trust the force that set me on this mission.*

The lightning sensation eased, a dull throb beat at the base of my neck, and a calm like I'd only known when in the presence of Cerys came to me. The chanting stopped. Images in the room blurred. All that remained was the light sensation of floating in a quiet pool. Silence, pure and golden, closed out all other filtered sounds. The only feeling, gliding on the ether. The relaxation Tarsamon promised. Kevin's face drifted in and out between that of the small child with auburn curls. *I tried. I tried for us.* A tear ran from the outside corner of my eye to my temple. *Will you forgive me, my darling love?*

19

"She's here somewhere," Jade said, scanning the area. "Goddamn spiritual leech," he added under his breath, referring to the necromancer who'd taken Sara.

"Why can't you trace her energy?" Kevin asked.

The rest of the team had caught up to them and were now trying to follow the path Jade had set in search of Sara.

"The same reason that bracelet you gave her isn't working—a force is blocking it."

"Then how can you be sure she's here?" Aria asked.

"Every few seconds, there's a sensation that matches her energy. It's damn frustrating because it's never in the same spot. Like some really irritating game of hide-and-seek."

"Where would the spirit take her and why?" Juno asked.

"To Tarsamon," Kevin said. "Sara told me she'd had a dream with him in it. She woke with a small laceration on her arm from the encounter. He'd mentioned something about a spell, from the *Book of Spells*, that would keep her alive."

"That's not possible. Nothing can break the power of the keys."

"Tarsamon struck her, not terribly hard, but enough to draw blood."

"So?" Juno said.

"A necromancer has unique abilities to manipulate energy from human DNA," Jade replied. "They spend eons learning what the best way is to extract a soul near death from its body. They know what keeps a soul intact and what helps it to leave."

"With the proper spell, her blood would work similarly to Lady Mara's magic when she creates the weapons specific to our abilities."

Kevin shifted uncomfortably beside Jade, itching to stop the chat and keep searching. Every word spoken about the trouble Sara could be in was another bite to his recently peeled raw nerves.

"But Tarsamon wouldn't want her to die," Elise said.

"No. But the filthy leech spirit would create a spell if there was something more valuable in it for him."

"Like what?" Aria said. "Keeping her alive should be all he wants to preserve his forces."

Matt glanced to Kevin. "What would a spirit who deals in souls want with Sara?"

"A powerful one on his side," Topetine replied. "Not for Tarsamon but for Aqen."

The tension had grown as heavy as the humidity in a Florida summer.

Kevin clenched his fists. "We're wasting time with the lesson. How do we find them?"

"We'll need help from Norul." Horus's misty shape shifted into a visible human form. "There are sound waves in the area, distracting Jade's and my ability to track Sara's energy. Like Jade, I can't locate the exact coordinates, either. Once we have the vibrations toned down, we should find her quickly."

"We'd better hope that's all that's throwing off Jade's tracking ability," Juno said.

"Tarsamon can't manipulate the power in this underworld as he might in Ardan."

"Why not?" Aria asked. "He's had no trouble tracking her in the past, in the Mayan underworld."

"He has no control here," Horus replied. "Tarsamon has no free will here, like he has in Ardan. He's joined with Aqen for strength.

He needed the necromancer, for God's sake, the lowest form of energy available…"

"Not this one," Jade added. "He was stronger than most I've encountered."

"That may be so. And if it is, Aqen and the necromancer are who we need to fight. Why?" Horus said before anyone could ask. "Under Aqen, he is bound by certain rules, namely not to try and command the spirits in the City of Souls. They, in turn, agree not to attack the necromancer. I'll return shortly with Norul."

Kevin's restlessness grew. Time was no factor to take for granted. The only good thing about Tarsamon having Sara, if he could even say so, was that he didn't plan on killing her. But what if the necromancer was successful? What would he do to her while she was alive?

"Keep trying to track her," Kevin said. "'Shortly' is too long for Sara to be in the hands of the demon lord, even if he plans on keeping her alive." He angled himself toward what looked like a doorway that had been cut out in the brush. "I'm going to search this area," he added, lifting his chin toward a cluster of palm trees.

"It's no use," Jade said. "I've covered the area."

"If she's close enough for you to pick up on her energy, I might be able to detect it, too. I can't sit around waiting for Horus to return, not with a necromancer holding her."

Jade was one of the universe's best energy trackers. The fact that he couldn't locate Sara meant the powerful conjurer of souls had gotten the best of him and the team. In a single moment, all they'd worked for was teetering on a crumbling ledge. There was a better-than-average chance he wouldn't be able to locate her, either, but he had to keep trying.

God, what he wouldn't give to be out with her again, in that little Italian restaurant he'd first taken her to. The way she'd traced the rim of her glass, wondering about him, before she remembered anything about such evil and this quest. To see her again in that dangerously low-back dress, all in black, feel the silkiness of her skin under his fingertips. And later, when he'd finally felt her beneath him. His anger grew with each passing moment.

"Don't do that to yourself, man," Jade said, suddenly appearing beside him without a sound. "That's sheer torture. We'll find her."

Had he forgotten to block his thoughts? He couldn't afford to be careless, not now.

"Norul is the best shot at finding Sara," Jade added. There was little he could say to make a warrior feel better when he was out of options.

Kevin nodded. "I can't sit here and wait. Those intermittent sensations you're getting, tracking her energy, will eventually to lead us to her."

The longer he considered what was happening, what could happen, the more he thought it would take sheer luck to prevent her from the harm that could come from a Dark Lord *and* a necromancer. Add the help of a god and… He shut down the rest of the thought, unwilling to let such negativity consume him. It didn't make sense. He'd never before allowed such dark images to mask rational thought or prevent action. Soldiers fought. Warriors didn't shy away from challenge.

"Track the darkness," he said to Jade. "Forget the light, the energy you use as a path to track." He started off in another direction with the realization he and the team were exactly where they should be.

20

The power of silence, of stillness, was stronger than I could ever have imagined. Nothing was visible. No sensations. No voices. No movement, even in the currents around me. No foul odor from the necromancer. And the temperature in the room was no longer cold.

I must have died. I waited. Would guidance come? Was I still holding the keys? I hadn't felt the energy leave.

I listened ever so closely, until the void of sound itself was deafening. I had to know if I had passed, if my heart was still beating in my chest.

"Sara."

I know that voice.

An unintelligible whisper, sinister in its flow, followed my name as it broke through the quiet.

I narrowed my eyes at a movement a few feet ahead. *A man with a dog-like face?* He appeared in front of me like a dream. A cloud of mist swept below his feet and followed him as he stepped toward me, then lifted above our heads and vanished. Behind him, more darkness and the faint outline of trees with their long, leafless arms and their sturdy trunks, gradually came into focus.

My recollection of Egyptian gods had the name Anubis on the tip of my tongue. Powerful spirits in many realms were well-informed about the keys and what they could do for Earth. But what power, if any, could they have in death?

"Have the keys been released?" I asked.

"I cannot say. I cover the passage of spirits into the City of Souls. I don't know if the keys have had an effect on or what has become of the place you call Earth."

"Well, are there more humans crossing over into death?"

"No more than usual."

I scanned the ground, which came into clearer focus, as though the world was being created in fragments of time, and lifted my gaze. The landscape started to resemble the world we had traveled into with C-05, before he'd been struck down by the dark angel. The snow had begun to fall, calm and quiet still, in a soft, thin blanket. I didn't feel the cold upon my cheeks as I had the last time I was here.

"If I'm here with you, then I must be seeking passage into death like the others you bring with you, those who reside here forever. And what is that annoying whispering?" I turned my head, trying to locate the sound that continued in the same slithering lilt.

"You hear the necromancer whispering to you from where your body remains, in the temple where you left it. Your spirit seeks passage to the City of Souls. But I'm not here to transport you to the underworld, Sara."

Did the serum really separate my soul from my body?

Why was I surprised? I'd been dealing with immortal spirits well-versed in their roles since beginning the quest. Why not one who deals in a soul's transition from life into death? A serum and an irritating chant would likely have been easy for a necromancer to create.

"Has my heart stopped? It's the only way to know for sure the keys have been released."

"The experience is, in a way, like being in a coma. Your heart can beat there, but your consciousness, your spirit can wander."

So, no. I shook my head and flattened my palms to the sky. Seeing the transparency of my form only agitated me more. I was here but I wasn't. "I need to know if I've died."

"The only way you arrive to meet me and enter the underworld is if your spirit is seeking to leave another world, as you are. But as I've told you, I cannot let you pass."

"Why not? If you're not here to guide me into death, why are you here?"

"To help you. I've received no communication that you are to be brought into the City of Souls, into death itself." The man slammed the point of his staff into the ground, causing a rumble and blaze of fire that turned into a wall of blue flame. "You aren't meant to be here. The spell created by the one whispering to you was interfered with. You must go back."

"How do you know about...? Wait a minute. How? By whom? No one had the chance to change the serum once it had been administered, after the necromancer took me from the palace." I stared at him. "Who are you? How do you know about the spell?"

The corner of his mouth turned up. "Not all is as it appears to be in the eyes of a human. They see only what they wish. Including you, Sara." He waved a hand over his face and pulled across at the air. The dog-like mask faded into the sky, as though it had been an illusion all along.

"Impossible!"

C-05's smile lifted more. "This image, known by some as Anubis, is my spiritual equal. I wasn't at liberty to share the information until now, now that I've finished my mission for the Soltari."

"I don't understand. What mission for the Soltari? You went against them."

"Your mission. For the keys. I've fulfilled their request and have agreed to remain in the underworld. You, however, aren't finished. You see now why I can't let you pass?"

"No. I don't. What happened? You exchanged your life for mine? Your death instead of mine? I won't let you keep me from finishing this job."

"I don't work against you, Sara. I'm on your side. I always have been."

I gasped out a breath. "That's a leap, given all that you did to prevent my path to the keys. If that were so, you'd let me pass now."

I tried again to cross the fiery barrier. A shield of light, the same electric-blue color as the powder Horus had blown in my face, extended fiery-tipped fingers from the flame toward me, holding me at bay. The memory of the tiny flicker in Horus's hand returned.

I looked at my palm, as if to find an answer hidden there. My skin was not as translucent as when I'd first arrived. The answer I sought was clear—the longer I stayed in the underworld with C-05, Anubis, whatever he chose to call himself, the longer my spirit would remain. "I have my answer."

"You think so. But you don't. You don't have much time, Sara. And you sure as hell can't afford to doubt what I say. Not now. This quest of yours was planned at every stage, to prevent any chance of interference by the dark forces."

"*Any chance?* You were once part of those dark forces." I glanced again at the wall of fire and to him. "I'm not leaving without knowing the keys have been released."

Where a void of sensation existed moments ago, there was plenty to fill it now. Plans surrounding this mission had been made without my knowledge if he was telling the truth. Rage at not being informed of all the decisions that impacted my life, and death, seethed within my soul, clawing to the surface, like the flames barring me from passing. I was so close to finishing all that I'd fought for and struggled to hold. That fury collided with the constant impediment C-05 had been since the beginning of this mission. I pushed forward again, only to be denied once more.

"Don't fight me anymore," he said, angling his staff toward the flame. "If you were meant to cross into the City of Souls, this barrier would have been a path welcoming you. Your energy here grows weaker by the second. Your soul cannot pass and it cannot remain trapped between realms." He lifted his chin in the direction of the flames. "That is protection. Given to you by Horus."

"If this"—I splayed an open palm—"is part of the plan, there must be a way for me to let go of the keys."

"Of course there is. You can choose to refuse what I have to say, but understand I only speak the truth."

"You've lied plenty of times. Capable enough once, and certainly again. I'm sure."

He shook his head. "Never in death." He wasn't misleading me with a lie. I felt his truth.

C-05 took two steps toward me. "Goodbye, Arwyn. I'll see you again." He wrapped an arm around mine as I struggled to get free.

"No! You can't do this." I writhed in his grasp. "If you are with Horus, then you understand."

"Horus gave you the lapis lazuli to keep your spirit safe against passage. There's your proof."

I stopped my struggle and glanced again at the fire that still burned with such fierceness. As though it sensed my frustration, it lifted higher, daring me to challenge it.

"Why won't you answer me? Were the keys released?"

He tapped the staff again, causing a thunderbolt of electricity to extend in multiple directions beneath our feet. His grip on my arm tightened and the ground disappeared beneath us. In a blink, we'd changed locations. Land appeared beneath my feet, rooting me to the ground once more.

"Go," he said. "The answers you seek will come. And not at your demand for them."

"I don't trust you."

"I know. But that doesn't change what is and what must be."

"If you can't tell a lie in death, tell me one thing—why did you help Tarsamon? You know, back when you held me prisoner in Ardan, when you..." My words trailed off at the memory of him crossing the line in an unsuccessful attempt to claim the key. "You delivered me into his hands!"

"I'm sorry about that. Really. So many methods were required to convince him of my loyalty to him."

"What?"

"My life for yours. It had to be that way, to make you believe, but more importantly so the Dark Lord would trust that I meant to join him."

You didn't?

"In the end, I had to lead him to his death."

"What death? Tarsamon is in a temple with a necromancer and Aqen, making sure I don't fulfill this mission."

"You don't believe my only role at the onset of your quest was to lead you and your team to the keys, do you?"

"Yeah, actually. I don't know what to believe. All I know is that you won't let me finish this quest and release them."

"See that tree?" He angled the top of the staff forward. "You remember it, don't you?"

"I guess. But I don't recall from where."

"The triskeles. The artifacts that gave you clues to finding the keys."

"The tree of life."

"Yes. The answers you seek are there." He glanced to the tree and then to me. "Go. You only have a small window of time remaining to get back."

"Get back to what?"

And with that, he shoved me toward it. I stumbled forward and pressed out a flattened palm to brace for impact. But instead of landing against the rough bark of the tree, a doorway opened and I fell into an empty, dimly lit space with a single thought—*when will the labyrinth of passages that move me from one realm to another end?* I clawed at the air, grappling for tree roots just beyond my reach. My hands slipped over the inside bark of the tree. Roots disappeared and transformed into the smooth walls of a tunnel.

"Do you want to live? Can you withstand the strength it will take? Where does your loyalty lie? Who will you love?" A myriad of whispers joined in a mixed chorus of sound as I fell. Louder and louder they grew, closing out the chant of the necromancer and his spellbinding words, until I couldn't take it anymore.

"Take the keys, goddammit! I've fulfilled your task! I give them to be released into the world, however they were meant to be used! I'm finished! Do you hear me? I want to live!" I shouted the rage to the order that set me on this mission. The fury and frustration that had built up inside joined with a forceful fight for life and pressed their way beyond my ability to hold them any longer. "Set me free!"

The sensation of falling ceased and the tunnel filled with a blue light as the walls faded away. *Finally.* I started to shiver, colder than I'd ever felt. The snow was still falling, but instead of a thin layer upon the ground, the blanket of powder now covered my feet, ankle deep.

It's so dark, so quiet. I glanced up. *No stars. What happened? Where had I landed? God help me, not back to the evil that waits.*

21

Sara's team covered their ears against the sound waves Norul used to reveal the hidden pyramid temple behind numerous snow-laden branches and the spell meant to camouflage it. The lucent shade contrasted against the dark sky, reminding Kevin of the white, sandy beaches on the coast set against the backdrop of deep blue and gray storm-filled skies before a heavy downpour. Norul continued an unintelligible chant to undo the barrier while Kevin pressed into the force, until Norul had reduced it to nothing more than a mild vibration.

Spells were not his forte. The elves were the experts in such magic, not the warriors of the realms. With varying degrees of energy that could affect the different types of matter, it was nearly impossible to be an expert in every field of otherworldly powers. Such energy was specific to the strengths of the immortal. Kevin wondered if Norul had spent time with the elves, learning their specific magic to enhance the powers she carried. How else had she been able to rework the spells the necromancer created to block the strong connection he had with Sara?

With a clear path to the temple and Kevin unable to tune into Sara's energy, he raced with Jade toward the entrance, steps behind Horus and Norul.

Upon entering, Tarsamon and the necromancer lifted their gaze from Sara to meet Kevin's murderous stare. The necromancer attempted retreat but was quickly prevented midway through another disappearing act by the surprise connection of Norul's hand at his back. He cried out as she slammed the cloaked skeleton into the waiting grasp of Horus. In the hands of a god gifted with the power of the sun and moon, Horus held him in a tight squeeze. A light as bright as the sun's rays cut through the smear of black until no trace of his shadow and skeletal outline could be seen.

Norul turned her sights on Tarsamon.

"The serum prevented her death. Check with the one who leads the dead into the City of Souls. He'll confirm it," Tarsamon said. He'd already withdrawn from the rocky surface they'd carried Sara to after she'd become unresponsive.

With Norul's strengths to detect the most sensitive of energies and the intentions that drive behavior, Tarsamon suspected she was aware he and Aqen had worked together to replace Sara's soul with another recently transitioned spirit. Aqen, however, had vanished once the spirit wasn't able to settle into Sara's body. He'd chalked up the error to a mistake in the formula created by the necromancer, or a misstep in a line of the incantation. As Tarsamon glared at Norul, he put odds on her having some hand in the failure of their plan.

"No need. I'm well aware of what occurs in the realm I govern." Her eyes scanned him. And with the same speed she'd used with the necromancer, she clamped a hand around the throat of the demon lord. "Aqen wouldn't be caught with you," she said. With her other hand she spun a cloud of gray. "You crave evil? You can remain in the darkest dungeons of the underworld with the god you *thought* would help you."

Tarsamon gripped her arm with claw-like fingers and spun out of her grasp, transforming into the thick, black fog he preferred when not the grim reaper he often utilized. His voice bounced off the walls of the temple, "You can't contain me any longer."

Norul thrust the gray cloud at him, only to have it miss and drift away across the rocky ceiling, as Tarsamon's form escaped through the doorway of the temple.

"I'll track him," Jade said.

"No. Don't." Norul's arms fell to her side. "His powers should not have worked here, which only means he has become stronger. Likely a gift from Aqen. If so, he'll have trouble leaving the realm. What's important now is this one." She turned to the platform where Sara looked to be resting.

"The necromancer—" Jade started to say.

"I know," Norul said, stepping beside Sara. "Horus informed me he transported her here in the same manner you track energy. They hid this temple using magic from the *Book of Spells*. A source that has caused more problems than it was ever meant to."

Kevin was at Sara's side the moment Norul attacked the necromancer, his physician instincts at work frantically scanning for a sign of life. He squelched the feeling his heart was telling him. His fingers went back to her neck. *Still no pulse.* He placed a hand on her heart. *No heartbeat. What happened to Tarsamon preventing her death?* His lids closed together as he struggled against unleashing the tears that somehow suggested he'd accepted her death. He didn't. He couldn't.

"Kevin," Matt said.

He felt a gentle tug at his shoulder but shook off the hand trying to urge him away. Every sensation was on Sara and whether he could feel anything from her. *She's still warm. If she truly hasn't left, I can get her back.* He leaned over her and started CPR, just as he had once before, when she'd been introduced to this mission and nearly died.

A reaction he'd not expected to feel flooded his system. *Keep going.* There was the chance she had to give up her life for the keys. He thought he had accepted the fact when they'd brushed over it in conversation. It occurred to him in this fragile moment that maybe he'd just chosen to ignore the idea of her leaving until it was actually a reality. With that time here, something else reached deeper for her, screaming at him not to stop his effort. He'd be damned if he was going to lose her, and certainly not to the Dark Lord, after all it took to get her to this point. Tarsamon's last words gripped his heart and squeezed tight. *She's still here. She's still here.*

She and Kevin might have made a deal with the Soltari for her to release the keys so they could keep eternity together, but now that the time had come to fulfill the ultimate sacrifice, he couldn't imagine living the rest of this life without her. The damn governing order was tainted, anyhow. She'd promised to fix that. He *couldn't* let her go. He wouldn't let her go over malign decisions that might have altered her path and a decision to leave him he was sure she had nothing to do with.

With every breath he gave her now, he recalled each sweet kiss from her, urging him to force life back into her body. Memories flooded him—the first dinner he'd shared with her before she realized who he was, her curious gaze, and how he'd wanted her the moment he first touched her… No, no, no. He hadn't even been given the chance to say goodbye. It was more than unfair. More than a bitter pill he was expected to swallow. He couldn't imagine a life on Earth without her, couldn't wait however long it would take for them to share eternity once he finally passed. The compressions were exchanged with breath, back and forth, again and again.

Norul put a hand over Sara's mouth, stopping the next round of effort. It was all Kevin could do to not rip her hand away. And before he did, she said, "You can't heal her that way. Not here. Her energy, her life-force is depleted."

Deep, heavy breaths came in and out of his chest from the struggle to bring fragile life back to the strong, soft form in his arms.

"Step aside," he said. "I won't give up on her, and I won't let anyone stand in my way."

Norul smiled softly. "Of course you won't." She touched his cheek. "Allow me to help you." Without waiting for his answer, she put an arm in front of him and gently pressed him away. To his surprise, he let her, taking two steps backward. She lifted her hands to the room, as a slow murmur fell from her lips.

Would she be fast enough to save her? he thought. What if Sara needed more breaths fed to her? Time was a critical factor. It always had been.

A familiar hum started up, silencing his gasps for air while bringing comfort to the tense feelings he could feel from the others in the room. A singular low note shifted to another frequency, playing several tones up and down, reminding Kevin of the deep sounds of a wind chime that resonated longer notes before settling on two that continued intermittently.

The air changed. Cleansed in an ionized scent, almost like purified water, lifting on the currents that gently swirled first around Norul and then Sara.

"These particular vibrations can restore the energy of life to an ailing body," Norul said.

"What about death?" Kevin said in a cutting tone that pierced the room. "Can it restore life from death?"

"Time will reveal the truth in what is to be. There is nothing more you can do for her."

He doubted that. He'd saved her once before. Maybe he could again.

Tiny trails of what appeared as white smoke entered Sara's mouth and nostrils, hopefully, he thought, on a path to her lungs.

His eyes lifted from watching for the rise and fall of Sara's chest and settled on her face, pale in color. A gray-blue tinge had fallen over the usual light pink of her lips and cheeks. Had her lip twitched? Had he missed it? He lunged past Norul. But she gripped his arm with such force to stop him before he could reach Sara's face to be sure.

"Not yet," she said. Her attention shifted to Jade as she nodded once.

Jade placed a hand on Kevin's shoulder.

"Like hell you're tracing me away from here. It'll be the last thing you do." Sheer, toxic rage filled Kevin's eyes as he glared at the man who'd fought beside him across so many battles.

Jade's hand dropped. They'd been friends for centuries. A woman, no matter a lover or underworld god, wasn't going to change that. Not if he could help it.

Kevin turned to Norul. "I'm not leaving her. Got it?"

Norul stepped closer to Kevin. "If you go near her now, any chance of survival can be undone. You will interfere with the time she requires to decide."

"Decide? Decide what? If she released the keys, she had to die. I'm not leaving her on some platform and saying goodbye. You might claim her spirit, for a time, but I'm taking her back with me."

The sound of the humming shifting between soft tonal vibrations reminded him of the *hush-click* of the ventilator she'd been on when she'd arrived in the ER following the car accident that had set her on this quest. That night, he'd stayed as close as he could. It turned out to be a room beneath hers where physicians seek a little shut-eye during a long shift. Day after day, while she healed in a medically induced coma, he'd promised her he'd stay, while also considering ways to win her heart once more in yet another lifetime. A promise was more than a few words spoken, it was a solemn declaration, a contract he held with her in the bond they'd created long, long ago. Nothing would break it. Not then. Not now. Not ever.

"If she isn't dead, if you can bring her back, we aren't finished with this mission," Kevin added. "Including my role in it as her protector." He let out a heavy sigh, feeling the weight of failure.

How could he have known a filthy necromancer would try to take her from Jade? The man was a military commander as fearless and every bit as strong as he. The Chamber of Tombs, too, was supposed to have been secure. And yet, he hadn't been with her. He'd trusted the Powers That Be to keep her safe on some level. He wondered if having experienced such broken trust over time, over a course of several missions, was where Sara had developed her own hardened distrust of almost everyone.

Kevin looked up and across Sara's body. "The rest of you can go if you'd like, if there's nothing more to do here."

But they wouldn't leave him, not without the answer they sought nearly as much as he about the release of the keys.

"We'll wait," Jade said. He chose a spot near the entrance of the temple, folded his arms across his chest, and leaned against the wall.

Aria leaned into Elise. "What do we do about Tarsamon?" she asked. "We can't leave him to wander. He'll be back."

"Likely with stronger forces," Elise added.

"There's a place for him," Norul replied, hearing them. "Among the undead. A death for the living."

"We should see if Jade can track where he went so we can hunt him down."

"Jade's not going to make it," Matt said, closing the distance between where he and Jade stood. "There's movement, a shadow, coming quickly through the brush in this direction." His eyes drifted past Norul's shoulder, into a vision of the future containing a large black form angling right, then left, pressing through the denser areas.

"How far away?"

"A mile at most," Juno said, tuning in to the same foresight that he and Matt shared.

"If it's that filthy necromancer, he's mine," Jade said.

The team drew their weapons.

Elise stepped beside Juno. "Can you tell if they are searching for Sara or the Dark Lord?

"Unknown," Juno replied. "There are no sensations tied to the energy."

Matt shifted positions outside the door. "I think he's alone."

"We can't leave her here," Aria said, referring to Sara.

"We'll need to meet what comes out there." Horus moved to Jade's side, just inside the entrance. "Whoever it is won't enter with the vibrations. They'll wait until it's quiet."

The team stepped from the opening into the bitter cold, breaking off in separate directions. Topetine had already shifted into her jaguar form and remained beside Mac, close to the entrance.

"We've got to get Sara out of here," Kevin said to Norul and Horus, who were the only ones still inside. "We can't risk that the vib—" He stopped talking at seeing Sara's fists clench and release. He ignored Norul's warning and pressed his fingers against her throat, searching for the pulse that assured him she was still alive, still his. He closed his eyes in relief at finding a faint but steady rhythmic beat.

"She may not be healed enough," Norul said.

"There is care for her that can be given at the palace," Horus said, returning beside Norul. His eyes flicked to Kevin. "She can't go back if she's chosen to stay with you, and she can't remain here. I'll give instructions for the team to leave as soon as we move her."

"Wait," Kevin said before Horus could leave. "Back to where?" Kevin's gaze shifted from Horus to Norul.

"The undead. A place where the soul is trapped, neither passing into the City of Souls for permanent residence nor returning to the living." Norul put a hand on Sara's forehead and let it slip away. "The Guardian of Souls, Anubis, would not let her pass."

Good. He'd have to thank him if he met him.

"How do you know?"

"I told you. I'm aware of everything that happens in this realm, especially when this one"—she nodded to Sara—"has such important business here. I paid a visit to Anubis, knowing there was the chance she could die. Isn't that right?" Norul turned to Horus and smiled softly. "Your Light Carrier here, she's been watched over throughout her journey. In the end, the choice to stay or go had to be hers."

"You might've mentioned that earlier. The information would have been very useful to both of us."

"It's closing in!" A shout from the entrance, sounding like Matt's voice, echoed off the walls.

"We had to protect the integrity of the mission at every possible turn." Horus's words were rushed. "Still, Tarsamon managed to get to her."

Kevin felt the sting of failure touch once more.

Sara stirred again, her fists clenching and releasing.

"Jade," Horus called. "Take her back to the infirmary. You know the place?"

Jade nodded.

"Has the power of the keys been released into the world?" Kevin asked.

"With the stopping of her heart, it should have," Horus replied. "We won't know for certain until we return to meet the Inner Society and confirm the changes we expect to have taken place. Should be pretty visible once we arrive back in New York."

Sara's neck strained in one direction. Eyes still closed. Her body began to shiver violently.

"Sara. You're safe, now," Kevin said. He wasn't sure if she could hear him.

What of the child?

Kevin's gaze lifted to Horus. "What did you just ask?"

22

A glaring light filtered through my eyelids, as though I was staring into the blinding white and painful rays of the sun.

"My God, why is there so much light?" I asked of no one.

At least I wasn't cold anymore. And whatever it was I was lying on was billowy soft and contoured against my body, as opposed to the previous bed of stone in the temple. *How long ago was that? What happened? Pain, Anubis, and the dark. Where am I now?*

Soft ringing sounds like those of wind chimes playing in different keys stopped.

A hand slipped under mine and squeezed gently. I blinked up at a face thankfully blocking most of the bright light.

Kevin.

"You came back," he said.

I squinted against the harsh flood of light from behind him. "Or I never left."

He let out a breath with a smile. I felt relief from him as the lights dimmed. "Is that better?"

"Yes. Much." I glanced away from him, scanning a room that hummed like the Soltari when they were about to provide an answer to a question. My instincts told me the room was some sort of medical place, but it had none of the machines I would have expected to find. No monitors, no noisy beeping or a blood pressure cuff that would have gripped uncomfortably every few minutes. There wasn't even an IV.

"What is this place? Where are we?" I moved to sit up, as Kevin let go of my hand, and found the only attachment to be a small tape-like strip on the top of my forehead. I peeled it off and tossed it on a shelf lit with a softer beam of light in cerulean blue.

"It's… a hospital of sorts." He waited. "An advanced medical facility where they practice the art of healing using techniques more advanced than any we've yet to see on Earth."

"There isn't even a pulse monitor."

"Everything is energy, remember? The energy of the room is being monitored. It's able to pick up your pulse, heart rate, even the state of emotion."

I nodded, recalling the Professors that had helped reintroduce me to the facets of the quest, explaining that devices of creation all stemmed from thought, right down to the materials constructed to make them. "That last item is a little intrusive."

"The facility uses all energy, the magic from the Rules of Wishes, vibrations, light, otherworldly abilities, and pulls that into a practice. The tape you removed monitors your electrolytes, oxygen, and temperature."

Something told me the individuals operating out of this "medical facility" were more like scientists than doctors. That it made me nervous after all I'd witnessed and experienced in other realms caught me a bit by surprise. Maybe it was because I'd grown used to the rudimentary practice of medicine. Or maybe these *scientists* were more knowledgeable than doctors I'd known. This was still an advanced realm, after all, right?

"Are we still in the City of Souls?"

"The palace outside of it, yes." He brushed a lock of hair off my cheek with his fingertips. "But even spirits grow tired and worn down."

I suppose I'd never really considered whether they did or didn't. Being human was all there was, unless I was fighting Tarsamon's demons and shadows, or his alliance with an angry god or necromancer.

A medical facility inside the palace. Just how big is this place? "Whatever it is, it's the strangest center I've ever seen." I tossed back the sheet and the blanket, glowing in a warm, yellow light and softly vibrating. I was wearing little to nothing in a short, almost sheer white covering.

"How long have I been here?"

"A few hours. Are you sure you should be moving so fast?"

"Why not? I feel fine, except that I'm starving."

"I'm glad you have your appetite. Let me help you." He pushed the rest of the covers away from my feet and took both of my hands, helping me to stand.

"Your eyes still have that unique sparkle."

"Oh my God, the keys. Do I still have them?" I yanked my hands out of his and lifted the gown I wore, looking for the almond-shaped image of an eye with a flame in its center that had been branded into my skin, like a tattoo, following deliverance of the first key from the Druid priests. It was still there on my abdomen, but faded, like that of a scar after a few years.

"Do you feel any different?"

"No. But I never felt anything much after I'd received each one of the keys." *Mild discomfort from the small singed flesh markings by the Druid priests, a breath of life from a supernatural serpent deity.* Those were the only memories and feelings I held after receiving them. I placed a hand over the faded image. "These markings are the only indication I ever held them. That and the gift of a bit more protection to call upon if needed. I can't imagine I'd feel differently that they are gone."

"Horus is confirming the release of the keys," Kevin said. "He went back to New York, to our time, to see if the effects of ridding the shadows and bringing daylight back have occurred, and to ensure a pathway exists for our return."

"That's right. Leahnan. She and the Inner Society must have opened the portal. That means they've been released into the world."

"Horus doesn't need the portal. As a spirit, he can move to any time or place at will."

"Okay. But while he confirms that the energy is doing what it's supposed to, we will need to be sure the passage is opened. And what about Tarsamon? You, the team, killed him, right?"

"Slow down. First things first. Let's get you some food. There's a lot to talk about. We can take care of Tarsamon after Horus returns."

"I knew it. I just knew it. He's still alive." I frantically scanned the room for a shred of clothing.

The door to the room opened and a man entered, effectively stopping my search.

There's no way I was staying and no way anyone was going to make me. *Too much to do. Tarsamon is still alive. I have to be sure the keys were released. If I'm alive, that can only mean one thing—I didn't die as I was supposed to.*

"Your heart stopped, yes," the man answered, evidently hearing my thought on the subject. He held a device that blinked blue, then white and stopped. A second later it repeated the sequence. The reflection flashed off his white coat.

"Excuse me?"

"Sara, this is"—Kevin took in a quick breath—"Dr. Erol."

It was unlike Kevin to pause over something minor. *Doctor...* I let the sound of the term linger. *No, that doesn't seem right. Scientist?*

"Though it's not a term used much anymore, *scientist* is the term you'd most likely associate with the practice of molecular quantum mechanics and human biology," the man replied. "You're asking if you died?"

"Yes, I suppose I am."

"Then technically, yes, you did for two minutes and forty-three seconds. Exactly."

How is that possible? My gaze floated to the floor and a reflection of C-05 saying the lapis lazuli had interfered with the serum was returned as a memory.

"The energy you carry as an immortal spirit coupled with your will and desire to live were strong. The compressions along with the temple holding your oxygen levels within an acceptable range managed to restore your brain and heart function quickly."

"Once Norul arrived," Kevin added.

I glanced to Kevin. "What's he talking about?"

The man in the coat stepped closer. "You're here because after you were brought back to life with his help and the vibrations in the temple, clinging to it, as a matter of fact, you needed to become stronger. I suggest you lie down a while longer. We can heal you quickly, but even our advanced knowledge can't heal you as fast as you'd like. We must assess your condition further. Your body hasn't had the proper amount of time to fully recover."

"Time. It's always been a factor, and more like an impediment for immortals." I flashed a tiny smile. "With all due respect, I feel fine. I have important work to see to."

"Yes. I'm sure you do. But for your welfare as well as—"

"I'm sure all is well," I interrupted, suddenly remembering the secret I kept from Kevin. He had to be unaware or he would have said something, right? I turned to Kevin. "I'm ravenous."

"What would you like?" the man replied.

A mere thought and anything was possible. Hopefully, that didn't apply to the preparation of food in a medical facility. But I wasn't counting on it. The magic in this realm was greater than any I had experienced in the other locations for the keys. "Nothing's really coming to mind."

Dr. Erol waited a moment.

Please don't fight me. I put a block in place so Kevin couldn't read what I was thinking.

Kevin locked his gaze with mine, a sure indication he was aware of the block and assessing my thoughts or attempting to.

"I'll see what I can find for the short term," Kevin said moving to the door. "And then you'll be getting a proper meal."

The door closed behind him and I waited another second.

"Look, I'll let you do an assessment before I leave, but I would rather have it done alone."

"Whatever you prefer. But you should know the man who just left this room is aware of the child you carry."

My jaw dropped open. *He hadn't said anything.*

"Are you sure?"

"Yes. He brought you in with another man in a hood, embellished with knives. Before we'd detected two heartbeats, yours and the child's, he said you might be pregnant. The chest compressions he administered saved your child."

How did he already know? "I have to go then. I need my clothes." I searched the room, the one cabinet that might contain anything resembling what I had been wearing but found nothing. "A mere thought?" I said to myself, "Let's hope so. Clothing. Pants, long-sleeved shirt, coat, boots, preferably," I said, thinking of the last items I wore. I turned my back to the man and stripped the one-piece garment off and was being wrapped just as quickly as when I came through a portal.

"I highly recommend you stay, at least until we can be sure you and the child are well enough to make it through the passage back to your world."

"Sorry. There's no time. We're fine. I can't explain how, but I know it in the depths of my being."

"The serum you were given by the dark forces that serve Tarsamon altered your chemistry. We can remedy it completely with a little more time. But"—he paused—"I must admit you seem strong. Our team would just like to be certain."

"I can't. Not this time. Thank you."

I flashed a smile and slipped past him and out the door, looking for Kevin. I couldn't risk any other delay. I wasn't ready to talk about a child.

As I darted out of the building, the brisk air and clouds hit the small amount of exposed skin and seeped past the thinner layers of my shirt. An icy chill ran the length of my spine. My breath fell out in a ghostly cloud as I realized the walls were of the same texture and color as the palace we had entered upon our arrival. *Could it all really be part of the same place?* I started scanning the property. *Second story.* I looked across from where I stood and lowered my gaze to the courtyard below, spotting a set of stairs off the side of the building. From this higher level, the palace appeared like three temples facing each other, a courtyard as its center. Smaller buildings were scattered like tails extending from the larger structures. Was the whole place a small village with everything necessary for survival at our fingertips?

Where to find Horus? If he managed to get to New York, to the Inner Society, it won't take him long to return, spirit that he is.

I headed for the stairs and turned in the direction of where I'd last spoken with him, and what seemed to be a favorite spot of his—the floral garden. How anything was still in bloom given the drop in temperature was as baffling as all of the other magic and mystery we'd encountered. All that had been presumed to work one way, before this quest, inevitably had been turned upside down to become my new "normal." If I didn't find Horus there, I would truly be stuck having to explain everything to Kevin, tail tucked between my legs.

I felt guilty for having left him at the medical facility. But if he was aware of the pregnancy, there would be no way he'd let me find Tarsamon. And while I understood his reasoning, I'd spent far too long on this journey to not see it finished to its very end. If this child wanted to be here now, it would have to go along with a mother who had a duty to fulfill. But first, Horus and the confirmation I sought of the release of the keys' power into the world.

My heart had stopped. That had to mean the keys were gone. I didn't feel the loss of the energy, and that made a little reassurance sound all the better. Besides, I couldn't get back to New York without the help of the Inner Society, after the passage into this world had closed to protect reentry of any evil. Horus would have the location if he'd met with Leahnan. He could also provide enough information to find the Dark Lord and in plenty of time before Kevin would find me. Maybe, I thought, I could persuade help from the team and put him at ease.

I skimmed the tops of greenery and found the area still brimming with crystalized blooms in an array of color. Ivy climbed the rocks, softening the contoured edging. The tips of their leaves slightly browned. The scene was both foreign with its contrast of spring and winter and lovely as the perfect escape for solitude. *This would be a good place to hide if my energy couldn't be detected.*

"Sara." Horus's misty form swirled around me as the whisper of his voice lifted over the air currents. "I didn't expect to see you quite so soon. Happy to see you're feeling better."

"Much better, yes. I need to talk with you a moment."

He slipped into the form of a human, making it easier to converse, and began strolling past a cluster of lavender.

"I'm always listening. By the way, do you think you should have left in such haste?"

"What? From the medical facility?"

"I feel your tension. The pull of your decision to do so."

"I didn't think I had much choice. Kevin mentioned you were confirming with Leahnan the effects of the keys being released."

He waited a breath and turned to me. "Yes. It's done. Even now, daylight exists where it didn't when you left New York. You should see how the awakening is shifting the dark shadows from Earth and clearing the fear from the minds of the humans. I could only glimpse it, though, needing to return quickly while you recovered."

I nodded, trying to imagine what he described, and saw a brief image skip through my mind that he shared. "Good." I heard the sound of relief in my voice. The tide was turning.

"You've also had the gift of your strengths returned to you," he added.

Really? Short of utilizing the additional defenses that came with the keys, a stronger shield and an energy to keep the Dark Lord from touching me, I hadn't ever felt their presence. "My strengths? You mean, the ability to feel what others feel, to hear the truths of their thoughts? Those I had before we set out on the quest?"

"Yes. You were born with those. I'm talking about your shield and shifting into the hawk." He reached for a red rose. "Though, the latter won't be possible in a couple of months, with the child you carry." He continued down the path, taking a detour around a patch of anise, with me close behind.

"How is it that there are still blooms on the branches?"

"They'll fade soon," he replied, melting ice crystals with a wave of his hand over the rose. "I like to see the full cycle of life as much as the brilliant height of it.

"How far did you expect to get when you chose to evade the Last Great Warrior, Kevin?" A slight laugh caught in his chest. "Or do you prefer to address him as Cerys for the eternity you'll share together, my lovely Arwyn?" He continued his path through the garden, never looking back at me.

"I think I'll refer to him as Kevin in this life. I've got an eternity to call him Cerys." The thought of forever with him was pleasing, peaceful. How strongly it contrasted with who I was before I'd met him, never wanting such a connection. Preferring, instead, to keep my independence and desire to be alone. Now, a void I was certain would ache deep in my soul if I were to lose him had replaced the need to be alone. "As for how far I'd get, well, as far as I choose, I suppose." I thought I heard him chuckle to himself again. "I'm sorry, I don't have time to languish in our success with the release of the keys, not just yet, anyway. I must know what happened to Tarsamon."

He stopped his stroll. "He escaped from the temple. But with the keys' release into the world, there will be little he can do to harm the people of Earth."

"The serum Tarsamon created with the necromancer wasn't successful." My mind trailed in thought of how he had planned for it to happen. A bloody rope, DNA, and magic strong enough to alter human chemistry to the point of affecting the rhythm of a heartbeat, to keep it beating, in fact.

"It might've worked if Norul hadn't intervened with her strong connection to Anubis, and the power of the lapis hadn't been carried by you. It created the fire barrier preventing your spirit's path into the City of Souls."

"You did that. The lapis lazuli was meant to deny my entrance into the realm."

"Protection against your will, you might say. We, mainly the members of your team, when planning, had to take into account every possible way the Dark Lord could have interfered in your quest. The one change made after the quest was in motion was to give you wings to fly, should you need a way to escape when your human body couldn't. The lapis lazuli was always part of the plan, to counter any spell in the

Book of Spells. You know as well as I, you would have risked crossing any barrier if you thought it would release the keys. The blue lapis is a protective force in the underworld. Norul countered the negative effect the necromancer's serum had taken on your breathing. If he wanted to keep you alive, you needed more oxygen than he allowed with that serum. Probably an oversight on his part. We sent you to medical to be sure your chemistry was balanced completely."

"But how did she know about the serum? No one but Tarsamon, Aqen, and the necromancer were in that temple with me."

"Anubis." He handed me the rose he'd plucked from its stem. "He works with Norul. I was on my way to get her help in locating you when she found me, after Anubis discovered you were trying to cross into the realm."

"C-05." He'd saved my life twice—once from the dark angel and again from the necromancer.

"Yes. Norul monitors rhythm and vibration in relation to life and death. No one can enter permanently without her knowledge. We weren't sure if her timing, however, to alter the course the serum was taking would be quick enough. But here you are." A smile spread across his face.

"Yes. But this isn't finished. I can't rest as long as Tarsamon exists to recreate his wrath."

"Norul has the matter of Tarsamon under control, my dear. You need not worry."

"You said yourself he escaped. How much control can there be if he's able to get away? To find Norul, I'd need to go where I left C-05, near the Nile, right?"

"Yes, but—"

"Thank you." I turned without waiting for his approval or argument, dropped the rose, and fled the ice garden. I felt his energy shift from a state of peace to discontent and heard a sound I'd not heard from him before.

I needed my team, or at least Jade, who could trace me from any real danger if it was necessary. He would also be able to trace our path to the Nile. But would he agree to go? Perhaps, if I told him I was seeing Norul. I headed for the Chamber of Tombs. The silence along the path was eerily quiet. Where was everyone? I rounded the corner, flew down the steps, and slammed into a solid form in the darkness.

"Where are you going in such a hurry, love?"

Kevin.

He captured my wrists in his hands. "I'm sorry. I know you don't like being handled, as you once put it, but I can't risk you shifting."

"You don't understand."

"Possible, but not likely. I'll let you explain it to me when we get back to our room. Let's go."

23

"How could you possibly have known where I was headed, anyway?" I asked, as Kevin opened the door to the room we shared. Silence had been a heavy weight I dragged with us back from the Chamber of Tombs, with his hand still clasped around my wrists, like a prisoner.

"Juno," Kevin said, closing the door, his tone flat. The sensations coming from him, however, were anything but. He didn't try to hide the anger he felt behind a block. And was that hurt, too, I detected? He released my hands. I rubbed away the pressure and pressed behind me the irritation at being stopped from my task.

"I didn't anticipate his ability to view coming events to be working so well." I actually hadn't considered it at all. My mistake. How slim a chance it would be that I could do anything without the mind readers and otherworldly abilities my team possessed.

"Lucky for me, they are," he said. "By the sensations Juno was picking up, he thought you were in danger. He detected urgency. And given the way you flew out of that hospital, he was right. But there was more. Because I detected it, too, as soon as you hit the entrance to the Chamber. What was it, exactly, leave me behind or find Tarsamon?"

Both. Sorry.

"I guessed as much," he said, hearing the thought. "Why would you consider going alone when all I've ever done, my only part in this mission is to protect you?"

There's the hurt.

I felt his eyes on me and forced myself to meet his stare. "You wouldn't have let me go. You can't deny it."

There was no escaping him to finish my task or to be free of the conversation, for that matter. How could I convince him that I couldn't leave this realm without being sure Tarsamon wouldn't try to retaliate?

"I think before we talk you should have something to eat. Besides, I've worked up an appetite, too."

"Fine. Yes." At the suggestion, my stomach woke to the previous forgotten demand for food and growled loudly. "But understand this, I'm not giving up on making sure Tarsamon is disabled permanently."

"Oh, I know. When you get something set in that busy mind of yours, there's no stopping it or the stubbornness that drives it. I've come to know that well enough."

On a small table against the wall was a perfect setting for two. The scent of tantalizing herbs, roasted potatoes, and warm bread found my senses, distracting me momentarily from my argument to wonder if it had been there when we'd walked in.

I sat down and put a napkin on my lap. "Will you help me finish this task?"

He lifted a pitcher and in silence poured a glass of what looked like tea for each of us. *No wine. We always had wine at dinner.*

"It's a blackberry blend," he said. "One of your favorites, right?"

I watched him. The guilt of leaving him in the hospital and the feeling it had been the wrong decision settled over me, pressing my reason to do so aside. The awareness that it was a selfish choice had also come to light with the filling of those two glasses, despite what might be very sound reasons. Every complicated conversation we'd ever had always came at his pace, causing me to force patience from the depths of my eager soul.

He set the pitcher down, and I swore I saw a smile creep from the corner of his mouth.

"How long have you known?" I asked, referring to his knowledge of the child I carried. The man had felt every sensation I ever tried to keep from him since the moment we'd met. Why should this be any different?

"After we rescued you in the temple." He cut into a bite of food.

"Are you pleased?"

A long minute passed as he finished chewing, swallowed, and met my stare. "More than you probably can feel from me."

My heart skipped a tiny leap of joy and settled.

He had always been good at blocking his emotions. He was hurt. "But?"

Timing. Risk. Those two words floated between us unspoken and still as thunderous as if they'd been shouted.

"My goal. My reason for being here with you has never changed and doesn't waver with this new revelation." He sat back in the chair. "I must protect you and the life we could have together." He paused. "It's something we've always wanted…in other lives we've shared."

Flashes of memory, his, winked in my vision. They were so quick I had only a split second to feel them, even less time to see them from his point of view. The gist of which was repetitive pain at the sheer desire for a child and the loss.

"Will you help me, then? Help me defeat Tarsamon?"

"He'll be banished from Earth having lost all power with the release of the energy found in the keys, Sara. There's no justifiable reason to hunt him down."

"He could try to hurt us. Maybe not now, but another time."

He shrugged his shoulders. "Doubtful. You also carry more power now than you have before. His energy cannot be sustained without the lives on Earth. I don't see him coming for you, us, again."

"What do you mean? Is that a yes or no?"

"Because Horus wants you to lead the Soltari, you won't have to ask for any strengths or protections on any mission. We have the protection of a very powerful force for eternity backing us."

"So long as, I believe, the governing entity still exists to aid us. The Alliance, however, must be wiped clean. I can't trust anyone after

Jade confirmed infiltration." I picked up my fork and cut into a large piece of potato, unable to deny the hunger pangs any longer. "We can't have such evil roaming the other realms. Look what happened when Tarsamon was banished to a small area in Ardan. He still managed to grow his forces and gain entrance into a world, to Earth, to claim it and destroy its people."

Kevin leaned forward and took my hand in his. "Sara, I love you like no other, ever. I was terrified to hear you were pregnant, when you were hardly conscious. So, I'm not going to let my happiness over the news take hold just yet." I pressed my lips together, half in a smile at his "happiness" and half in frustration at feeling as though I'd denied him the full joy. "And if you thought I was too protective of you before, you haven't seen anything yet now that you carry our child." He released my hand and continued eating.

"You'll go with me then?"

"If the Dark Lord is still in the underworld and we can access him, yes. But not until I see you eat."

What? Just like that? No fight? The corner of my mouth turned up at the possibility.

"I'm not going to fight you," he said.

"Always listening." Once, not so long ago, he'd said that to me, and I never forgot it.

"One, because it will do me no good. You'll find a way to go to the darkest places where evil hides and face it head-on, no matter any effort I put toward trying to prevent you. Two, there is much more at stake since I've become aware that I'm to be a father. That said, I don't need anything, and I mean anything, harming you since you have come back to me." He took another bite of food and swallowed. "But we're going to need much better weapons than the abilities we possess to destroy a soul as powerful as Tarsamon's permanently."

"And so the hunter becomes the hunted. Where do we get such weapons?"

"Juno and Matt will know. Something tells me, though, they aren't the kind we'd be familiar with."

24

"You must be out of your mind," Juno said. "You want to hunt down the one of the most powerful forces in the realm?" He stepped away from the large table we'd gathered around to discuss our plan. "We don't even know for certain the keys' power has affected Earth yet."

The room was stale with sweat. Fatigue winked in the eyes of every member of the team.

Juno glanced down at the floor deeper in thought. Always considering every angle, every risk as a military specialist would.

"I do," I replied. "Horus has already confirmed it."

"Then we've fulfilled the quest. It's time to leave. Tarsamon will have no power on Earth."

"True. But do you want to fight this fight again on another mission, in another realm?" I asked. "He came to stop me and he failed. With the keys released, he will have no other option but to go into hiding, unless we put an end to him once and for all."

"Where would he hide?" Elise asked. "With this universe and others open to him, he could go anywhere."

Aria leaned her elbows on the table. Her bright blue eyes and flaming-red hair reflecting the same fervor of the conversation. "She's right. Look, I want to be done with this as much as the rest of you. What I want more, though, is to never have to hunt this Dark Lord down again."

"I can't go back if Tarsamon is hiding in this realm," I said. "He could be waiting to slip through with us."

"Norul said she has plans for him," Matt chimed in. "What more is there to handle?"

"That's exactly why we have to find him. If Norul has him handled, there's nothing more for us to do. If not, well then, we… It can't be left alone. There's no way he's going to let Norul hold him as a prisoner. He'll have to leave."

"Or kill her," Juno offered.

Elise shifted beside him. "Is he able?"

"Not unless he had help. Possibly from Aqen."

"Kevin's right." Jade flipped a blade, tip to hilt, back and forth in his hand casually. It was a move I'd seen Juno do when he was in deep thought or concentration, analyzing a situation. "If we don't see this through to the very end, we'll only chase the Dark Lord through the realms and never be finished with him." He clutched the hilt and slipped it neatly into its compartment in the jacket he wore. "And I don't know about the rest of you, but I need to see him permanently put out of commission. Only then will I be able to have a chance at finding some well-earned rest."

"It's your decision," Kevin said, all eyes on him. "Mac, you have a family waiting for you. Your part in this mission is complete. That goes for you, too, Topetine. Your tasks have been fulfilled as guardians of the keys. If you want to go, we wouldn't think any less of you."

"And Horus?" Elise asked. "Will he go back to the Soltari?"

"I don't know," I answered. "His task as guardian of the third key is complete, but he also wants to see more change in Ardan. That's got to include the elimination of a dark force such as Tarsamon."

Mac nodded. "I've trained for this mission my entire life. If I see that it's fulfilled, by way of what New York looks like, I'd like to get back to my family. Mind ye, if I'm needed, I'll follow ye to provide the protection."

"That goes for me, as well," Topetine said. "I'm an elder to the people of my village. I'm sure they would like me to return. But if I can help, I'll stand beside you."

"The rest of us can help." Matt put a hand on Mac's shoulder. "If we run into difficulties, we know we can count on both of you," he said, looking at Topetine. "I can't imagine the additional protection would be necessary, though, given that Sara has confirmation of the release of the keys. In the meantime, our supply of weapons isn't sufficient for carrying out a hunt on a demon lord with many places to hide." He looked at Juno, who nodded, aware of the location their special stockpile of weapons would be found.

"We're going to need that portal opened from the Inner Society to get Mac and Topetine back to their lives in present-day Scotland and the Yucatan while we search for Tarsamon." My gaze darted around the circle. "Does anyone know for sure if he's still in the realm?"

"There's no passage out yet. He'd have to be," Juno said. "If Horus was able to glimpse the effects of the keys, his forces on Earth have to be dwindling as we speak. The shadows he placed there would be destroyed. The only human casualties would be those who were too weak to sustain the takeover. Which may be more than we expect. But there would be no reason at all for him to return to Earth."

"Who would hide him?"

A silence rolled between us.

"Aqen might help him," Horus said as he entered the doorway. "He's the only one willing to risk challenging Norul." He shifted into his human form and stepped between Jade and Kevin. "But to do so means it would have to be worth his effort and the risk of losing his place in the death realm. Norul is tracking both of them. If you're going to hunt Tarsamon, you'll need to get to him soon. He has no lasting power in this realm without help, and I'm quite sure there's little of that left for him."

"We can always find him in Ardan," Elise said.

"He'll have no power there, either, with the removal of his forces. When the keys were formed, the power was set to seek out all of his specific brand of evil—the shadows that feed off the energy of the humans, the faceless demons, and the dogs that hunt such energy. He'll have no choice but to hide, if he can."

"Any chance another passage out of this realm exists without the help of the Inner Society?" Aria asked.

"There is if you're a spirit belonging to the light," Horus replied. "The only other way out I'm aware of for a demon would be through a transformation. A much darker, condensed energy form is all that would allow transport for Tarsamon out of the realm of souls. Without holding any power in the realm, his evil could attach to that energy."

"Dark matter?" Jade said.

"Exactly."

"That's impossible to hunt."

"Difficult but not impossible with the right tool. A tracker such as yourself couldn't find energy that connects to dark matter, but a seeker could. They have the ability to hunt specific energy patterns, especially hidden types."

"There hasn't been a seeker in, well, as long as I've traveled the realms," Jade said. "That's nearly a millennium."

"They exist, albeit very few."

"We don't even know if he's still here," Aria said. "The portal should be open if, as you say, the keys have been released. If we can find that, we could start there. But what if Aqen already helped him out? Could he pass through before Sara?"

"The doorway back to Earth, created by the Inner Society at the release of the keys, should be active, yes. But passage through it is coded only by the algorithms Sara carries. The same ones given to her by the orb before all of you left the Society's underground haven. It won't open for anyone but her."

"Which means Tarsamon is still here," Juno said.

"If he hasn't transformed and combined with dark matter," Jade added.

"What is this 'dark matter' you keep mentioning?" Elise asked. "I haven't run into this."

"It rarely shows a presence. I've only encountered it twice in my existence," Horus replied. "Dark matter is a force of energy that contributes to movement of a particle. It's matter that does not interact with light or the electromagnetic spectrum but exists everywhere at all times. Jade uses the energy from the spectrum to follow a trail or path left by someone in order to trace such energy from one place to another. But if Tarsamon transforms his energy into dark matter, he becomes invisible in the spectrum. Trackers like Jade can't find him. However, when dark energy and dark matter combine, it constitutes a total mass energy content greater than ordinary matter."

"And that means we should be able to find him, right?"

Horus shook his head. "Not necessarily. While the particles are larger, they hide in the gravitation and weak force of subatomic particles. Jade can't trace that. Only someone with the ability to detect subatomic particle distance, where what is known as weak interaction takes place, can find dark matter."

"Jesus." Jade blew out a long breath. "Without a seeker, Tarsamon could hide for a long time."

"Exactly."

"And you're sure a seeker is the only person with the ability to track that type of energy?"

Horus nodded.

"Let's just cross our fingers he hasn't melded into dark matter yet," Aria said.

"And if we catch him, assuming he knows of this dark matter and it's before he transforms, how can we hold him?"

"The spell of Tascia," Juno replied. "Eldor gave it to me before the mission, when we were preparing. He said it was a tool I *may* need that only the leader of the elves himself could create. It can hold the Dark Lord long enough for the elves to cast a spell more permanent, or until it can be determined what to do with him."

"Why didn't we use it before now?" Elise asked.

"We were only concerned with protecting Sara from the Dark Lord's forces," Matt replied. "Using the spell wouldn't have done enough to hold him while his army was still hunting Sara."

Horus slipped away and appeared beside me. "Sara, we need you to open the portal back to the Inner Society in New York to let Mac and Topetine go back. But we'll have to close it until we've found

Tarsamon. I don't want take any chance of him slipping through the passage under cover."

"And if we don't find him, we'll still need to open it again," I said.

"Yes. It's a risk we'll have to take. We're not likely to find a seeker to hunt down dark matter in this realm."

"True."

Juno looked in my direction. "I think you should stay here."

"I bet you could guess my answer to that."

"She's not safe alone," Kevin said. "She's safest with us."

Juno shook his head. "If anything happens to her and the passage back can't be opened because the one holding the algorithms is dead then—"

"That's not going to happen," Kevin interrupted. "The chance for that has passed. You know it as well as I. Tarsamon's focus will be leaving the realm, and possibly using her as a means for escape."

I hadn't thought of that. Perhaps that's why I wasn't in charge of protection on this mission.

"She stays with us, protected as if she still held the keys," Kevin added.

"She sure as hell holds the key out of here," Jade said. "Enough wasting time with talk. Let's see if we can even find the demon lord."

"We need to find Norul first," Matt said. "As the ruler over the realm, she'll have the best line on Tarsamon."

We moved through the palace, toward the Chamber of Tombs.

As I crossed over the threshold into the room, a sparkle, followed by several others, glimmered in the corner, across a large, pale, flat stone with markings carved into it.

"There," I said. "That's our doorway." I pointed to the same wall we'd passed by on our way into the City of Souls. One of the last things Leahnan had told me before I left was that her team would be able to track us after the keys were released, to aid us in opening a path to return to New York. "The Inner Society must be able to see our location because that wall was as unremarkable as sliced white bread until tonight." The sign of assistance was a small comfort.

"Hopefully it will be there when we get back," Jade said.

"First, we return Mac and Topetine. Juno and Matt will then need to access additional weapons if we end up encountering Aqen or anyone else Tarsamon might have aligned himself with."

"We have the necessary weapons here in the realm to battle Tarsamon," Matt said, picking up his pack and slinging it over his shoulder. "Just need to make one quick stop. Other than that, Norul is the weapon we'll need if Aqen wants to battle." My gaze rested on him, finding confidence in his assurance. "A soldier is always prepared."

I turned toward the corner and to where I'd last seen the glimmer on the stone, and set my focus on finding the mechanism that would sync to a code, or something I carried that would make the connection. Holding my hands in front of an object that would recognize the ring I wore and give us clearance to finding the keys had worked before to open a passage, but not this time. I traced a hand, one at a time, around the faint outline of light winking back at me in no precise pattern. Nothing. *Slower.* I tried again, holding my breath and cursing at the finicky nature of such an important passage. *Time. Always the impediment.*

"Maybe the working of it requires finesse and patience," Juno said.

"Maybe it does," I gritted, lifting my eyes to meet Juno's before refocusing on the passage. The frustration in my tone bordered on the brink of sarcasm. "Not a good time to suggest the obvious." I bit back the next thought on the tip of my tongue. We were all tired. We'd had enough fighting—fighting against the evil, fighting to protect what was good, fighting for the keys that could end the takeover of Earth, and now to open a passage.

"Got it," I said in a low voice. I heard a few exhales of breath behind me.

The sparkling on the wall came together in one central point above my hands and connected with a faint lighted energy from the engraved silver band I wore. My hands moved across the wall in one direction, then another and back. At each touch of the wall, a rectangle illuminated, raised from the flattened stone, and changed into a specific hieroglyphic pattern. I didn't know what any of it meant, only that the action felt so much like a living puzzle I had to solve.

"There. That's it." I stepped back, finished with the work my hands had been guided to create, and saw the pattern illuminated as a whole. I'd never studied hieroglyphs, nor had I retained any knowledge from the experience in the Mayan jungle, but I could read the message, gilded in silver metallic:

Upon the passage of the Light Carrier and those who follow, the door to the keys shall be closed forever, and the world called home shall be rid of darkness. The birth of a guardian will remain in each lifetime as a gift to aid the light that protects the world.

I read the last line twice. *Birth*…must mean a human, right? Could the message mean the child I carried?

"Do I have to go through it first?" I asked.

"No," Horus replied. "You've activated it by unlocking it."

Mac stepped forward. "We'll say goodbye to ye here, then."

"Thank you." I threw my arms around him, then Topetine. "Tell your lovely wife, Aggie, to expect that invitation she wanted to one of our charity dinners. And your boy, Ian, more chocolate."

"Goodbye, my dear," Topetine said.

"Not goodbye. I'm not good at those. I'll see you soon!"

She held my face in her hands, stared into my eyes, and smiled. "You've done well."

"I'm not quite done yet. None of it could've been done without either of you." I smiled back as she touched her hand against my cheek.

"The portal was created to return all of us to New York," Horus said. "Leahnan or a member of her team will meet you."

I pressed a flat palm against the wall, causing the stone to fall away, disappearing into the center of the passage that would return them to present-day Earth. In its place was a black hole, a crackle of electricity passed down the length on either side as far as my eyes could see.

Mac nodded and stepped into it, followed by Topetine.

A slight sensation of sadness, followed by relief for their safety, came and went.

"I don't suppose there's any way to close it in the unlikely event Tarsamon finds this before we get to him?" Elise asked.

"The palace is secure," Horus replied.

"It might've been once. But since it's been breached, I'm not so sure," I said, at the same time considering the defenses available to me—shield, the hawk, guns—should there be a dark angel we had missed.

What if the passage isn't open when we return? If the codes don't work…

"No reason to overthink it, Sara." Horus swirled around me. "The Inner Society would never have told you the doorway would be open or given you the algorithms if you weren't meant to unlock the passage, even if it's more than once."

I nodded. "Of course not." But I'd also trusted the Soltari once upon a time, too.

25

We didn't have to go far to find Norul. A commotion had drawn our attention to the riverbank of the Nile. Her long hair streamed down across her shoulder, touching the top part of her arm, as she struggled to free herself from the binds that held her suspended between two sturdy limbs of a tree.

Swords drawn by the team along with the white-blue fireball twirling in my hands were stashed, with no obvious threat present. She met my gaze and shook her head.

What?

My senses sharpened to the energy around us and found its target a short distance away from the tree.

"He's here."

Tarsamon had actually taken a risk to go after Norul? But how had he managed to capture the powerful god?

As though in answer, a rush of small, shadowed children came out from behind the brush and surrounded the tree. Their faces resembled Tarsamon's, black with yellow lit eyes. The only difference was there was no identifiable jawline. Who had created them? Aqen? The necromancer? Any forces Tarsamon brought with him would easily have been dominated by Norul.

I drew the shield of light around me before igniting another flaming sphere. The swish of blades being pulled sounded as we held our positions.

Aria stepped beside me and leaned into Matt. "What other weapons do we have?"

"The bullets we brought with us were created specifically for the dark angel. Still," he said, loading a sleeve of ammo, "if they're strong enough to kill a demon that powerful, they should be able to handle this crew."

"They're the hollows of the dead," Jade said lifting his voice. "They steal souls."

"Which means…" Juno said, loading his weapon.

"The leech who commands them is nearby," Jade added.

The answer to the source that brought the dead forward revealed himself. The necromancer stood in front of the hollow children, like a parent ready to protect them. Or, I reconsidered, a general ready to lead his soldiers. Other spirits he'd called to the location appeared from thin air—his loyal dead. Permanent residents of the City of Souls that had chosen their loyalty to Aqen. Illuminated transparent forms of all shapes and sizes filled in the gaps between the hollows and spaces of night. Their hate-filled expressions screamed death, murderous rage their intent. It took less than a second to determine we'd been thrown into a battle with not enough manpower on our side to fight and win.

"Got anything else in that pack?" I asked, my gaze locked on the number of forces that had accumulated, and guessed the count to be approaching a hundred, give or take a few. "Those bullets won't kill what's already dead. I've tried it. Once."

"We're going to need reinforcements," Aria said.

I glanced up, past Norul and further still beyond the tree. "Leahnan, if you have the ability to track our movement or to see what's in front of us, we're going to need your help." The only evidence I had that she and her team had a second sight was the passage back to our world that had appeared in the Chamber. But that could as easily have been provided because Horus had gone to check with her about the release of the keys. Either way, without help, a blatant fact stared back at us in those yellow eyes—our souls might be trapped in this hell. It wasn't a consideration any of us would allow ourselves to reflect upon. We'd come too far and were too close to the end of this long journey to be denied a path home to where we belonged.

Where's Tarsamon? I felt his energy close. Too close. *Must be hiding.*

"Sara," Kevin said, reaching for my arm and pulling me beside him.

"I've got to get her down from there," I said, glancing to Norul. "If she's freed, she can rectify this mess. I'm sure of it."

"Find Tarsamon," Juno called out from several feet away.

"We'll get her down," Kevin said, "but stay close to me."

I'd learned over time and through stubborn perseverance that this man I loved didn't get his Last Great Warrior title from doing much wrong when it came to battle. This time around, as much as I wanted to disappear to free Norul or find the Dark Lord, I had to trust Kevin's instruction.

A movement beside the necromancer's forces drew my attention, but when I looked, there was nothing. "Why haven't they attacked us yet?" *What are they waiting for?*

"They're protecting him, Tarsamon," Kevin replied.

"I need a path a path to Norul." I said a prayer and released the fireball, sending it sailing toward the center target, where I thought Tarsamon might be. The flame died on landing. Streaks of gray smoke lifted and scattered as though I'd tossed a smoke bomb.

"How did he do that?"

Are we all defenseless, or just me?

Thought after thought of desperation blanketed rational thought. *Think, think, think.*

Jade rushed to my side. "We've got to go. There are too many and you're at a bigger risk being here."

"Who do they owe allegiance to, the necromancer or Aqen?" Kevin asked.

"I don't know where their loyalty lies. When a necromancer calls upon them, they work for him."

From behind us, opposite the riverbank, the sound of drums

filled the unusual stillness, causing the waiting hollow children and death spirits to advance slowly. Did they want to push us back?

The rhythmic patterns grew louder, but I couldn't identify the source. As the sound drew closer, weapons appeared in the hands of the hollows, and the transparent hands of the dead shifted into points, like daggers.

The thought of losing Kevin or the child entered my mind and, with little effort, caused my body to shift into the hawk without the intention of doing so. Jade and Topetine had warned me on different occasions I'd need to control such images associated with thought. The shift didn't feel like the usual fear or rage that caused me to shift. Instead, it had felt like a defense mechanism.

"Shit," Jade said as I lifted higher, my wings carrying me to the tree where Norul was bound. From above, I saw what approached from behind us—the lean figures and stern faces of the elves, armed with bows and arrows. Behind them, and unarmed, the source of the rhythmic sound revealed a second row of elves.

"Neeah!" The necromancer shouted the call to advance his forces at battle speed. The death spirits responded with a shrill cry and lifted into the air, charging full force toward the team.

Their too fast. The sound of Juno and Matt's guns tore through the cries. I glimpsed Horus's form as a bird gliding across the sky. His wing tipped into another of the transparent forms, instantly causing it to fall, robbed of it's soul even in death. A pointed arm of a spirit reached inches from my face as I settled on a branch close to Norul. Faster than the arm had reached me it was gone as Kevin's blade slipped through the transparent form, causing the violent whisper of white to fall like smoke through the branches to the ground. *He'd followed me to the tree? Thank God for his otherworldly speed.*

Arrows outlined in a silver glow lit the sky as they flew across the air above our heads and landed at most of their targets. The small dark figures of soldiers fell into black pools where they stood. The spirits that took an arrow cried out and spun into glowing funnels, their color a sickly yellow-green that lifted high into the air like toxic, radioactive fumes. Still others fell in place. With no obvious threat of another spirit, Kevin went to the aid of the team.

I turned my attention to Norul. The bindings around her wrists and ankles glowed red, speaking of every sort of danger I shouldn't touch.

She shook her head, slowly this time.

I couldn't hear her thoughts in the chaos around me to understand what she was trying to say. Instead, the bothersome sound of small movements filtered to my keener senses.

The razor-sharp vision I held in this form pierced through scrub only a few feet away. I centered my attention on a small area with no snow. *My target.*

Abandoning any sense of desire to free Norul, and overcome by the fierce, innate sense to track and kill, I flew straight for the source resonating every bit of attempted deception, a play to hide I couldn't resist.

Everything in my body tingled at the sensation of pinpointing the prey and going in for the kill. As I lifted my wings and sank my talons deep within the bundle that shifted violently beneath me, the energy felt nothing like the creatures Jade called hollows, and instead more like what we'd come to know well—the Dark Lord.

My claws locked onto the movement. A scream ripped across the sky in a high-pitched alarm as if the dark angel herself had felt the sting of piercing talons, driving the force of my hold deeper. The mass within my grip moved more violently, throwing me off-balance and causing me to bear down tighter on what sought to be free. The object rolled to the side, taking me with it. I flapped wildly, trying to regain balance and maintain control over the object. The sound of my own shrieks mixed with the screams, surprising even to my ears.

"Jesus. Hold on," Juno's voice said from somewhere closer than he had been, as I bumped and toppled. The rhythmic sound of hundreds of footsteps marching in time, along with the fighting I could hear around me were not going to deter me from holding tight to my opponent.

The figure and I rolled out of the brush. It was Tarsamon. I was sure of it. I fought to right myself above the bundle, tossing the icy white powder that had collected on my wings.

The sound of unintelligible words from the elves added to my frustration at the difficulty in concentrating. Why had I gone after the Dark Lord in this form? Had pure animal instinct driven me? Or was it the feeling of being threatened over the last several months? I had to be more powerful as a human than a hawk. And yet, there was no way the strength in this form was going to stop the Dark Lord entirely. Not without help. *Where's Juno with his spell?*

A bright light flooded the landscape, rolling across the ground and beneath the cloak. The object I held stopped moving and went flat with the ground. *What? Wait.* I held firm to what lingered in my claws. As I lifted one foot, then another, only a clump of black, half the size of what I'd held in my clutches, remained. Was the cloak all that was left?

"Sara," Kevin called from behind me. The only voice that mattered pierced my focused attention. I lifted my head. Seeing Juno with Matt close behind, I released my grip as I flew to the branch for a better look. One small part of the form I once held, a flattened black mass, slipped beyond the bulky cloth and drifted away, defeated and powerless as a shadow across the snow. And yet, I fought the instinct to chase it. The rest of the form remained unmoving beneath the cloak. Had I killed him?

Juno was standing on the other side of the brush, the bundle of cloth pinned beneath his boot. An elf stood beside him. I flew to Kevin, landing on his extended arm, covered in the same protective leather Jade wore.

Where did the hollows go? The necromancer?

Scattered across the blanket of snow were the remaining death spirits that hadn't lifted upward, their glowing forms fading across the landscape. The silver-lined arrows lay in the center of most; other tipped points were strewn across the landscape, abandoned by the elves and fading spirits.

"Damn it," Juno shouted.

Matt took off running in the same direction as the shadow across the snow.

Anubis stood beside Kevin, staff in hand, still emanating the same color of light that had rolled beneath the form I'd held in my clutches. Had he been following us?

"How are we supposed to free her?" Aria said, referring to Norul.

"She's bound by dark magic," the dog-faced man said. I angled my neck to see him better. "Her energy has a connection with mine. When it suddenly faded, I tracked her path here."

Is he the same as the image C-05 took the shape of? Is this C-05?

"Are all the little creatures gone?" Elise said, her breath puffing in and out from a recent chase.

"They can't exist in the light of Ra," Anubis answered, lifting his staff slightly. "And the death spirits, they can't withstand the arrows constructed with the same energy."

"Ah, that's what that light was," she said.

Without the painful thoughts to hold me as a hawk, I left Kevin's arm and went to the ground, shifting back into my human form behind the cover of another tree. The clothing began to wrap and cover my body as I crouched protected mostly from view, shivering as the icy air reached the areas not yet clothed. *Warmth.* "One could get used to calling the necessities of survival to fruition with a mere thought," I said to myself.

Fully draped in wintery attire and more comfortable, I turned and walked the few steps to meet the rest of the team standing together. Matt had returned, shaking his head and talking with Kevin and Jade. As I approached Kevin, I saw a stream of blood trailing from his forehead along the side of his face. "You okay?"

"What?" He saw my eyes flick to the side. "Oh," he said, swiping his temple with the back of his hand. "Lucky shot. It's nothing."

"She has numbers running through the bands around her wrists and ankles," I said, lifting my gaze to Norul. "What does that mean?"

"It means anyone who tries to free her will die with her," the dog-faced man said.

"C-05?"

His brows closed together in a puzzled look. "Anubis," he said, nodding once.

"How many men named Anubis are there in this realm?"

"One."

"I thought so." Did the others know that Anubis was the spiritual manifestation of C-05?

I glanced back to Norul and the more important matter of freeing her. Her deep brown eyes filled with tears. But it was rage, not sadness, spilling from her in waves of vibrations that reached me. Her mouth had been bound, too.

"The ground has been shaken by the staff of Ra. The energy chased off all but what Juno has collected." Anubis angled the staff in his direction.

In a gloved hand, Juno held a large cage radiating electric-blue light. "You caught him as he was shifting," he said to me. "The elves will take him back," Juno said. "I'm not sure how long the spell will hold." He handed the cage to the elf, who started off in the direction the rest of the elves had come from.

"Tarsamon, right?" I said, glancing at the form within.

I watched for a moment as his form faded to no more than an outline.

"Right," Juno answered. "The spell wouldn't have worked if it wasn't. I wasn't sure but had to chance it. How did you know where to find him?"

"I heard sounds coming from the brush. Why was he hiding? Why didn't he fight with the rest of them?"

"He's tired," Anubis said. "While the forces of the dead can be numerous, the power the elves hold in battle and healing is often unstoppable. He's been in a realm where the weaker energy of darkness exists. That same force in death drains energy from the living. Life isn't meant to be sustained here."

"What did he want with Norul?" Kevin asked.

Aria stomped her feet against the cold. "Why don't we get her down and find out?"

"It's not an easy task to remove her," Anubis said. His eyes flicked to Kevin. "He wanted power." "After what Tarsamon and Aqen attempted with Sara, neither could exist with Norul as the ruler over the realm. Together, they must have joined their energy. It's the only way they could exert enough strength to restrain a god, and then mark her to destroy anyone who tries to unlock the power holding her."

"I think I can free her," I said.

"And what if you're wrong?" Kevin asked. "We didn't come this far to have you killed, again, by a spell or some other magic from the Dark Lord or Aqen."

"The codes. Those numbers are like a lock. A lock that needs a special key."

"It's a kind of specialized magic, Sara," Jade said. "Not a lock. Don't be foolish about this. You're risking too much. But what else is new?" he added under his breath.

"Just let me get a good look at it, will you? Then you can judge the situation."

"We need to get back to the portal, and now," Juno urged. "Our energy is dwindling in this realm."

"We can't leave her up there," Elise said.

"Is this a power you can release?" Kevin asked. He glanced from me to Anubis.

"I don't possess the specific energy to attempt a release of that magnitude. She'll need a force I don't have access to."

"What about the elves?"

"They would have freed her if they held such a power," Horus said. "Maybe the Soltari would be willing to—"

"There isn't time," I said. "We all know it. If Aqen and Tarsamon can combine their energy to create a hold over a god as powerful as Norul, there would be a time limit in place to be sure we don't free her. If there's a chance I can help her, I need to try."

Without waiting for a reply, I turned and headed for the tree. Kevin didn't try to stop me. I looked over my shoulder at him before taking the last steps to reach Norul. His face was unreadable. But even as I climbed, I felt the emotion from him and whether he should try to stop or trust me. He opted for the latter, remaining fixed, eyes never wavering.

Climbing was as effortless as when I'd practiced in Ardan for the challenges I'd face, where I didn't have to fight gravity, and the angles over and around branches were already known. The only difference was the climb was slower. Juno was right, our energy was fading. *All I need is a little longer to figure this out. The passage back home is already open. God willing, it's remained that way.*

I scanned Norul first, head to toe, assessing which branches were perhaps weaker, where she might slip if her foothold gave out. "Why in God's name did they put you in a tree?" I said more to myself than to her.

Her gaze followed me. She was gifted with powerful magic. How were they able to get to her? *Must have been a surprise attack.*

The band continued to glow red. *Is it electrified?*

"Sara," Juno called from below. "We can come back for her."

"Just give me a minute," I said quietly as I scanned the binds for any clues. I shifted my gaze to her eyes. "I'm not leaving you." All evidence of tears had been replaced by sheer determination. To live? Retribution, perhaps? Likely both.

Digital numbers scrolled over the illuminated bands in a sequence, followed by an upside down *U*, a swirl, straight lines and a group of swirls, and then a *Y* with a pound symbol over it. Roman numerals I understood, but patterns? Why the added complication of hieroglyphs? Must have been a successful system to transfer from one location in Egypt to the more current Mayan culture. Topetine might've been able to translate. *Why did we send her back early again? Because we were expecting to find Norul.* With some luck, we'd found Tarsamon, too. Item one, check. Item two, check with a caveat—a battle and a riskier situation.

Got to code them together. Bring them together.

Was Norul speaking to me in thought or was some other guidance at work directing me?

"Don't touch it, Sara. You don't know what its power is capable of," Jade called.

If everyone would just…let…me…figure…this…out.

I reached for the band at one of Norul's wrists, no wider than a watchband, and closed my eyes, letting the guidance lead me to the next step.

"Jesus," a voice said a short distance away.

No electricity. And because I was not ejected from the tree, still holding tight, I had confidence in that guidance. A certain calming sensation filled my head. *No interruptions.* I half hoped everyone would be quiet long enough for this to work, despite the urgency I felt growing from Juno.

A certain stillness moved over me, stifling the fear that so easily wanted to take its place. An icy breeze blew from the direction we'd come from to find her and settled again. The numbers I'd seen scanning across the band filled my head and streamed in synchronized deadly form, daring me to conquer the power it held. In seconds the numerals began to organize, shifting their pattern to follow what I could only guess was according to the direction of one of several algorithms given to me via the Inner Society. With my eyes still closed, my fingers slipped to each end, connecting and locking onto the energy with my own, as my index fingers moved across the face, left and right, a tap to insert a break. The sensation of light stinging in the tips of my fingers was the only mild discomfort as they rearranged the pattern to match the one in my head. Faster they moved, then slowed long enough to catch the new sensation of heat. Could the energy that had once denied Tarsamon's touch on my skin also be the catalyst now shifting the numbers? I didn't dare open my eyes to find out and risk losing the pattern. What if this made things worse? The vision of the pattern in my head stopped moving across the mental screen.

Did it finish? Or, God help us, did it break?

I opened my eyes to see the numbers were indeed not moving and in a different pattern than when I'd first viewed them. Some held a few numeric identifiers, along with the hieroglyphs, and still some had changed with only one numeral.

"Sara!" The call from Juno was more urgent this time. "It's too dangerous. Leave her!"

I yanked my hands away as part of the band caught fire and fell from her wrists. Kevin raced up the tree and pulled me back against him, just in time, as the binding at her mouth and ankles followed the same fiery destruction. The minute it sparked at her face, she tore it away, fury behind her lashes.

"Thank you," she gasped.

With Kevin at my back, we climbed quickly back down the tree. Anubis extended a hand to Norul.

"It'll take time to restore your energy," Anubis said to her.

"Yes." She angled her head to me and the team. "In the meantime, you'll need a seeker that can track down the energy that broke away from the form you captured. Aqen helped Tarsamon shift into dark matter, as Horus thought he might, in order to hide. The rest of him can't escape the underworld. He's got to be here."

"But where's Horus?" I asked.

"He was here when were trying to figure out what to do," Aria replied. "Maybe he went to find the remaining dark matter."

"He'll find his way back to us," Juno said. "What's important is getting back to the passage that'll return us to New York."

Norul rubbed at her wrists. "The rest of you can follow me. I can get you back faster than you can travel through the realm, except maybe you, Jade." She flashed a smile at him. "I've got a lot of work to do here. There's a great deal to make right again." Brief images of vengeance flashed in my head from her, cutting through the relief from the rescue.

Norul started to chant in a way that sounded like the elves, *"Aru day. Son deaude..."* as a bright light crossed my vision and everything disappeared.

One moment we were standing in the wintery open air of a death realm and, another, staring across at each other in the Chamber of Tombs. Horus stood beside the same wall where I had opened the passage for Mac and Topetine. For a spirit, void of lines to give away his expression, he looked solemn.

"What happened?" Jade asked.

Horus shifted into the image of a man and shook his head. "The remnants of Tarsamon, the dark matter he changed into, found subatomic particle energy."

"Where?"

"Through the passage."

"What do you mean *through the passage*?" I asked. "I thought the evil could only enter after I'd gone through, following my energy. That's how his forces had followed us in the past." *Except for this realm.* C-05 had made it through because he had the coordinates. He and the evil entered from the last location in the Yucatan, after our team. "But how can dark matter return?"

"Subatomic particle energy exists everywhere. You need to pass through first only if another self-contained energy, one that can't combine with another, like you or me, will want access. Having joined with subatomic particle energy, Tarsamon no longer fits into the self-contained category."

"And?" I said.

Jade stepped closer to Horus. "And dark matter attaches to the subatomic particle energy for movement, including unlocked passages because…"

"Everything is energy," they both said.

Horus raised a brow and angled his head. "Exactly. Humans are at the infancy of discovering the mechanism for its workings through what they call the quantum field. In the planning of the keys, with Sara and the rest of her team being human, the Soltari never thought a method to prevent such a transformation would have been necessary. It shouldn't have been needed, especially through a portal."

"A loophole?" Jade said, letting out a breath of frustration.

"But how would Tarsamon have known to find the exit here?" I asked.

"As dark matter, his sole existence would be to track subatomic particle energy to stay alive. He would be looking for your passage, this doorway leading back to Earth. He can then choose to hide in your universe or escape it."

"How much more dark matter is in the universe?"

"Infinite." It wasn't the answer I wanted to hear. "It's responsible for connecting all forms of energy. From the creation of stars and galaxies to the very substance that makes up the particles of the physical realm."

"But it wasn't necessarily evil until now," Jade said. "Is that what you're saying?"

"Essentially, yes."

"Let's hope Tarsamon is just using his new form as a means of transport," Jade said, "to escape from this realm and Norul, rather than a plan to expand into another type of energy. For instance, a contaminating disease."

Aria pressed between me and Jade. "Once Tarsamon shifted, Juno captured most of the dark matter, shipped it off with the elves. Whatever is left of him that escaped can't be strong enough to cause harm, right?"

"You're right," Horus replied. "He'd have nothing substantial left of his energy to cause harm. It would take years, in fact, to build up to the same mass he was before he shifted. With the elves holding most of that energy, well, I imagine he'd want to regain that energy and become even stronger."

"How?" Elise asked. "He'll never be able to get close to where the elves hold his remaining energy."

"He'd collect subatomic particle energy and combine with dark matter spread throughout the universe," Jade answered. "Then, what the elves hold of him wouldn't matter."

I felt my gaze drift to the floor, suddenly consumed with the thought of my child surrounded by a family of immortals and a looming threat before ever being born. How could I raise a child in a world where the Dark Lord that had hunted me once might be roaming about? Would he seek revenge? Because if roles were reversed, I might.

26

My fear had come to fruition. The passage returning us to our world, to New York, was indeed shut when we returned to the Chamber of Tombs. After a few comments from Jade about locating a seeker to hunt down the dark matter, a few deep breaths, and reminding myself to have faith in what led us, the last click thankfully sounded the final connection, following the same pattern I'd used to open the portal for Mac and Topetine.

Gold flakes fell over sand. Amun's words when we'd first set foot in the Chamber returned. "Gold is reserved for the afterlife."

Let's hope not in this case.

A glass cylinder rolled out from a crevice at the entry point. Encased within, a swirl of white mist intermingled with vibrant blue.

"You must break it," Horus said. "It sets in motion protections for our arrival."

Did Mac and Topetine need such measures?

"The Inner Society is waiting," Horus added.

I swung the cylinder at the wall, shattering it. The pieces of glass were sucked into the mist as it expanded into the hazy opening and rose into the air, tripling its size and hovering over what was once a doorway.

An icy breeze blew into my face. The chill sunk beneath the surface of my exposed skin, as the sensation of pointed fingertips danced down my spine, causing gooseflesh to erupt across my covered arms and the need to take a half step backward.

Kevin's hand slipped into mine.

An ionized smell lifted on the current, like the one I'd detected when I'd first entered Ardan.

"This seems different." I looked at Horus. "You're sure this returns us to New York?"

"Positive. There isn't time to discuss it."

I took a deep breath and, with the team behind me and Kevin at my back, extended one arm into the mystical passage to be sure I didn't feel a wall blocking my entrance. Free to pass, I stepped in all the way. Kevin's hand pulled from mine as the energy separated us in its tunnel, a passage created with every intention of ignoring time and space. The dizzying feeling returned and a rush of images blew by on either side of me—ancient and modern, creations from past and present, hieroglyphs and numbers, pools of blood and skulls, like those I'd glimpsed in the magical Mayan caves. I tumbled through the wormhole as I'd done before, fully awake and wishing I wasn't. Experience moving through the portals had not made travel any easier as my stomach lurched at the too-fast pace and flood of stimuli. I couldn't see anyone else who'd stepped into the passage with me, just the image of Leahnan's face. It floated past as black consumed my vision, signaling the approaching arrival.

I woke to flakes of snow kissing the bridge of my nose and eyelids. Had I landed in Central Park again? The sky was black, with only the residual glow of a streetlight hidden behind the bare arms of branches nearby. Where was the daylight Horus had said was starting to show? Was it evening?

"That's it. Over there," I heard a distant female voice say. But whose?

"Kevin," I tried to say, but his name slipped off my tongue in a whisper as light as the falling snow. "It's so cold. So cold." My teeth began to chatter. Had the clothes I'd worn not come with me? And if so, where was the cover that always draped me after crossing into another time?

As if in answer, a large sheet of heavy fluff fell across my body. I turned my head and lifted it to see Leahnan placing a blanket over me.

"Kevin," I said through chattering teeth. "Where is he? The team?"

"We've got them."

I nodded. "Okay. Are we safe?"

"Everything will be fine. You've done well."

Will be?

She slipped a pair of thick, soft slippers over my feet. "Can you stand?"

"Yeah. Of course." *I think.* "I can't get warm." My body shook violently, and I was so tired. "The tunnel had some unusual effects upon returning this time. I don't understand why or what was different."

"It's okay. Stand up with me," she said, slipping an arm beneath mine and across my back. I pushed up with her help and saw the once grass-covered landscape now blanketed in a fine layer of fresh snow. There were no obvious signs of humans wandering with vacant stares, as they were upon my last arrival.

"First snow," she said. "A sign of your success. Let's get you in the car and warm."

With words too difficult to speak, I nodded and walked with her to a waiting car. The heat was on full blast and I scooted across the seat beside Kevin, his arms extended as he brought me closer, draping a large tartan cover over us. Beneath it, I caught the faint glimpse of denim and a bright white T-Shirt. Not his usual attire. The door slammed shut and Leahnan jumped in the front seat beside the driver.

"Is it supposed to be so cold?" I said.

"You've forgotten New York winters, love?" Kevin replied, wrapping an arm around me.

I smiled and leaned my head against his shoulder. "Can't say I've experienced them without clothing…" My words trailed off.

"We have clothes for you, right here."

"Sara, stay awake. Okay?" Kevin said, setting the clothing on top of the tartan. "Put these on. You'll feel better."

"In a minute. Just need a minute."

With one arm still around me, he leaned forward and quietly but with intensity said something to the driver, causing the car to burst ahead with the same sense of urgency in his voice.

"Forget that," he said, still speaking to the driver. "Take us to the nearest hospital."

I looked up, wanting to protest, but the need for sleep was winning out. There was no more fight left in me. I forced my eyes to stay open but was losing the battle.

A flash of light blew past my limited vision, eyes at half-mast, and stopped for an instant at the window long enough for me to recognize the figure as Jade, blades brandished for a fight.

"What?" I tried to sit up. "S-s-t-top the c-car."

Kevin's arm came around me.

He leaned into the front seat again. "What's happening? Why aren't we headed to Lenox? It's the closest hospital."

"We have the necessary accommodations to help her," replied Leahnan.

"She's experiencing hypothermia. We need the closest facility to help her."

He reached for the clothing and began slipping a pair of pants over my legs, followed by a hooded sweatshirt. My body continued its violent shake.

Why am I not warming from the car's heat?

"Try to breathe slower, Sara," he said, rubbing my arms. "Stop the car. I can get us to safety faster."

"We're here," Leahnan said. The car came to a sudden halt. She opened the door and jumped out. Kevin didn't wait as he pushed the door open and lifted me out, then followed her.

"What is this place?'

But Leahnan didn't answer, only nodded as a large metal panel opened, revealing a wall of glass. Guards at the sides slid open the doors and closed them and the metal panels as soon as we were clear.

Kevin followed her into a room.

"Place her right here."

My eyes had closed and all I heard was the sound of Leahnan's voice. Kevin set me on a table that was, to my pleasant surprise, heated, and lifted my head as a pillow was slid beneath it.

"You awake?" he asked, stroking a hand over my forehead. "You'll feel better very soon."

I blinked open my eyes. "I am. Better, that is." I was still shaking but at least my teeth had stopped chattering and my breath flowed more comfortably in and out of my lungs. My gaze drifted to an arbitrary metal plate screwed into the side of the wall. The words I began to speak flowed in unclear single notes with multiple syllables.

Leahnan was in conversation with someone nearby.

"What happened?" Kevin asked. "She was just speaking. Why is she chanting?"

Leahnan turned. "The power of the keys works quickly. But the world has not yet been rid of all the darkness, the judgment, its cruelty." She paused. "She chants from an ancient text known as the Vedas. It's one of the oldest known scriptures in the world. Wait." She paused. "She's talking about Prakriti. She's calling upon the forces to bring about, wait, to move energy through the darker corners of the universe." Kevin watched as Leahnan leaned in closer. "Dark matter." She shook her head. "She's asking for help." A few more seconds passed. "She can still hear you."

"Sara." Leahnan's voice filtered through the unintelligible words I muttered in an unwanted interruption. The trance-like state faded, the chanting ceased, and a calm, sleepy sensation replaced it. "You asked about your team. They've arrived. They're here, with us. Jade and Juno, however, were headed to Ardan, to confirm the dark matter is in safekeeping. Jade was stopped in his effort to trace into Ardan with Juno."

"Stopped by whom?" Kevin asked.

"Some residual dark energy that remains on Earth. We expect it to fully clear in the next day."

"Does he need help?"

"We've called the elves to aide both of them."

"Where can I find Jade?"

My hand clamped around Kevin's arm.

The tension from Kevin not being able to handle the business of seeing to the safety of every member on this mission flowed into my hand. He needed to go. I was safe in the hands of the Inner Society that worked to protect us. I released my grip and felt the resistance leave.

"Be careful," I said. "We aren't sure how many shadows remain."

"I will. You're sure you're okay?"

"Of course. Go. Do what you need to."

He kissed the top of my forehead, pressed his lips to mine, and lifted them ever so slightly. His eyes locked with mine, fire alive in those gold flecks. "I love you."

"And I love you." My fingers stroked across his cheek.

His hand glided across my abdomen before rushing off.

An emptiness I had purposely avoided by keeping people at a distance came to visit like an unwanted stranger. Small price to pay, I told myself. The walls that he'd shattered for me to allow him to be close far outweighed any fear of loss, or momentary emptiness, for that matter.

Jade had told me once shortly after I'd met him, on our last quest for the second key, that he and Kevin had been longtime friends. I didn't recall this, nor had there been a chance to ask Kevin about it. They were friends, sure. But Jade was exceptionally skillful in the art of defense, as much if not more so than Kevin. That knowledge gave me a sense of calm that they both would return. And yet, I still wondered, with Horus's form a mist, helping Jade had to be easier for an immortal who could easily pass between worlds. Faster, too. Horus wouldn't have needed rescuing by the Inner Society, not like my team and I. Where had he gone, anyway? There was only one way to find out.

27

Light. Everywhere there was light in the depths of Ardan that had once been consumed in hues of blue and black of a forever evening. The only exception was the moment I'd met Cerys at the beginning of this quest. The memory filled me with joy even now. I stopped hiking along the path I'd arrived at shortly after I'd fallen asleep, to take in every sensation. A warm, comforting illumination invited passage through the realm of the immortals. The way it had once, long ago. I recalled it now, as I did all of my past lives and experiences that had been returned to me with the acceptance of Kevin's gift of the thousand-year-old ring, still as brilliant and beautiful as ever. All the memories I'd lost had been returned with the ring and the release of the keys to heal the toxic effects of Tarsamon in Ardan and on Earth—certain books of magic I'd paged through, quests I'd been on, the many meetings I'd participated in as a member of the Alliance. All in Ardan moved faster, too, unencumbered by time and the physical nature of being human.

I had a home here, as well. A home I could always come back to. But could I recall where it was? I hadn't visited it in what felt like a hundred years. I paused to consider. Yes. A place of tranquility, so contrary to the life I'd been born into, before I'd met my adoptive mother, Mary Ann. This home was filled with only those things that brought comfort and peace, the lit flame of several candles, trickling water, books upon books stacked where the shelves were already full, comfortable corners to stretch or curl up into, and stillness. I shared it with a love that spanned many lifetimes, including this one.

But what was it that had brought me here shortly after falling asleep? The silence filled the space and with it the recollection to find Kevin.

I set off in the direction he might have gone, near where the elves resided. Juno had mentioned Eldor had a spell to hold the power that Tarsamon had shifted into. Kevin had been in search of Jade, which meant he couldn't be far. But had they made it to Ardan? What if—

"Sara," Horus said, interrupting the thought. He took a human-like form beside me.

"Did you pass through the portal with us? I didn't see you when we arrived in New York."

"You were in safe hands with Leahnan. I returned here, to Ardan, to organize a new plan going forward."

"To lead the Soltari?"

"Yes." He paused and tilted his head slightly. "My god, you are lovely. I'd almost forgotten what your true form looked like."

"What do you mean?" I held my hands out in front of me, noticing a paler-than-usual tone.

"Here." He swirled away and reappeared once more in front of me, this time with a mirror. I looked into it and didn't recognize the "me" I'd come to know as Sara Forrester. My skin was lighter than the toffee color it had been. Like the shades of gray that had departed, so, too, had the dark hair with red highlights. My face shape was all that was the same—angular, with high cheekbones and relatively pointed chin.

"Oh my," I said, drawing my fingers lightly over my cheek. "Will I stay like this?"

"In Ardan, yes. But you'll look the same to those you've come to know on Earth when you wake. You've come into your full being, free of the burden of the keys and a quest unfulfilled. This"—he waved a hand in front of me—"is who you are."

I looked again more closely. The palest skin, as smooth as

porcelain. Long, wavy hair flowed down the middle of my back, white as the snow I'd left in New York. A stark contrast to the darker hues I preferred. My eyes, however, framed by white lashes, too, were still jade green with a sparkle, perhaps the same one Kevin mentioned seeing not so long ago, that lit every few seconds.

"That may take some getting used to again."

"Not long, I'm sure," he said, stepping to the side. "You've come for Cerys, yes?"

"I have. But to be sure he made it safely to the elves, to Eldor specifically." I looked around for the telltale sign he was near, the yarrow with its little red flowers dotted with yellow centers. "This place is so different, so alight. The colors so vibrant."

"Vibrant to you but muted to some. It all depends on the eyes that see them, the world they wish to create when they are here."

I nodded as though I knew. Because, I suppose, while I didn't see what anyone else in Ardan could see, I understood what Horus meant. People of Earth had a similar phrase that they would see the world as they chose to.

"I feel like this is the right area but I don't see the houses in the trees, where the elves resided when I first arrived."

"Think back a little more," Horus said. "You'll remember the houses were in the trees only when you were introduced to the quest as a human, until you could adjust to or transition to your true self, your spiritual being."

My gaze dropped from his and my thoughts drifted further to a city, a place with waterfalls and streams, a world of mist reminding me of clouds lifting from a cold Colorado mountain in the early morning. The hillside and paths, the buildings melding into the scenery were both vivid and muted in a blended luxury of color like I'd never recalled. As I shifted my gaze back to Horus, the world behind him mirrored the image etched in my mind. We'd travelled to it by mere thought.

"You remember now?" He paused. "I'd like to see just how far you'll get."

"What do you mean?"

"Do you recall the dungeons and the room where the elves create certain spells to aid the warriors who fight for balance in the universe?"

The location was difficult to recall at first, but then I saw it. The same place where my sword had been created for this mission, bound with the spell protecting it from being handled by another soul, immortal or otherwise.

"I do. Though, I must admit I never thought myself to be a believer of magic. I do remember it, however, as one of several functions the elves serve, as protectors over Ardan."

"Their work is specialized in the manipulation of energy. Since everything is energy, the creation of spells an manipulation of energy is a common practice in the effort to dispel darkness. It's how the elves aid in protecting the warriors on their quests, where energy makeup varies across multiple realms.

"I remember it." I glanced around the room we'd arrived in, traveling again by thought. "But this isn't where the elves keep someone like Tarsamon."

The scent of herbs and florals lifted into the air, and the sound of a recent chant resonated off the cream-colored porous stone in the very space I'd crossed into.

"They'll never keep an energy like that here for very long," Horus said, referring to such evil. "It's like a poison that seeps slowly into the energy that holds it, where the strongest spells are unable to contain certain evil. It's why an area of Ardan was sectioned off to keep Tarsamon."

"Before he extended his boundary and grew stronger than any of us imagined until he needed to venture further into Earth."

"Yes."

And with a little more concentration, I made my way well beyond the doorway of the next room, with Horus at my side.

The unpleasant sensation of the Dark Lord filled my senses, closing out the beauty that surrounded me.

"He's here," I said more to myself than to Horus. I walked deeper into the room, down a set of steps, and into a more confined space, where I saw a white transparency of a wall, whose border sparkled. There was no sound from it, but I could sense the electricity-like sensation that warned not to touch.

A smile spread across Horus's face. "I can't believe you found him."

I peered closer behind the transparent flickering wall to see the cloud of black, nearly invisible, moving from one corner to another in constant motion.

"I don't think you should get any closer to him." Eldor's voice came from behind me. "He's quite angry, as I suppose anyone who'd been captured and held against his will would be." I turned to see the leader of the elves approaching from the other side of me. "We'll need another place for this energy Tarsamon has shifted into, away from Ardan."

I smiled at him in greeting and he took my hand. "It's good to see you again, Arwyn."

"You, as well. In better times, too."

The last I'd seen of Eldor was when Ardan had been breached and the invasion had begun along the borders by Tarsamon's demons and shadows, just as Earth had. The only exception was the defense by the wolves and the elves against further attack, holding a new yet highly guarded boundary.

"How did you know to find Tarsamon here?" Eldor asked.

"Juno said his capture would be held by you."

He nodded. "No one but the elves know of this specific location. We've built an energy to hide him from Aqen, or anyone else trying to find him. So I must ask again, how were you able to track him to this exact holding cell?"

"She's carrying the next seeker," Horus replied, "to be born into their world, Earth, as the next guardian."

Eldor angled his head toward Horus.

"You're sure?" I asked in disbelief.

"I wondered myself," Horus said. "But I wasn't sure until you brought us through the passages to this very cell. It's what I meant by seeing how far you would get."

Eldor looked from Horus back to me. "If that's so, you'll need to guide him carefully into his role."

What? No role. "I don't want him, *or possibly her,* to have to experience the same that we did on this quest, to feel the burden of guardianship of so many lives."

"It's what we do, Sara," Horus said. "We guard the light in all realms. Earth is one of those locations set aside for development. It, too, needs protections against the imbalance created by certain types of energy with the aim to upset that equilibrium."

It had not escaped my attention that he'd switched to using the name I'd been given on Earth. Was it a way of indicating I'd slipped into my human tendencies, forgetting the spirit I am? *What happened to that spiritual being anyway?* My thoughts drifted back to a time when I'd seen someone who looked like me speaking with Kevin, once on a return trip to Ardan, long before we'd found the keys or before I knew anything about my history with the Soltari.

"Your spirit reconnected with your mortal body the moment you sacrificed your life for the keys. The lapis lazuli was the protection preventing passage of your spirit."

"That was such a brief moment, though." *I think. How long was I speaking with C-05, or Anubis, when I tried to get past the blue wall of fire, anyhow?*

"It was the loss of the breath of life that allowed you to join together. Don't you see? You are whole again."

Did that explain the change in my appearance?

I paused, considering the idea, until the memory returned. "Of course. We are only a fraction of our being when we are born. A portion of our spirit comes into this mortal life. And when we leave, it joins with the higher self. But I didn't think I had died."

"Humans aren't meant to remember all the truths of existence. Including you, Sara. It would be exceptionally overwhelming."

"I suppose it would." I looked back to the cell. "There's only one potential problem with this containment. Does it house the entire dark matter that Tarsamon shifted into?"

Eldor shifted his attention to Horus.

"Tarsamon split his energy when he shifted," Horus explained. "Probably in an attempt to make sure he could survive."

"This cannot be. The spell created to hold such dark matter was on the basis this was all there was." He extended a hand toward the shifting matter. "The power this spell holds will only work once. There is more dark matter from this source loose in the world?"

"Yes," I said. "Just before Juno could contain all of the energy with the spell you'd given him to hold Tarsamon, it scattered. Horus and Matt set off to track it."

"But that's—"

"Impossible? We thought so, too," I added. But with help from, Aqen Tarsamon managed to do it.

"More work is needed, and quickly," Eldor said. "I would encourage you to seek out the other members of the Soltari and have a plan constructed to address this issue. I don't have a seeker to provide you."

"We have one," Horus said. "He's just not ready to trace the energy trail yet."

I felt my eyes widen. "There must be someone else, someone with the experience to track such a force," I said. The sudden reliance on an unborn child put into any sort of complex situation, especially one associated with Tarsamon, was reflected as rejection in my tone. I couldn't help it. This was my child they were making a plan for.

"What if you're wrong?" I asked. "What if this child isn't really a seeker? Besides, we can't wait for him or her to grow strong enough to fulfill what I think you have planned."

"We may not have to," Horus said. "You tracked this matter directly to its location in the depths of the dungeons, fully protected and concealed by the elves."

"No. I didn't. I was called to Ardan to find Kevin. You led me here by discussion."

"I simply had you recall what all immortals know—the place where spells are created. You found the dark matter in a region previously unknown to the rest of us."

Though it might be true, I still felt as though I'd somehow been tricked.

"Let's see if the members of the Soltari have other options available," Eldor said, "before nerves become frayed any further."

"Frayed." That was an understatement. I'd be damned if my only chance in several lifetimes to have a child would be hinged on providing humanity with a guardian. The Soltari may have called me to the quest for the keys, and yes, I had issues about decisions that had been made about my task, but they would not put my child in harm's way. Never. Not for any cause.

28

Horus swirled around me and upward into a mini funnel-shaped cloud as I waited below, calling to order the entity that governed the equilibrium of force in the universe, of which I was now supposed to be the director.

I couldn't shift into mist, being that I held a mortal human form on Earth, still sleeping in the place I'd left in Leahnan's safekeeping.

Within moments, the massive white cloud that made up the Soltari surrounded the empty space and the mist faded, leaving only the transparent floating faces that looked toward me. The group as a whole, however, seemed to be comprised of fewer members since I'd last spoken to them.

The sound of footsteps behind me had me turning to see Aria and Matt, Jade, Juno and Elise, along with Topetine and Mac arriving slightly apart from each other. A touch at my arm revealed Kevin at my side.

"Thank God you're okay," I said to him.

He smiled. "Of course I am. You were worried?" His fingers reached for the ends of my hair. "I've missed this look. So lovely."

Horus slipped to my other side. "I call to order the meeting of the Soltari. Directing this and all future decisions and meetings is Arwyn, keeper of the light in all the realms."

I leaned beside him and whispered, "What happened to the others? There are not as many."

"Our first order of business is the declaration of new members and to announce the release of souls that have been determined to be working against the force of light governing the realms."

Released? Released to where?

"To the city of the undead, the City of Souls," C-05 replied, hearing my thought. I turned in the direction of his voice as he approached from behind Matt. No sign of the mask of Anubis. "Where they can be managed and no longer trusted in such a powerful role to oversee our warriors."

"Arwyn," Horus said, "These are the members who support your path, your light, your direction. They have proven themselves worthy of a place away from the Alliance and on your council."

When did Horus have the time to weed out the reliable souls? I scanned the group, transparent faces followed by the line of allies that had traveled with me on the quest, my team, and having every confidence regarding each member, with the exception of maybe one.

I stepped toward C-05. "I thought you were committed to reside in the underworld. Wasn't that part of your agreement with the Soltari, in exchange for them setting you free to help us on the quest for the last key?"

"I'm not being punished as you might think. But yes, I agreed to remain in the underworld, guiding souls as they cross into death." His gaze drifted across the rest of the team. "I will remain as Norul's assistant in the underworld." He paused. "It's a risk I took," C-05 said. "Going to the Dark Lord and leaving you to doubt my inentions."

"To say the least," I replied.

"It had to be done. If you don't see that now, you may see it soon enough," C-05 said, glancing to Horus.

"I haven't had time to reflect upon it yet."

"Understood. Horus?"

"His betrayal was always part of the plan, Arwyn," Horus said. "It had to be. We needed an insider."

The information hit my senses and sank slowly, in a most

uncomfortable way, deep into every encounter, from the lies, the initial blow I'd taken from the shadows, to the pain inflicted at multiple turns.

"It didn't really work out, though, did it? And this last time it nearly killed me in the process. Had you been successful, the mission would have failed, and this would be a very different conversation."

"I was there to keep you from transitioning fully into death. That, too, was part of the plan."

"It couldn't have been. How could you have known a serum would be used?"

"I didn't. But Horus guessed the *Book of Spells* would play a part in Tarsamon's effort at some point." He turned to face Horus. "Good choice in selecting the lapis lazuli."

"What about the dark angel? There were a few attempts on my life, before this last quest. Had she been successful—"

"She was never instructed to kill. She wouldn't have gone that far for fear you'd release the power you'd collected from the first two keys. I convinced Tarsamon to put you in my charge when we captured you. Only once when we lost control of the dark angel in the Mayan jungle were you at risk. But the team you have, especially Jade, was at your side to see that you were protected."

I shook my head. "I've said it before, you were lucky."

"Indeed, I was."

I turned to Kevin. "You're the only one I trust with everything. Did you know of this plan?"

His eyes locked on mine with that intensity I'd come to know, trust, and fall into. "None of us who protected you knew. I swear it on all that we hold close between us."

I scanned the rest of the group, those I'd come to trust, to see the same look of determination. "In that case," I said, angling my head to C-05, "you're forgiven. But I don't want you as part of this team."

"Sara," Aria said, "he has always been."

"Not anymore. Not while I'm Sara Forrester in this life." I pierced C-05 with a hardened stare. "Part of you enjoyed what you did. I felt it from you. You can't change that. The night in the dungeon after I was captured by the shadows and the weight of the hold you kept over me. Or the room prior to the blast of light and before Kevin pulled me from your grasp. There was no one watching you then. No one you had to convince of your loyalty."

"I was human."

"Not nearly a good enough excuse."

"Fair enough. Perhaps in time you'll see, once you've had a chance to reflect, that the sensations the Dark Lord could pick up on were much stronger than what you could feel. And though you may not believe me, I want you to know it was a very difficult role to assume."

I felt some pain emanating from him over the experience. An emotional burden, but not too heavy. It wasn't that I wanted him to suffer. Well, maybe a little for the attempt to force himself upon me. But I'd never considered his efforts as part of a "role" he'd been asked to assume, to convince the Dark Lord he hated me, or to help him believe he could win this battle of darkness over light. Every move from C-05 had to be convincing, so much so that perhaps he took steps that were necessary despite the possible repercussions. I couldn't decide that now. Everything happening was too fresh. I had a child to worry for, a dark force that might hunt him or her and what life meant for the family I wanted to create going forward. The new information would require time to settle, time to quell the raw nerves that remained.

"My loyalty will forever remain with you," C-05 said. "For now, I have agreed to stand beside Norul and direct the passage of spirits into the City of Souls, as Anubis."

"That was you," Aria said, "with Norul, while Sara freed her from that tree. I felt your energy, familiar as it was, but didn't understand the whole dog image. It makes complete sense now."

"Thank you for your loyalty going forward," I said. Only time could shed light on whether it would be true or not. "I'm curious, have you found your partner, the love who was taken from you by the previous members of the Alliance?"

Surprise drifted across his face. "She lives. That's all I know."

"If we could find her, would it be useful to you?"

His eyes drifted down and returned to mine. Sadness linked with hope reflected in them. "I wouldn't be able to live in this life with her, but"—he paused as though he'd never considered the idea until now—"I could visit her when she sleeps, reconnect with her, possibly make plans for another life together."

"My first order of business," I said, looking to Jade, "is to set free the armies that fight for our order of balance in the realms, to release punishment previously set forth and going forward. The burden that accompanies loss will not be placed upon anyone, spirit or being, who chooses to work to diminish darkness in an unbalanced state. That sort of pain comes without purpose and has no place in an immortal world. All freedoms previously held are to be restored effective immediately." I felt the space around me become calmer, more at peace, and attributed it to the mood of Jade, Juno, and Matt, the warriors who had, over time, taken the brunt of the penalties inflicted.

"My second order of business is for the location of this spirit's love, his partner across lifetimes, to be revealed." I felt Kevin's hand stroke the back of my arm. By granting C-05 his most deeply held desire, it was proof I'd forgiven him, and perhaps might serve to strengthen an alliance with the realm of death. A world that had no reason to consider life until Norul's immortality was on the line. "No one shall be bereft of their chosen eternal partner, ever, for any reason, so long as they agree to remain together. These two rules stand for eternity to be unchanged by any vote of an Alliance or other governing order." The sound of my voice surprised me as it fell out with all the strength and determination of a command rather than a request.

A weight of such enormity lifted with the utterance of those words that I felt nearly as light as the faces that floated beside me.

"One more thing," I added. "We, the order, will maintain a blend of pure immortals and beings who, like us, choose to exist as mortals outside of Ardan." I swept a hand in the direction of my team who had followed me on this quest. "As members of the Soltari, this blend will act to maintain a collective balance. There will be no need for an Alliance that could change the course of action by vote. Instead, the

Alliance can be utilized to consult on matters pertaining to missions, but never to be the sole decision makers for immortals."

"Arwyn," Horus said, "we have the issue of the remaining dark matter. We can't have any piece of Tarsamon lingering in the realms."

How could I have forgotten? My child, the one Horus wanted to seek out such energy and the suggestion that it be done even before he or she was born.

"Absolutely not," Kevin said. He'd listened to my recall of the memory of the conversation with Eldor. Nothing could be hidden in the immortal world. All secrets and lies were revealed for their truths. This was the way to the path of honesty and love. Secrets and lies were what bred darkness and the very energy we'd put an end to with the release of the keys.

Horus moved closer. "Would you agree to consider that when you're ready, we might utilize the ability of the seeker you will raise, with all the same protections given to you for your quest? We could put them in place now, to protect your unborn child."

I looked to Kevin. "I don't see that we would be ready for anything of the sort, so long as another seeker exists in the realms. You'll need to exhaust every effort to find him or her."

"Sounds like a possibility to me," Juno said. "Or as good a one as you can get right now."

"Sara!" Mary Ann's arms flew around me in a bear hug. "My God, it feels like forever since I saw you last!"

It felt so good to hear her voice and hug her. The fresh, familiar scent of her hair wafted over my face and I smiled at the memory.

I'd only been in the new location Leahnan had brought Kevin and me to a few hours. After a little sleep, a hot shower, some clean, comfortable clothing, I'd been invited for breakfast in the courtyard, and a "surprise."

"Let me look at you," she said, stepping back, her hands at my shoulders. "You look...different, but good."

Hopefully my eyes weren't sparkling in a weird way that would cause me to have to explain anything more than she already had been informed—that my team and I had set off to see if we could set right the darkness in the world and rid it of the nightmares she and I had been having. Of course, those shadows and demons had come to life for me but, to my knowledge, remained mostly hidden from Mary Ann. The Inner Society had done a good job protecting her from the worst of the ugliness. They had invited her to come stay with them for a short time, when the daylight hours had grown darker and for longer increments and the people, many of whom became unresponsive, were changing. I don't think she realized the full truth of the situation and the consumption of life by the darkness. A good thing, too. There was no need for her to know. I was certain Leahnan would have kept that knowledge between her and the select few members of the Inner Society. Fortunately, I had been able to say goodbye to her before leaving for the Egyptian underworld, giving Mary Ann reassurance she could trust Leahnan while I was away.

"You look so rested," I said. "So beautiful. Here, have a seat. Coffee?"

"Oh, no thanks. I've had plenty," she said, sitting in the chair opposite me. "I feel rested. This place, your friends, Leahnan and everyone, are so kind. They provided me anything I could want while we waited for you to get back. And isn't it pretty here?"

The ground was covered in small patches of melting snow. I lifted my gaze to the sky, a bright blue, sunny but wintery day, and smiled. Tinted glass surrounding the enclosed courtyard suggested the possibility of some privacy. A small flowering plant lifted its leaves to the sun, thriving in a tiny blue and white pot in the center of the table and the dessert plate and matching coffeepot with a tiny light blue and gray floral motif on the side felt homey. "Yes. It really is beautiful." *I'd like to get a better view and venture beyond the metal gates we came through last night.* "I'm so relieved to hear your time here was good."

"Well, your being gone has me reconsidering my responsibilities."

"What do you mean? You're not thinking of shutting down the

Forrester Foundation?" I lifted my cup and inhaled deeply the rich, dark-roasted aroma of coffee, reminding me how I'd missed a good cup of British tea. This morning, however, I welcomed the necessary stronger brew.

"No. Too many people benefit from the support it provides. I'm thinking about letting go of other responsibilities, like the work I was doing for Robert, and focusing more on family."

Robert, Mary Ann's husband and my adoptive father, was a man I'd never really grown close to, who had been away on business acquiring a company in Europe when I'd set off for Scotland on the quest for the first key. I'd always felt like another business deal to him—get me married off to a wealthy man who he wouldn't worry would take the family money. That meant a man of his choosing, who, in the end turned out to be a narcissistic, egotistical choice I'd happily dumped before meeting Kevin.

"Family," I said, "is good. Where is Robert, anyway?"

"He was stuck in England, too ill to travel when I was hunkered down in this place." She glanced up and around. "I got a call from him a couple of days ago. He said he's well enough to travel and will be back tomorrow."

I nodded.

"Which is perfect, because I'd like for him to meet Dr. Kevin. Maybe we could have dinner?"

"Sure. Dr. Kevin, huh?"

"He said I could call him that." She smiled.

"I haven't seen him this morning. You've already talked with him?"

"Yes. He was in a rush. Said something about being back soon but wanted to stop by the hospital first."

"Oh, okay."

Wonder what that's about.

"He says you have news to share." She tried to glance at my left hand, which I had kept in my lap since she'd sat beside me.

"I suppose there is news." I lifted my hand for her to see the ring.

"It's just lovely, Sara." Silence filled the space as she held my hand. "You've been through so much, and now this."

I tilted my head and looked into her eyes. "*This* is good. Are you crying?"

"Of course it's good. It's the best news I've had in a long time. Crying would be foolish," she said, looking up at me. "The cold air is making my eyes teary." I smiled. "Listen, I've got to finish packing my things. Leahnan said she would take me to go see my home, to be sure everything is okay before I head back permanently."

"That's fabulous news, too."

She flashed a smile and put a hand on mine. "I'm really so happy for you both." She leaned closer and hugged me. "I'm so glad you're okay," she said, standing. She put a hand on my shoulder. "I was worried a bit, but Leahnan kept telling me you were fine."

"I was." *For the most part.*

"I'll catch up with you later today. Dinner tomorrow, yes?

"I'd love that."

"Leahnan thought it would be good if I stay here a day, just to be sure nothing is still, you know, weird out there." She wiggled her fingers at the sky.

I nodded. "Good luck at the house."

After Mary Ann disappeared through the glass doors, I downed the last sip of coffee and listened to the air around me. The currents always hinted at what was happening and things to come.

The thought of Mary Ann needing to be accompanied to her home suggested all might not yet be resolved with the shadows. I'd have to see for myself. Exactly how long could it take for the energy of the keys to correct the landscape, rid the people of the darkness that had consumed them? I'd better go and find out. Would I need a weapon?

Hands came around my eyes in another surprise I wasn't expecting. I lifted a hand to peel them away but at the touch recognized them as Kevin's.

He let his hands fall. "Ready to find our home?"

"Our home," I repeated. "Seems somehow strange to say that."

"Second thoughts?" he said, sitting on the edge of the chair in front of me and taking my hands in his.

I shook my head a little. "No. It's just…"

"It feels like the days before we set out on the quest. Your fears of sharing your life with someone are returning."

"Perhaps, for a second. But I have you beside me, and I realize they aren't real fears, but an illusion."

He stroked his hand over mine. "Together, we'll bury those illusions forever." I nodded as he held my eyes for a second more. "So?"

I smiled. "So, we're having dinner with Mary Ann and Robert tomorrow."

The corner of his mouth turned up and he nodded. "She found you, huh?"

"Yep. She said you were at the hospital."

"Ran a few errands while you were still asleep."

"Like?"

"To see about a job at the hospital again. I might have also taken a detour around the 'hood to check out the surroundings, and, if I have a soon-to-be wife, a possible location to live."

"If?"

He shrugged a shoulder and a grin tugged at the corners of his mouth. "These fears pop into her head now and again, and I've already had to tear down so many walls."

I let out a deep breath I hadn't realized I'd been holding. "I'd marry you today if it would put your mind at ease." I stood and held my hand out to him. "C'mon. Let's go find out what you had in mind for our home."

29

"Where'd you find the car?" I asked as Kevin settled behind the wheel and into the buttery leather seat of the McLaren. "I believe this is a rare model."

"It is. It's *vintage*. A 2014 MSO 650S. They only made fifty of them." The car purred to life with the sound of a black leopard's growl. "Connections," was all he offered in answer to the earlier question. He turned to face me. "It's my engagement gift to you. For your collection."

If it's still there. "So very thoughtful of you. How about I drive?"

"In a bit, if you don't mind? When I turn this over to you, I'm not sure I'll be able to take the driver's seat again." He leaned forward with every intention of a quick peck. I stroked my fingertips along his jaw and held him in a gentle grasp, pressing my lips to his, extending the kiss. It had been a good while since I'd felt his clean-shaven skin. While I liked it, I had a slight preference for the rougher side of him.

"Thank you," I said at his lips.

He eased back. "I want you to see the impact the keys have had."

"Okay."

As he pulled out of the drive from the safehold under the watchful eye of Leahnan's team and turned down the first major street, the initial effects of the keys were clear. The light had restored the darkened skies from the previous state of continuous dusk and, at times, total black in some areas. The city streets were almost empty, as though they had been wiped clean. There were no longer people wandering with no purpose, burdened by shadow children causing them to be slumped over with the additional emotional weight that sponged off the negativity they held, feeding off them like a succubus. Had they all been freed, granted another chance to live on in a happier state of being? Had some been consumed by the shadowed spirits, too far gone to be healed? If so, had they fallen under the illness of such energy, perhaps to meet C-05 in the City of Souls? Either way, the world felt good. Fear had released its captive hold, allowing room for growth and the rise of the human condition to higher levels.

We headed deeper into the city, seeing more people milling about the streets, and yet not nearly the sea of foot traffic I was used to. I searched those who'd ventured out to find the twisted faces of anger, the pain in their eyes, and shouts of ugliness, but there was none to be found. Streets that had once been filled with the bustle of busy people, minds filled with tasks to finish, errands to run, were replaced by the bright eyes of a sudden awakening. Instead, a new light reflected in the eyes of the faces that looked at one another, bouncing off my gaze at times. The feelings I sensed from those same people seemed as though they cared less about their tasks and more about where they were and what existed around them. It was a look that mirrored the clearing of a blinding storm, replaced by the brightness of a new day and sudden clarity.

"Is this everywhere?" I asked.

"From what I could see, yes."

"It's remarkable."

"I thought so, too."

"Are they kind?"

"I was only out for a bit, stuck mainly to the hospital, but yes. It was just a glimpse, though."

"Your job?"

"Looks good. They've filled my previous position. But they are looking for a new head of pediatrics.

"Off to a good start."

"We'll see."

"The rest of the team is safe? I didn't see anyone this morning except Leahnan, so I assumed all was well."

"Yes. Everyone is anxious to get back home. You must have just missed them. Juno and Elise took an early flight back to Juno's home in California to check on things. We're supposed to get together tonight for dinner with Matt and Aria before they leave."

"Flights," I said. "Good. The world is chugging back to a normal flow. Any word from Mac or Topetine?"

"Arrived safely, according to Leahnan. I still want to make sure. I'm planning on calling Mac sometime today."

For the first time, I felt the weight of the responsibility to deliver the keys finally ease. I took in a long breath and released it as I scanned the landscape, absorbing the reflection of light off the buildings as we drifted onto the almost vacant highway leading out of the city. The overall brighter beauty was a welcome sight after so many weeks of growing darkness. Despite the colder temperatures and lack of light that had turned the grasses brown, the illuminated backdrop of the city whispered of hope, like a mirage in the heat of the desert. The darker days of evil that shadowed our world had been wiped away in a fresh start at life.

"Wait a minute. Juno and Elise went *together* to his home?" My voice resonated with complete disbelief. "She was so annoyed with him."

Kevin flashed a grin. "She softened."

"Come to think of it, I felt a little more from her than annoyance with him. But it'd be going too far to call it enamored."

"She's good at hiding her true feelings. I picked up on her attraction, too. His was obvious." We both laughed at the thought of his tactic to gain her affection—a sharp-witted mind coupled with childlike playfulness.

Several minutes later, we were pulling into the expansive drive of my home. The last time we'd been here, the shadows had stalked and attacked me and my team, sending us rushing off to Scotland.

"I don't know if I want to go inside." On a call I'd made to Mary

Ann while in the Yucatan, she said most of the collections, historical antiques mostly, had been damaged.

"I think it's okay. Here," he said, giving me the key. "Mary Ann still had a copy of it. She asked me to bring you here when we got back."

"When was that?"

"At the dinner before we left for the last key."

I recalled the three of us had sat together for a farewell dinner provided for our team and hosted by Leahnan and the members of the Inner Society.

"Maybe she had repairs done."

I unlocked the door and cautiously stepped inside. Everything was in place. The damaged walls had been smoothed in a bisque finish, elegantly decorated in contrasting colors of taupe and navy. There were some missing artifacts, but otherwise it looked like it had before the attack.

"She found the detailed wooden boxes that you love scattered around, but didn't know where you wanted them. So, she left them in your office."

"I don't understand. When did she have time to fix the damage to the place?"

"She hired help while we were in Scotland. Said it was going to be a surprise for you. She had almost finished when Leahnan's team picked her up and asked her to meet you at their site, the underground facility."

"I've never known her to be able to keep a secret, especially from me."

"Are you happy?"

"Yes. Surprised, for sure, but happy, too."

"The cars are all safe, too. And she'll hire new staff if you'd like."

"I don't know what to say." I turned in a full circle. "And I think this decision is up to you as much as it is to me." I stepped closer to him. "Do you want to live here?" His gaze into my eyes was a rush of emotion that I tried to decipher.

He scooped me into his arms and pressed his lips to mine, soft at first then firmer, before lifting them away, leaving me desiring more. "I want to marry you. Where we live makes no difference to me."

I let out a small breath. "It, um, should be close to the hospital."

He smiled. "Whatever you like. Everything at my apartment is intact. I stopped by on my way back from the hospital this morning."

"Can I think about it?"

"Of course. But we also have the matter of a wedding."

"Small. I hate being the center of attention."

"Being part of a well-known family does pose an issue in trying to remain inconspicuous to the press. But I think we can manage it if you can convince Mary Ann."

"No problem." *I think.*

He lifted my chin with a finger and kissed me. "Let's take a peek at the garage to be sure everything looks as good there as it does here."

30

I woke to the sounds of branches scraping across the window. A vague memory of a meeting with Horus and a message received in my sleep dashed through my mind.

"Earth will manifest what each desires to see, be it light or darkness, good or evil. Choice is the pathway to alter the energy of the thought into the physical, tangible, or what one chooses or seeks to make real."

I turned to my side and blinked open my eyes to see the buds of new leaves of the season peeking out from the otherwise bare branches through the large paned picture window. Proof that winter had officially moved on.

A hand slipped along my hip, up to my waist, and paused before sliding across my stomach and resting there. At the same time, a leg pressed into mine, intertwining closer.

"You awake?" Kevin whispered at my ear, sending tingles running the length of my neck and shoulder.

I turned into him, my face at his neck, and tilted my head up. "Good morning," I said in a half whisper, half voice.

I reached a hand to his cheek. Rough, day-old whiskers covering an angular jaw greeted my touch. "I find this so sexy." The contrast I'd discovered early on with him, of tender and rough, had quickly become my weakness. He knew it, too.

He pulled the white down cover over us in a cloud of comfort.

"Well, I'd like to hear more about that but"—he paused—"I'd like to do something about it first." He kissed me behind the ear. Another wave of tingles chased after the last in a race to the ends of my fingertips.

"What if Mary Ann hears us?"

"She's so consumed with wanting to mother our child," he said, lips lightly touching my neck, "there's no way. Not in this mansion."

I smiled at the thought as my fingers trailed down his back. We could finally rest. I suppose I was still adjusting to the fact, though it had been several months since we'd completed the quest. Everything had been a whirlwind since.

The three keys had brought to the world the light of understanding, love, and acceptance of all things as they are. The reflection of which was apparent in a more peaceful way of life that I could see, even with people still very busy. Workers still worked. Bills still had to be paid. But along with the responsibilities that often weighed one down, a new respect existed for one another and the struggle that living could be. Help and patience were more abundant, as was tolerance for the differences in each of us. The Golden Rule meant something once more, but now didn't come with feelings of guilt and shame to drive such kindness that had been attached once upon a time and across generations. Neighbors were neighborly, and life overall was indeed much better.

Hurt existed, like that felt in the loss of a loved one or the breakup of a relationship. It never lasted long, however, at least not with the couples who visited with me in my practice, checking to see if they'd overlooked a factor, or several, in the relationship. Instead, with the sadness often came a level of understanding that someone with more suitable traits might exist. A bittersweet edge to the suffering. The varying degrees of emotional pain were temporary, as they really always had been. The difference was that more people could see beyond it, while others took longer to see. Anger had dissipated. The fear associated with loss, abandonment, being alone, which often drove that anger or sparked hidden memories, was a consideration, but nothing more. It wasn't watered with negativity of shame and guilt, left to grow out of control, and passed on to others like a weed from one yard to the next.

This sort of consideration for humanity was likely going to put me out of business as a psychiatrist, I thought, but then that wasn't entirely a bad thing, either. The idea of good mental health had sprung a new definition—feeding the mind a healthy diet instead of starving it and leaving psychiatrists to medicate the symptoms.

Life as I'd known it prior to the quest wasn't exactly as I might have hoped once. It was better. Improved. I was so glad to be back from the puzzling hieroglyphs, caves, and spells to simple comforts like a glass of wine, my home office and a dose of internet shopping, regular showers, and a fluffy down comforter.

Kevin and I, along with Aria and Matt, had a quiet dual wedding ceremony in Scotland, far from the attention of the press seeking coverage on the latest goings-on of the Forrester family and the philanthropic foundation. We had caused a stir upon our return to the States, once the Scottish media posted the news. The tabloids had managed only to capture a picture of our return as we'd departed the plane. I considered the "secret" a success. And doubly so after I'd managed to stay fairly well hidden during the pregnancy.

We kept the apartment in the heart of New York for when Kevin worked at the hospital and held on to the mansion we lived in most of the time, now that we were a family of three after the birth of our little boy.

Raen had arrived early but healthy. A head of auburn curls was starting to show, reminding me of the child I'd met on the quest for the first key and how he'd said his name hadn't been chosen yet. Even now, the encounter seemed strangely familiar, never to be forgotten.

As I stirred awake and right where I wanted to be in the gentle caress of the only man who ever mattered, I wondered how Kevin and I might protect the next guardian in this life. There was time, though. Horus hadn't asked me to track the dark matter while pregnant, not that Kevin would have let that happen if I dared to try.

I wouldn't feel truly safe until the part of Tarsamon that had escaped, after he'd shifted into dark matter, was caught. When the time was right, the Dark Lord would never be able to hide from the powerful seeker. Raen had already proven his ability before he'd ever been born, locating his position in the captivity of the elves. *What if I were to join our little seeker on his quest one day?*

"It'd be a cold day in hell," Kevin said, lifting himself over me and locking eyes with mine, "before I'd let you follow that little one without me."

He was still listening to my thoughts. What was different about it, however, was the fact that I didn't feel the need to hide anything from him to protect my feelings, or worry about his. We'd come far in a relatively short span of time with regard to his patience and desire to show me the strength a man could hold in the same space as the tenderness they often kept well hidden.

He stroked my cheek.

"I know better than that," I said. "I couldn't leave you out of anything. Ever."

A moment of silence passed between us. Were we actually considering the possibility of another mission? Would be silly, I thought, with everything as peaceful as it is, as it was promised to be with the release of the keys.

"That sparkle still remains in your eyes, you know, as though it's winking at my soul."

"Like the feeling I have with you? The intensity of you calls to me, whether far away or as close as this." My hands glided up his back, slowing at his neck, before extending my fingers into his hair, drawing him to me.

"I don't want to share you today," he whispered against my lips, reminding me of the busy day ahead with the team agreeing to fly in to visit us. Aria claimed "auntie" status the moment Raen was born. It was a reunion of sorts, with the exception of Topetine, who was too far removed in her village in the Mayan jungle, but said she'd be with us in spirit. Mac was visiting with his wife, Aggie, and son, Ian. I looked forward to seeing everyone. But with Mary Ann wanting time with her new grandson, I also had my sights set on enjoying a little of us.

"Take me then, while you have me." I lifted my head to meet his kiss and swept my tongue over his.

I pressed my lips to Kevin's and felt him grip me tighter, rolling to his back and letting his hands glide down along my sides and midway up my back.

"We've got eternity," I said, feeling his desire beneath me.

"I'm not waiting for that. I want you right here, right now. Everything else can wait." He lifted my hips to be right in line with his intention.

He tucked one side of my hair behind my ear, his eyes piercing mine with desire. I lowered myself to meet his lips as he unraveled me further with the stroke of his tongue across my lip.

I slipped farther to his neck and kissed once, then twice, and breathed into his ear, "And so it will."

The scent of his masculinity and the heat of his skin stoked my passion, fueling more of what we desired. As he watched, I was fully aware he had claimed me in more ways than one. A once elusive love now and forever only his. It was a promise to each other we could be sure this time would last for eternity, free from the burden of a potential shadow of sacrifice hanging over us in our roles as immortal defenders in a vast universe.

EPILOGUE

A certain stillness filled the air, mingling with the sound of a child's laughter every few seconds as I stood watching Raen engage Kevin in a game of chase. The new puppy, a floppy rescued Lab-mix Raen insisted on naming Butters, was close at his heels. I wasn't sure how the dog would fare with two trained Dobermans with names of strength.

The picnic we'd taken up to the ridge was almost finished. The scent of spring—green grass and the opening buds of the season's wildflowers—carried across the remnants of a cherry pie we'd brought and hardly cut into before Raen had run off. The small, strong legs of a three-year-old boy driving him up the hill were no match for Kevin's strength and speed, but he played along, letting Raen believe he was getting farther away.

A few billowy white clouds filled the otherwise bright sky and a mild breeze caught at the tips of my hair.

A perfect day.

Another feeling carried in a whisper on the current said otherwise. I had not needed to worry about the ominous sensation in so long. Not since the dark clouds had rolled in after I'd been summoned on the quest for the keys. I cast a glance up again. No. Not the same feeling as it was back then. The light was not threatened, nor this world, from what I could see and feel. But something was not quite right. I watched as Raen disappeared behind a cluster of trees, Kevin giving him a lead. Fast as he was, Kevin could catch him in a heartbeat. He looked back to me and waved before taking off after him.

I smiled and turned my attention to packing up the remaining food, the last bit of wine and juice boxes. Moments later, Kevin came out of the trees with a giggling Raen in his arms as he lifted him over his shoulder, his head facing the ground. By the time they reached the hill, I had everything loaded into the giant basket we'd brought.

"The boy's got a quick stride," Kevin said.

"Like you," I replied, thinking about the times he'd come to my rescue, moving so fast he looked like a streak of lightning.

"He couldn't catch me, Mommy. Did you see?"

"Oh, I saw you, little love. Daddy almost got lost." I winked at Kevin.

"Let me get that," he said, lifting the basket from my hands as we headed toward the car. "What's on your mind?" he asked, leaning into my ear.

"Nothing, really. Just thinking it was a perfect day. Loved seeing you two enjoying it."

There was a pause. "Okay. Later then."

"Later what?"

"Just because we're"—he waited as Raen carefully eased down the side of the grassy hill—"living as normal a life as we'd wanted doesn't mean I can't still pick up on your energy."

"Oh, I know. But you don't really have any reason to, with that whole matter of the keys finished three years ago."

"That's what concerns me. That I am, and that I'm picking up on a familiar vibe."

"You feel it, too?"

"A bit. It's weak, but there."

"I'll make a trip to Ardan tonight to check in with the Soltari. Make sure everything is being monitored. I'm sure it's nothing."

"Where are you going, Mommy?" Raen asked, overhearing.

"Nowhere, love. Just thinking about a place I like."

"Later," Kevin said.

I nodded and smiled.

After a long day of play, I tucked Raen in his bed and kissed him on the cheek. *So soft. So innocent.*

Butters was snuggled on the opposite side of the bed at Raen's feet. I patted his head. "Good boy," I said to him as I sat beside Raen.

"I found something today, Mommy."

"You did? May I see?"

"I don't have it, silly. I almost caught it but it ran away. It said it would come play again."

My interest careened with the feeling I'd detected in the air that day. "Who said, sweetie?"

"Not 'who,' Mommy. The dark. It talked to me. I found it when I was chasing Butters in the forest."

Alarm struck every nerve. Had Tarsamon decided to find our child before the Soltari even had a chance to call him to duty as a seeker?

He knows where we are. He's already connected with Raen.

I angled my head to see Kevin standing at the doorway. A gentle, closed-lip smile stretched across his face, but his eyes had all the seriousness I'd expected to find when I looked to him.

I turned back to Raen. "Because you're so fast you found the dark, I have a big-boy favor to ask. When Butters wants to play chase, make sure you can always see us, okay?"

"Okay. But why? Sometimes, Butters runs so fast."

"Because I wouldn't want to lose you," I said, tickling him at his waist. "Was this the first time you found the dark?"

"Yes. It said it couldn't play right now but would play another day."

"Can you tell me if you find it again?"

"Yeah. Hey, maybe we all can play."

Oh, you bet.

"What do you think, Mommy? Can we? Can we, Daddy?"

"We'll try," Kevin said. "But you have to tell us when you see it again so we know it's time to play."

"Okay."

"Good night, sweetie," I said.

"Night, Mommy. Night, Daddy."

I snuggled closer to him. "We love you."

"Me, too. And Butters, too."

I stroked a hand over his forehead, kissed him again, and kept the small night-light on beside his bed and the door, steps from our room, open.

After Kevin and I entered to our room, I made a beeline for where I'd stashed my sword, far out of reach of the curious hands of a little boy. I wouldn't be sleeping tonight.

"That explains the feeling I picked up from you today," he said.

"Yes. I suppose it does." I found the box holding my sword and lifted the lid. The blade came to life, lighting at the recognition of my energy. "Good," I said to myself, closing the lid. I went back to where Kevin was standing just inside the doorway.

Silence passed between us. Neither of us wanted to say what it was we were thinking, as if doing so would make it real.

Kevin stepped closer, stroked my arm, and pulled me into a hug. "I'll visit Eldor tonight."

"We've got to get some protection in place. I'll get with the Soltari, Horus, to see what he knows. He said he would be monitoring the realms and finding a seeker."

"It's going to be okay. We have a seeker in the other room," Kevin said, lifting his chin in Raen's direction. "We'll know if Tarsamon comes around."

I turned out of Kevin's embrace. "Not Raen. Not now." Not ever if I had anything to say about it.

I sat at the edge of the bed. "I knew he'd be back. I suppose the best place to hide, if you're evil, would be the least place anyone would expect you to be hiding."

"Right under our noses."

"Exactly."

"We don't know how strong Tarsamon is. All we know is that he found Raen. He can be protected by the elves."

"Tarsamon must know Raen is a seeker. He wouldn't have tried connecting if he didn't. Because of that, he couldn't be in more danger. We can't hide from dark matter. What if he can blend in with the energy around us? With our strengths in sensing the feelings of others, I'm not sure if we could detect him."

Kevin nodded, his silence a harsh reminder of the risk we faced. Every sensation told me he was turning over a hundred different options, from protection to escape.

"Maybe it's time to train him as a seeker," he said. "Show him the world of Ardan and have the elves teach him."

"He's so young. Trained or not, I wouldn't want him to face Tarsamon in any form alone, and certainly not by chance."

"Nor would I. Right now, I'm going to play camp-out with him, and get answers tonight from Ardan." He pulled a couple of pillows and headed for Raen's room.

"I'll see you there."

ALSO AVAILABLE IN THE THREE KEYS SERIES

Beyond a Darkened Sky

The balance between good and evil has been shattered, opening a path for a dark lord's demons and shadows to consume the energy found in humanity. To New York psychiatrist Dr. Sara Forrester, these nightmares become more than figments of a troubled mind when the Soltari—a powerful entity governing the balance of good and evil—calls Sara to retrieve three ancient keys hidden thousands of years earlier. But to find the keys she must unlock the gateway to each of them by way of three secret medallions.

A Light Within

Sara Forrester is plunged into the only role in life she was ever meant to fulfill—the quest to obtain three ancient keys hidden by a powerful governing order across the realms—the Soltari. She and her team race to Scotland to find the sacred Druid priests before the evil seeking to end her quest traces her energy trail and puts an end to mankind. But when Sara arrives, a powerful force lures her to a break in time and space, diverting her intended path.

Flight of the Feathered Serpent

When age-old myths of a lost civilization come to life, Sara suspects the very Order she serves might have other intentions—using her to achieve a separate and malevolent purpose. She's vowed that no matter who or what might be working against her and the immortals, nothing will stand in the way of achieving her vital goal.

**If you'd like to sign-up to receive exclusive content
and special offers, please visit Dana at
https://danaalexander.net/**

ABOUT THE AUTHOR

Dana Alexander is a summa cum laude graduate of Arizona State University who spent her career in Medicare policy, education, and audit before being compelled to write the story of two souls connected across countless millennia and held together by their duty to the Alliance. When she isn't creating scenes, dialogue, and realms for the series, her time is spent with family keeping cool in the ridiculously hot desert with their two huge, swim-loving Labs, Ryley and Brodie.

Connect with Dana at her website:
www.danaalexander.net